BLACK BULLET

RENTARO SATOMI, FUGITIVE

5

SHIDEN KANZAKI

ILLUSTRATION BY
SAKI UKAI

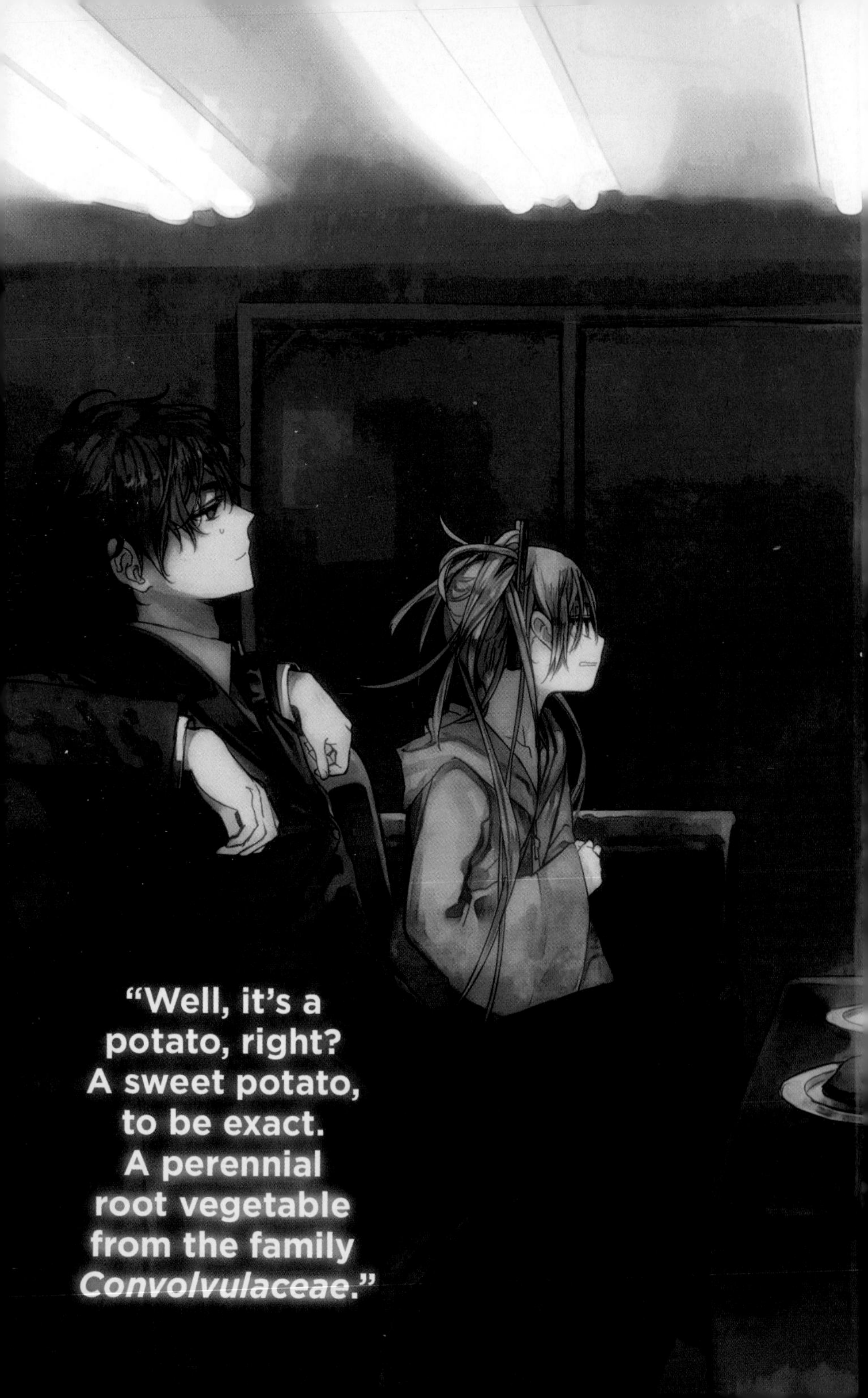
"Well, it's a potato, right? A sweet potato, to be exact. A perennial root vegetable from the family *Convolvulaceae*."

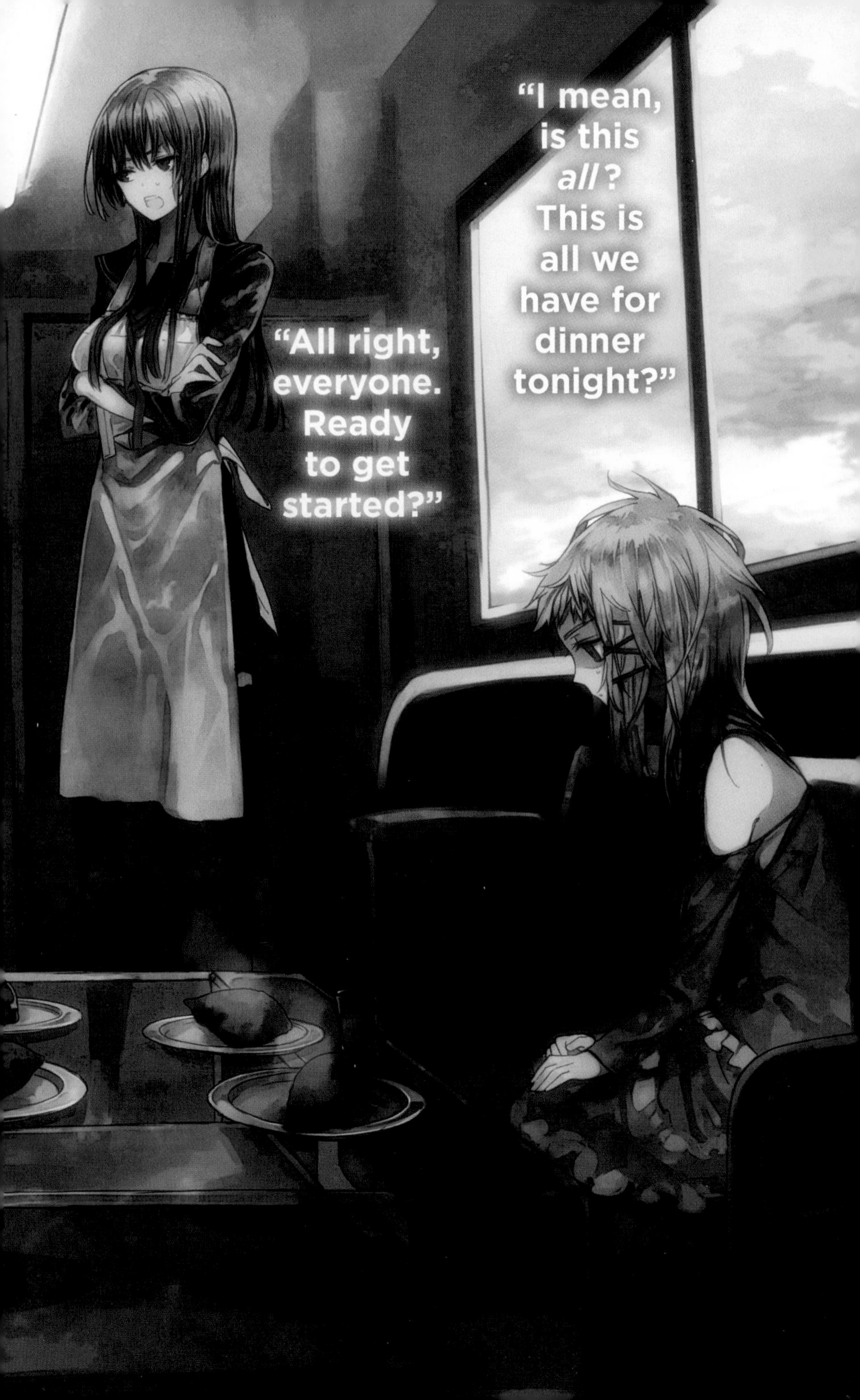
"I mean, is this *all*? This is all we have for dinner tonight?"
"All right, everyone. Ready to get started?"

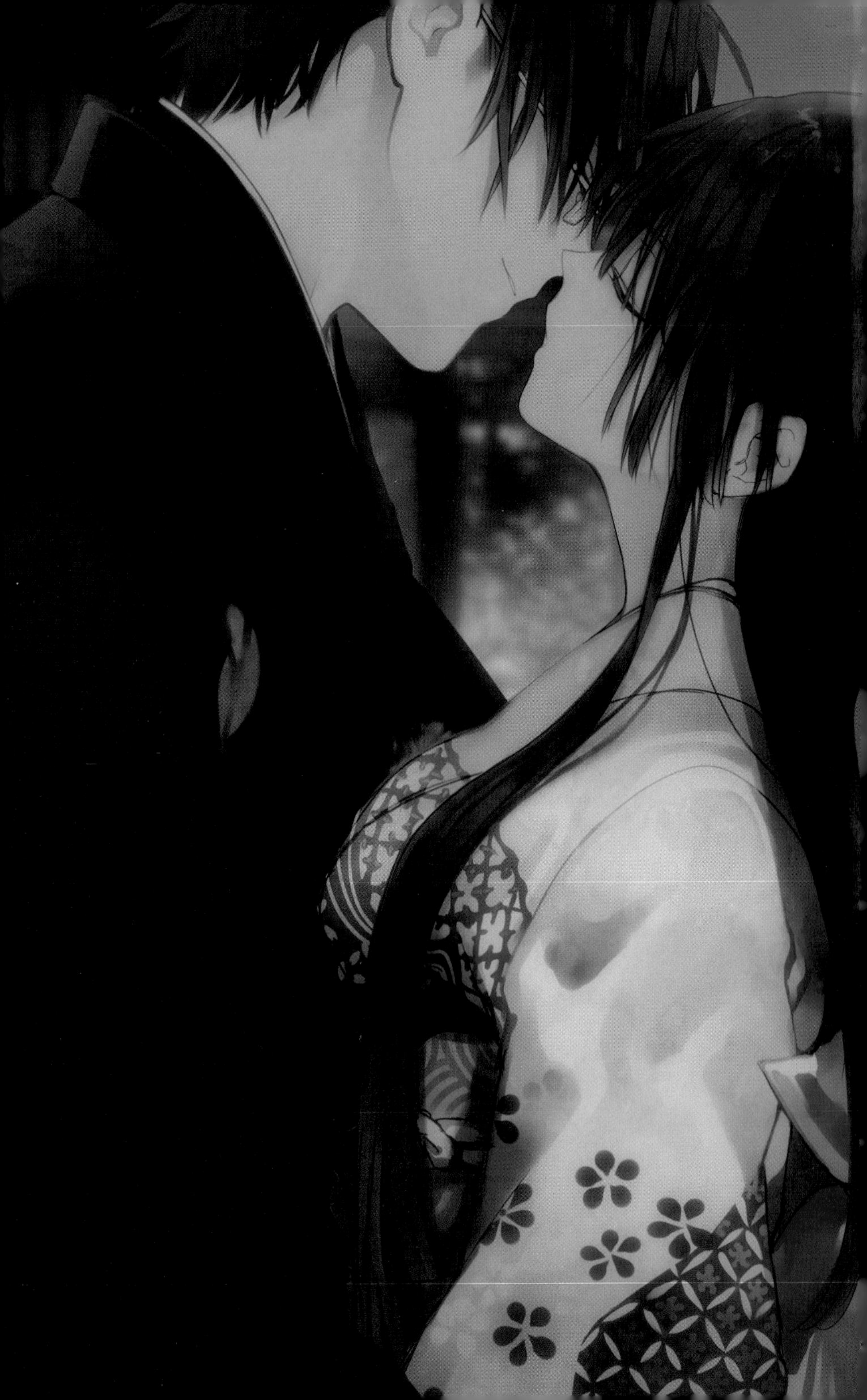

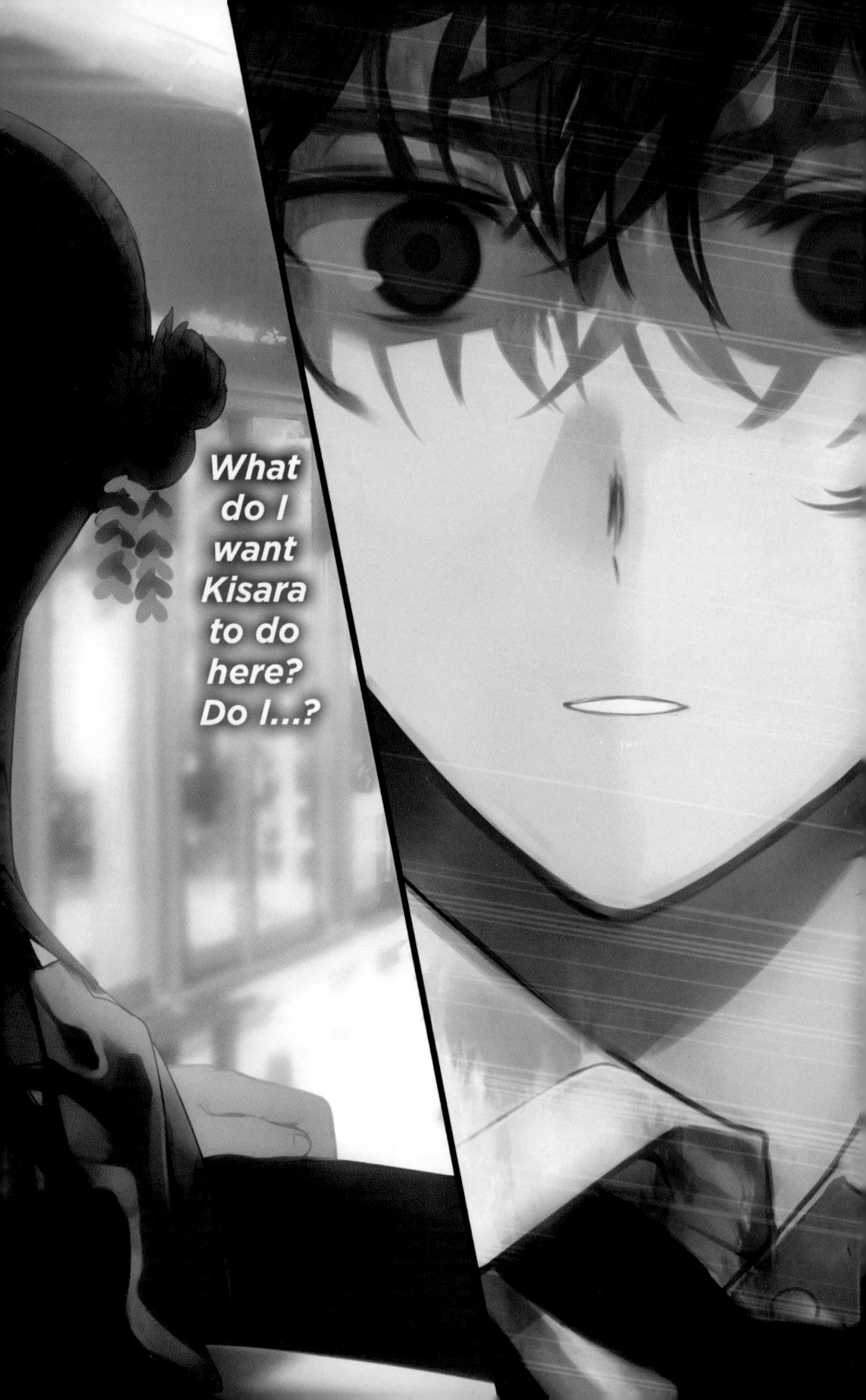
What do I want Kisara to do here? Do I...?

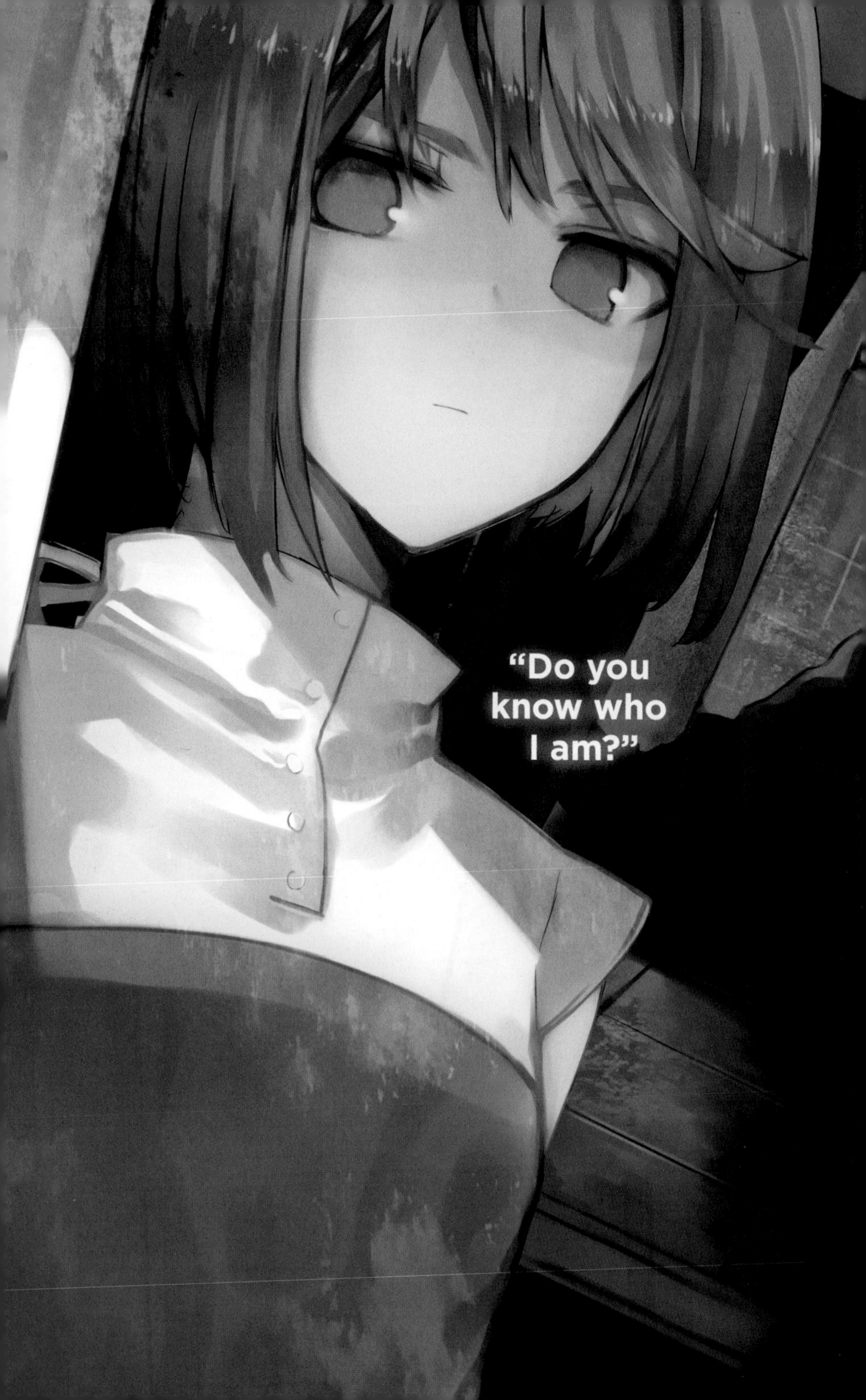
"Do you know who I am?"

"Hotaru Kouro... right? Suibara's Initiator."

**BLACK BULLET 5
CONTENTS**

BLACK★BULLET

RENTARO SATOMI, FUGITIVE

SHIDEN KANZAKI

ILLUSTRATION BY SAKI UKAI

YEN ON
NEW YORK

BLACK BULLET, Volume 5
SHIDEN KANZAKI

Translation by Nita Lieu
Cover art by Saki Ukai

BLACK BULLET, Volume 5
©SHIDEN KANZAKI 2013
All rights reserved.
Edited by ASCII MEDIA WORKS
First published in Japan in 2013 by KADOKAWA CORPORATION, Tokyo.

English translation rights arranged with KADOKAWA CORPORATION, Tokyo, through Tuttle-Mori Agency, Inc., Tokyo.

English translation © 2016 by Yen Press, LLC

Yen On
1290 Avenue of the Americas
New York, NY 10104

Visit us at yenpress.com
facebook.com/yenpress
twitter.com/yenpress
yenpress.tumblr.com
instagram.com/yenpress

First Yen On Edition: December 2016

Yen On is an imprint of Yen Press, LLC.
The Yen On name and logo are trademarks of Yen Press, LLC.

The publisher is not responsible for websites (or their content) that are not owned by the publisher.

Library of Congress Cataloging-in-Publication Data

Names: Kanzaki, Shiden, author. | Ukai, Saki, illustrator. | Lieu, Nita, translator.
Title: Black bullet. Volume 5, Rentaro Satomi, fugitive / Shiden Kanzaki ; illustrations by Saki Ukai ; translation by Nita Lieu.
Other titles: Rentaro Satomi, fugitive
Description: New York, NY : Yen On, 2016. | Series: Black bullet ; 5
Identifiers: LCCN 2016035659 | ISBN 9780316344920 (paperback)
Subjects: | CYAC: Science fiction. | BISAC: FICTION / Science Fiction / Adventure.
Classification: LCC PZ7.1.K29 Blae 2016 | DDC [Fic]—dc23 LC record available at https://lccn.loc.gov/2016035659

ISBNs: 9780316344920 (paperback)
9780316344999 (ebook)

10 9 8 7 6 5 4 3 2 1

LSC-C

Printed in the United States of America

PROLOGUE   THE QUICKENING NIGHTMARE

The beautiful soprano's voice, one with a wide, emphatic range used to sing professionally, is a portrait of constant change—sometimes high, sometimes low—as it exploits the finely tuned acoustics of a wide, expansive theater.

Kenji Houbara, reclining in his dimly lit seat in the audience, held his breath as he stared transfixed upon the sight before him. The players, dressed in the traditional seventeenth-century Scotland garb, sang their speech in a recitative manner as they pranced up and down the stage. To the side, a digital lightboard occasionally came to life, providing subtitles for the lyrics being performed. The intensity onstage was contagious, infecting the audience until both parties felt connected by a taut, groaning rope of emotion.

Kenji was taking in the opera *Lucia di Lammermoor*, an 1835 work by Italian composer Gaetano Donizetti. It tells the tale of Lucia Ashton and Edgardo di Ravenswood, two star-crossed lovers caught in a bitter feud between their respective families. Despite their attempts to quell the feud, Lucia's brother tricks her with a letter purportedly proving that Edgardo has another love, forcing her to agree to an arranged marriage to a rich nobleman instead. Edgardo, not knowing this, is so enraged at the news that he appears at Lucia's wedding and gives her a very public rebuke.

This causes Lucia, already brought to the mental brink, to finally go mad and kill her bridegroom, ultimately dying herself soon after. Learning the truth at last, Edgardo swears to follow her to heaven as he stabs himself in the heart.

When it came to classical opera, Kenji was strictly a Mozart aficionado. However, Donizetti—and *Lucia di Lammermoor* in particular—was one of the few exceptions he was willing to make. He could no longer count how many times he'd watched it, and he could now recite the plot just as surely as Lucia and Edgardo themselves, but time and again, he always found himself at another performance.

Reflecting for a moment, Kenji couldn't help but notice that most operas that stood the test of time seemed to be tragedies. Even true love's firmest bedrock could be quickly eroded away by tiny cracks of jealousy and suspicion.

Although he knew it was improper, he looked at the audience members seated next to and behind him. He made a glum expression. The New National Theater, with a capacity of 1,800, had failed to fill even a third of its seats. *But perhaps it was unavoidable*, he thought. Ten years ago, the Gastrea War had robbed the world of so much promising talent forever—both in film and in live performance.

Then he felt someone sitting down next to him. A sweet scent filled his nostrils as the sight stunned him into silence. A middle schooler, perhaps? Her wide-brimmed straw hat kept her face hidden, and a thin, shimmering dress accentuated her chest area like a stage light cast through a scrim. What stood out the most, however, was the pink teddy bear she had in her hands.

There are a million other seats in this concert hall. Why did she pick one right next to me?

Just then, with a thunderous percussion, the orchestral accompaniment burst into his ears. Lifted up by its ominous clamor, the soprano playing Lucia began to sing the so-called "Mad Scene" aria. He had been so lost in the performance that only now did he notice they were already into the third act. Lucia, blood-spattered and raving after killing her would-be groom, had suddenly thrown herself back into her own wedding ceremony from stage right, a blank look on her face as she began singing a fearsome, maniacal song. The bloodstained knife was still in her hand...

Then, Kenji's body reeled from a sudden shock, intense pain running across his body. He felt something foul well up from the pit of his stomach—and the moment he did, he began to spew blood profusely. Looking down, he found an unbelievable sight: a knife stuck into his own chest.

He had no idea what just happened.

Groggily turning his head around, he realized the hand around the knife's handle belonged to the girl in the straw hat next to him. She must have hidden the weapon in her teddy bear, the knife she had so adeptly just slipped between Kenji's ribs, piercing and ultimately destroying his heart.

"Wh...wh...?"

Why? Before he could ask, Kenji felt a hand over his mouth as the girl brought her face closer. "*Ssssh,*" she said, her index finger at her lips. She was like a slightly miffed arts patron, enjoining a nearby stranger to mind his manners while the performance was still underway.

His consciousness began to ebb away. Unable to even groan in response, Kenji slumped in his seat, then quietly expired.

The girl, her attention still focused on the opera unfolding before her, picked up Kenji's arm, making sure there was no pulse before standing up.

The final scene had just begun. With the orchestra playing solemnly behind her, she left the auditorium. The moment she left the climate-controlled theater, the sun's powerful rays began to beat angrily down upon her. In the distance, she could see hazy air drifting up from the cooking asphalt.

Then she set off, tapping a number into her cell phone.

"This is Hummingbird. Mission complete, Nest. Awaiting further orders."

In Saya Takamura's world, every day began by waking up her still-sleeping husband and son. She would always let the oak floors creak under her weight as she climbed the stairs, entering first her child's, then her husband's room, both adjacent to each other.

She was dealing with a couple of well-trained sleepers. A quick shake or two wasn't going to be enough. There was a certain trick to it, and that was to rip the comforter off the futon and leave the doors open. Once she left them alone and began making breakfast, her husband and son would jump out of their respective coffins, lurching like zombies toward the fetching aroma. Neither resembled the other very much, but this shared habit was all the evidence needed to prove they were family.

This morning she was mixing cheese into omelets, pairing it with some curried lamb mince from last night, along with toast. She spotted the rest of her family creep toward the kitchen table, then in time sent her husband off with a box lunch of salmon *onigiri* rice balls, and helped her son climb onto the kindergarten bus.

Now the real battle began.

Tying her apron tight behind her back, she checked the weather forecast as she dumped a nearby pile of dirty laundry into the washing machine, pushed the START button, and put on a pair of rubber gloves. Today, her main goal was to remove the mold staining the grout between the bathroom tiles, a task she had a tendency to put off for as long as possible. If she had time afterward, the toilet area could use a touch-up as well.

Despite her worst fears, the tile work actually went fairly easily. The high temperatures must have caused the dirt and mold to float to the surface. Kneeling there, spraying the walls with bathroom cleaner and scrubbing away at the grout lines, she couldn't help but notice how joyous the whole process was.

It was obvious that she cared for her husband and son. It was a given that she did chores like these. Ten years ago, a portrait of happiness she never could've hoped for was right here, before her eyes, between the tiles.

She stood up just in time for the washer to buzz its confirmation that the laundry was done. Both hands carrying damp clothes, she used a leg to open the sliding door leading to the rear balcony. The sky was an indescribably fetching shade of blue, liberally decorated with silent, puffy white clouds. The sun shone brilliantly upon her.

From this vantage point, Saya could only barely hear the front door-bell's chime. She hurriedly tossed the laundry on the floor and dashed for the front door, wiping her hands dry on the apron.

"Hello!" she said as she opened the door. Then she froze.

A man was standing there. An intimidating one. He was easily over 190 centimeters tall, and despite the summer heat, he was wearing a long trench coat. A short, well-maintained beard was visible below his round sunglasses. It was immediately clear that he wasn't visiting on any kind of legitimate business.

"Um..."

"You Saya Takamura?" the man intoned.

A miniature snowstorm of paper scraps flew toward her before falling to the ground. She lifted her arms up in self-defense before realizing she was "attacked" by several dozen photographs.

She was the subject of each picture. Hidden-camera photos, all of them.

"......!"

The moment she recognized what they were, Saya took a Glock pistol out from deep within an apron pocket. But the next instant, a gunshot sent her body reeling toward the wall behind her.

"Nhh..."

At some point, the man had readied a shotgun in his hands. A ribbon of hot, white smoke drifted out from the muzzle. The barrel and stock had been cut off, an aftermarket modification that made it compact and easier to hide.

Saya brought a hand to her stomach. The anti-personnel bullets had ripped through her lower torso, fatally wounding her. She let the handgun fall through her fingers and raised her face up high.

"Who...*are* you?"

She was answered by twin shotgun barrels placed between her eyes.

The man pulled the trigger and delivered a second salvo.

Not bothering to watch Saya's body as it slumped to the floor, which left a vertical blood smear on the wall, he hid the shotgun back in his coat and briskly left the home.

Some neighbors, noticing the gunshots, were already out scoping the scene by the time he closed the front gate behind him. Making sure he was a safe distance away from the scene, the man took out his cell phone.

"Swordtail to Nest. Mission complete. Awaiting further orders."

"So, like, getting back to the singles meet up I went to last night.... Right when we were all about to head out and pair up, the guys were all like 'You mind if we go Dutch on this tonight?' I mean, hell-*oooo*? They were all, like, ten years older than us! Can you have any *less* of a clue?"

A cacophony of unflattering laughter ensued, vulgarly echoing its way across school grounds through the wide-open classroom windows.

The place stank of perfume. Anyone could tell that someone had applied far too much. Whoever came up with the expression "too much of a good thing" must have been imagining this exact sort of confab. *I really don't like where this is going*, thought Yuga Mitsugi in a corner of his mind, but he shook it off as he approached his seat.

"Hey."

"Uhhh, yeah?"

He was greeted by the unruliest one of all. She was a second-year student here at Nukagari High School, and while her collar was folded down, it was badly bent out of shape, and her hair, which she swore to her teachers was real, was dyed a light blond. She always put her ear-rings back on whenever they were on break, and once the warning bell went off, she always took them off and pretended nothing was amiss in front of the next teacher. She didn't respect the rules—and in ways that did far more to annoy than actually cause any harm.

Yoshiko Kamuro, he thought her name was. If any girl in her school year crossed her, she and her clique would surround the offender, drag her into the bathroom, and conduct their so-called "punishments," one after the other. That the characters in her name literally meant "good child" was simply comical.

"Uh, that's kind of my seat."

"So?" Yoshiko replied, her ample rear end parked on Yuga's desk as she swung her legs in the air.

"Would you mind moving a sec? I can't get my textbooks out."

The request made the air in the classroom frigid. The boys and girls surrounding her swiveled their heads upward at him, eyes engorged with hostility. Yoshiko joined them, glaring silently at Yuga, then moved exactly half her rear off the desk. And no more. This was all she was willing to concede.

With some difficulty, Yuga proceeded to remove the textbooks he needed for the next class. He then left without another word, figuring a "thank you" for allowing him access to his own desk would be silly. When he made it to Shingo Kuromatsu's desk, his friend gave him a clearly concerned look as he waved.

"Oof. Not cool, Mitsugi."

"What's not cool?"

"What do you mean, what…?"

Kuromatsu gaped at him for a moment before sighing, realizing there was no saving him now. "Mitsugi, it's been three months since you transferred to this school, right? And we're friends, right? So I hope you'll take this the right way when I say, like, you gotta try harder to adapt to this place a little. I dunno what kind of social life you had over at Seishin High, but hell if *I* could imagine it."

"……"

Okay, so what was I supposed to do over there? He was putting forth at least a modicum of effort to act like any other student around here, but something about Yuga's behavior led the others to find him abnormal. And even if he revealed to his well-meaning friend that he had never set foot once in Seishin High School and that his presence there was strictly in name only—and even then those records were faked—it wasn't like that'd help solve the problem at all.

Besides, his past three months as a transfer student was all for the sake of today's mission. So maybe it didn't matter anyway.

"Mitsugi, look. I really hope I don't piss you off when you hear this, but sometimes you act like…you're really far away from us, y'know? Like you're a space alien from another planet and you're here to observe what life on Earth is like."

"Wow. That hurts."

"Huh?"

He laughed at his suddenly concerned classmate. "I'm just joking."

Then Yuga's cell phone rang. *Here we go.* Yuga pushed his biology textbooks against Kuromatsu's chest.

"Hey, I'm sorry, Kuromatsu, but can you take these to bio class for me?"

"Huh? Uh, sure, but…"

Before he had time to hear Kuromatsu's full answer, Yuga turned around and left the classroom, running past the rooms that lined the hallway and into an inconspicuous teacher's bathroom. There he pushed a hands-free headset into his ear and poked at his smartphone.

"Hey. This is Dark Stalker."

"Bad news. I got word that your target boarded the bullet train before the one in the plan."

Yuga's brows twitched a bit. He looked at his watch. "How long ago?"

"Twenty-five minutes. You got just five minutes until the train passes by you. Get to your post immediately."

He didn't need to be told twice. Flying out of the bathroom stall, Yuga clambered up the stairway next to the teachers' offices. At the landing, he made a quick twirl, one hand still on the safety rail. In an instant, he was behind the locked door leading to the rooftop. Taking out a previously made key, he stuck it into the hole and threw the metal door open.

Despite having "physically weak due to childhood illness" written in the special-comments section of his transfer certificate, Yuga had traversed the fifty or so meters from his classroom to here without so much as quickening his breath.

The warning bell rang just then. He could hear the students scurrying to and fro below him.

The door's hinges creaked as he opened the door, revealing bright light and seemingly boundless sky before his eyes. Yuga made a beeline to a spot behind the rooftop water tank, pulling out the thin attaché case he had stashed between the tank and the safety fence on the roof's edge. With another key, it was open, revealing a single rifle and the scent of gun oil—a DSR No. 1 sniper rifle, manufactured by AMP Technical Services.

It was a bullpup-style bolt-action rifle, one whose action—the mechanism that locks and fires the ammunition—was located farther behind the trigger in order to keep the barrel length down while retaining accuracy. It was a low-noise, low-light rifle, using .338 Lapua Magnum cartridges and an attached silencer instead of the usual flash hider. Its beauty lay entirely in its mobility—a sniper rifle not beholden to a single location, like so many before it.

Class must've just begun. From the music room directly below him, he could hear a low, heavy throb against his stomach as a majestic composition began to play. It was "Ode to Joy," the final movement in Beethoven's Symphony No. 9.

Yuga checked the time. Two minutes left. With expert concentration, he settled into a prone shooting position and turned his rifle toward the high-speed train line that deftly tore its way through the tangled mountains on the opposite side of his school.

Opening the flip-up cover on his optical scope, Yuga unfolded the bipod stored in the far end of the barrel jacket. Then, muzzle still pointed at the rail line, he placed the monopod stored in the shoulder stock on the ground, keeping the gun stable at three different points. Taking a box magazine from the holder attached to the front, he pushed it into the bottom of the action and operated the bolt handle, loading the first bullet into the chamber.

The scope he peered into presented him with assorted data, from wind speed to shooting angle. A Carl Zeiss company product, it was the newest 2031 model, boasting a calculator that provided real-time ballistic information at a glance.

The range to his target was 1,200 meters. It was already zeroed in on the right point.

"*Thirty seconds left,*" the voice on the phone said, unable to hide its alarm. "*It's coming!*" Yuga's face, meanwhile, was as calm and collected as the mirrorlike surface of a perfectly still lake. The background noise faded away; all he could hear was the loud beating of his heart. With several breaths to prepare himself, he placed a finger against the trigger and pulled it taut.

—Then he unleashed his cybernetic eyes.

A spinning geometric shape appeared over both of his irises as the CPU within his pupils came to life. They began to rotate, overclocking the miniature computer's thought processes to increase their speed by

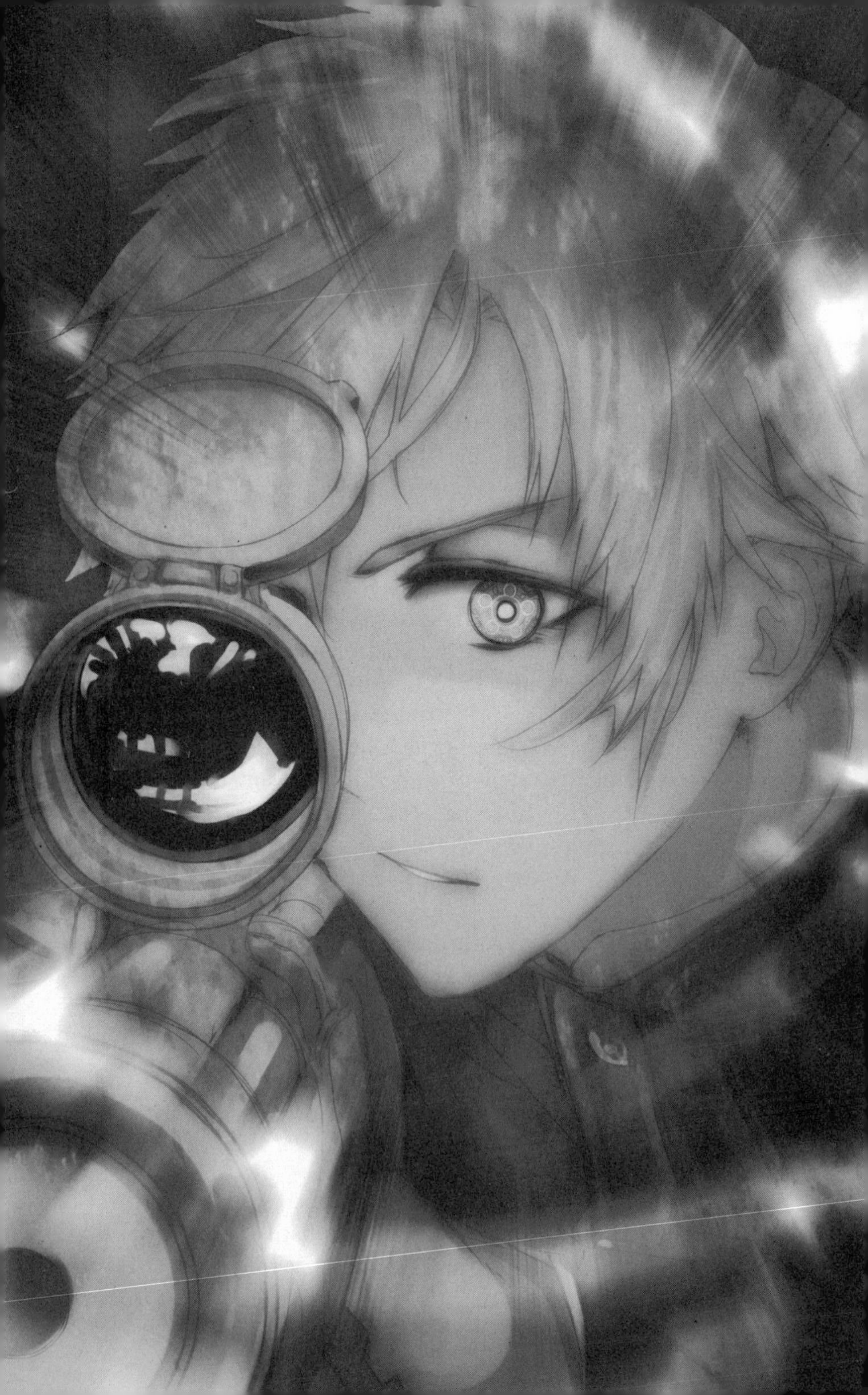

the hundreds. In tandem with this, the world around Yuga seemed to fall into slow motion. Beethoven's masterpiece became an indecipherable mishmash of bass noise, and the sunlight around him seemed to go two levels darker than before. The flow of all forces in nature slowed for him. Even the black kite bird in the corner of his eye seemed to stop in midair, its wings unmoving, as it lazily cruised the skies.

On the right edge of his vision, the bullet train sluggishly churned its way onto the scene. Normally it'd be here and gone in a flash, but now he could see everything down to the teeth on every individual passenger.

His dossier told him that the target would be seated windowside in a reserved seat in row twenty-five, as counted from the front. But if he boarded the train before the one he was scheduled for, that must have changed as well...

—*Found him. Still by the window, but now in row twelve.* A bald man, lips gnarled as he chomped at an expensive-looking cigar, a look of clear irritation on his face. Just like in the pictures.

Yuga's eyes completed their calculations, providing a formula that guaranteed him a clean hit. Narrowing them, he let the predator in him seize his body as he squeezed the trigger.

He could feel the spring inside bend, and before long, he had it completely pulled back. The firing pin in the attached bolt mechanism struck the detonator at the bottom of the cartridge, setting it off. A small explosion took place within the action, a dull, muted flash emanating from the far edge of the silencer. At the same time, the Lapua Magnum bullet made its way through the barrel, the internal rifling giving it rotational speed as it smashed through the air toward its target. A blunt firing recoil gradually pounded itself against his shoulder.

In a world where everything was slowed to near-statuesque proportions, only the bullet proceeded along at high speed. Yuga had given himself enough lead. He watched as the blast penetrated through the train window, broke the glass, and made a clean traverse through his target's temporal lobe. The target listlessly began to fall to his side and downward.

Realizing there was no point admiring his efforts any further, Yuga lowered his CPU's operational speed and returned his sense of time to its normal state. The instant he did, the explosive bombast of "Ode to

Joy" thudded against his ears as the remaining recoil force pounded painfully against his shoulder. Before long, the sun grew just as bright as it was before.

Standing up as he watched the bullet train motor along at top speed, he tilted his head toward the blue sky.

"You get him?"

"It hit home, yeah."

He even managed to camouflage the muffled gunshot in the overlapping sounds of "Ode to Joy" and the passing train.

Yuga sighed. "...So, Dark Stalker to Nest. Mission complete. Awaiting further—"

"—What...what *was* that just now...?"

Yuga whirled around, only to find a student—a girl—standing dumbfounded, clearly unable to believe her eyes. It was Yoshiko Kamuro. The wide-open metal door behind her instantly told Yuga why she was here. Maybe he was near the time limit and didn't have any wiggle room to work with, but he cursed himself for not even bothering to lock it back up.

Yoshiko, engaged in her usual boycotting-class habit whenever possible, must have noticed the half-open door and thought it was her golden opportunity for an hour or so of freedom. Not even realizing it'd cost her her life.

"You saw it, huh?" a detached Yuga said as he took a deliberate step toward her. Yoshiko took a step back.

"Wh-what the hell is up with that huge gun or whatever? Like, that's just...totally nuts!"

If she could've kept her legs from shaking, the half smirk she employed to accentuate her act just might have seemed convincing.

Yuga kept approaching Yoshiko silently. She continued to step back. Before long, she was against the metal fence that edged the roof.

"Are you, like, a hit man?"

"Nope. I'm an avenger." Yuga shrugged and looked up into the air. "Sorry, but if I let you live, that's gonna leave a black mark on the whole operation. I really feel bad, saying this to you after just three months—but die."

There was no excitement or passion—nor any advance warning— behind the heel of Yuga's palm as it hit home against her chest. The moment it did, there was a sharp crack as her torso cavity caved in upon itself.

It was a perfectly timed move, one that took every field of human anatomy into consideration as it so expertly destroyed the body before him. It was at a zero-degree-impact angle, working its way through her pectoral muscles as it shattered her ribs, ensuring the ruined fragments embedded themselves deep into her heart. Instant death.

What could have run through her mind during that one final circulatory cycle, the last time her doomed heart gave its mighty heave? He doubted her brain had enough time to comprehend her unsteady feet entangling themselves beneath her, or the meaning of the fresh blood bubbling into her mouth.

Catching her as she fell, Yuga spoke into his headset.

"Nest. Sorry, but I got an unexpected corpse here. I'm gonna sneak it into my locker on the stair landing, so make sure you have someone pick it up before the janitor finds it after school, please."

"Dehhh! This always *happens with you—"*

Yuga cut off the link before he had to listen to the rest. He laid down the girl's body, already embarking on its transformation into a cold lump of meat. Then, from the Nukagari High School roof, he took in the vista that unfolded below him. As the summer wind beat drearily against his cheek, he peered into his palms.

"I have all this strength. So why am I such a failure all the time... Professor?"

BLACK BULLET 5 CHAPTER 01

RENTARO SATOMI, FUGITIVE

1

The monster loomed large in his optically magnified vision. The single Gastrea, clambering an almost sheer vertical wall, looked like a crustacean-type at first glance—one with octopus-style tentacles growing out of it.

Its form, replete with a seemingly endless supply of sucker-laden feet, was clearly a walking mollusk. Its base core, however, was covered in a thick, almost helmetlike shell. Its head was directly attached to its chest area, making it impossible to tell exactly where its eyes or brain were, and as you went down the gentle plane of its back, you eventually came upon a long, sharp, spiked tail.

Just then, the Gastrea used its tentacles and arms to take another step forward, straight up the building, its entire body tensing itself at the effort. The sun, now halfway up the sky, kept it brightly lit as large droplets of sweat spilled from its eyebrows and down its cheeks. Its piercing, insectlike cry was extremely annoying to all who could hear it, and its skin was tanned so deeply that it seemed ready to catch fire under the sun's rays at any moment.

Even in this tense environment, though, Rentaro Satomi found a very different stress placed upon him. The Gastrea was climbing straight up Tokyo Tower's proud, bright-red iron frame.

"Big Brother, the wind's blowing at ten to thirteen kilometers per hour from six o'clock."

Rentaro pulled his face up from the scope on his sniper rifle to stare quizzically at the blonde girl next to him, lying prone on her stomach. This was Tina Sprout, and just like Rentaro, she had a sniper rifle loaded and ready, ignoring said "Big Brother" as she kept a watchful eye down her scope. The Bits that formed part of her aiming system flitted at regular intervals between her and the target Gastrea. Those were the infantry of sorts for her Shenfield, a thought-driven interface that, like so many buoys strewn across the sea, transmitted wind speeds and other pertinent sniper information directly into her brain.

She and Rentaro had set up shop atop a building not far from the Tower. Although he had a wet towel wrapped around his head, the punishing sunlight crashing down from above made him feel like he was taking a nap on a frying pan. Wiping the never-ending torrent of sweat from his brow, he tried to fight off the heat, strong enough to make his vision twist and warp.

But despite the clear afternoon weather, Tokyo Tower and the area around it was bereft of its usual activity. There were no resting children, nor any elderly dozing off into an afternoon nap. That was only to be expected, given how police had cordoned off the entire area, and every street around the Tower was crawling with patrol cars. A virtual army of officers sat resolutely at their positions, shotguns pointed upward.

Yet they didn't seem poised to take action. Ever since Gastrea-related crimes sent the police's line-of-duty death rates through the roof, responsibility for Gastrea incidents fell somewhere in between the police and self-defense force, right into the hands of the civil security agencies.

For a change, Rentaro and Tina were the first civsec group on the scene, earning the right to take out the Gastrea latched on to Tokyo Tower from their sniper nest's vantage point. He peered back into his scope. One hundred meters between him and the target. No sweat for any regular sniper, and the low wind speed worked to their advantage as well. He could get away with ignoring the wind effect on his shot if that kept up.

But despite all his efforts, Rentaro's vision kept blurring and falling apart through his scope, robbing him of any decent trigger chance. The sense of impotent irritation that resulted did nothing to calm his thoughts.

"Big Brother!"

The voice came tumbling in from behind him, pushing him to act. Throwing caution to the wind, he squeezed the trigger.

He felt a sharp kick at his shoulder. The Varanium bullet flew up and to the right, missing the Gastrea and pinging against the metal of Tokyo Tower.

There was no time to gnash his teeth in regret. The Gastrea, now on high alert, opened up its head/torso and deployed wings it had kept under wraps before.

—*Oh, great. It's gonna fly off on us.*

Quickly, Rentaro pulled the handle to load the next shot. Rapidly, he fired again and just barely missed, the bullet aimlessly flying through the Gastrea's former location.

Just as the monster was about to penetrate the police perimeter and make Rentaro question why he woke up this morning, there was a loud *crack* as a bullet cut through the Stage Two beast's core. It fell into a tailspin in midair, crashing helplessly to the ground.

Cheers erupted from the police officers nearby. It wasn't dead yet, but thanks to the Varanium bullet blocking its regenerative abilities, it was no longer in any shape to fight.

Rentaro looked to his side, noticing a wisp of smoke from Tina's Dragunov sniper rifle. She kept her eyes closed for a beat or two, perhaps so she could take in the remaining vibration from her gun, but a moment later, she looked up from her infrared-detector scope and wiped away the sweat with her arm.

"It's all right, Big Brother," she said. "That's how it is for everyone at first."

Rentaro hung his head in defeated shame. The nicer Tina acted around him, the more it seemed impossible to be around her a second longer. But he'd sound like a spoiled brat if he ever let *that* get out.

As both a gunman and a Tendo Martial Arts practitioner, Rentaro was just as much a close-range specialist as his Initiator partner, Enju Aihara. He felt it was his duty to provide some mid- to long-range cover when Enju's skills weren't a good match for the fight. As far as mid-range went…well, his pistol skills were good enough. But what about beyond that?

That was what drove him to ask Tina for a little instruction. Which was fine and all, but—and it really did hurt him, deep down—he wasn't progressing nearly as quickly as he had hoped.

Rentaro shook his head. "I can't do it," he said. "I have the worst time trying to focus on just one single thing like that."

And look at what just happened, besides. One more mistake, and that Gastrea would have gotten away. Who knows what kind of disaster that could've caused?

"Big Brother," Tina replied, "why did you want to master sniping in the first place?"

The force of her pure, emerald-green eyes overwhelmed him. "Because I thought I needed to," he said, averting his gaze. "I mean—I don't know. I just feel like I gotta make myself stronger."

"That's exactly it." Tina lifted a finger into the air. "You want to get stronger, Big Brother, but you can't clearly articulate *why*. And that's what's showing up in your marksmanship. It's making you hesitate."

"So you're saying it's all in my head?"

Tina nodded. "You've noticed it, too, haven't you? What being a sniper is all about?"

Rentaro groaned. *That* hit a little too close to home.

She was right, of course. As he had learned the hard way through training, shooting a pistol required a completely different skill set than firing a sniper rifle. There were the distances involved, of course, but more than that, a sniper had to reap his target's life before he even realized he was being targeted. To Rentaro, it felt a little too much like premeditated murder to wrap his head around.

If they were debating a gun battle between two hostile, engaged foes, he could at least explain that as a case of justifiable self-defense. But snipers didn't work that way. Rentaro still didn't know how to approach the connection between his pull of the trigger and the death that ultimately resulted.

This was somewhat doable with a Gastrea, at least. But Rentaro couldn't keep himself from thinking about it: *Could I will myself through the sniper process if this was a human opponent?*

"Can…can *you* deal with that?"

The platinum-blonde girl nodded brightly, eyes still on him.

"Sniping is the entire reason I exist. If I couldn't master this skill and manipulate this Shenfield the way I can, Professor Rand would've branded me a failure and I'd be disposed of like yesterday's garbage."

"Disposed of?"

"Yeah… Well, I heard all kinds of rumors, but I still don't know exactly what happened to the children who couldn't adapt to their machine bodies. If anything saved me, I think it's the way I shut off my imagination. That kept me from thinking too much about the future. That's how I mastered all the skills granted to me in pretty quick time. You can't kill another person unless your own soul dies, too."

"But that's not the way a *person* lives, Tina."

Tina fell into a shamed silence.

"Are you saying I need to kill off my own emotions if I want the strength to pull the trigger?"

"No, Big Brother. I'm saying you need to find a *reason* for yourself. One that'll make it seem worth taking *another* person's life. And that's something I really can't help you find. Or, really, unless you *do* find it, all the practice in the world isn't gonna make you any better, Big Brother, so you should probably give it up sooner than later."

When it came to this subject, at least, Tina wasn't one to mince words. For a few moments, she and Rentaro were silent, merely staring into each other's eyes. The lukewarm wind blew across the roof, gently tossing their hair around. Rentaro was the first one to speak again.

"You're a real slave-driving teacher, Tina."

Tina smiled through the sweat covering her face. "You've been teaching me this whole time, Big Brother. I'm just glad I have something to teach you back." Then she hefted up the Dragunov rifle and pointed downward. "The Gastrea's still alive. Let's finish it off before it hurts any citizens."

"Yeahhh!" a joyful voice bellowed out from below. "You did it, you bastards!!"

Startled, Rentaro and Tina tracked the voice to its source. At Tokyo Tower's base, they noticed a familiar civsec pair, both bedecked in some pretty authentic hardcore-punk fashion. It was Tamaki and Yuzuki Katagiri, two old comrades they had fought alongside during the Third Kanto Battle; they had already set upon the Gastrea Tina had shot down. It was clear their foe didn't have long to live.

Which meant—

Rentaro and Tina looked at each other and shouted in unison:

"They're stealing our bounty!!"

2

It was mid-August, and even with the Gastrea War decimating population figures worldwide, global climate change was still a serious problem.

The latest way it manifested itself was in the tundra—the eternally frozen land up north. Now that the permafrost wasn't so permanent any longer, the animal and plant carcasses caught under the ice were starting to decompose, unleashing an astonishing amount of methane into the atmosphere and further accelerating the warming trend. The media were on it like hyenas, of course.

The human race was releasing only a tiny fraction of the carbon dioxide that it used to, but they were still inheriting the cost for all the excesses of generations past. For all anyone knew, it was well beyond the point that anything could be done about it.

Even when operating at full blast, the air-conditioning unit back at the office could do little against the 39 degree Celsius temperature outside. The droning of the cicadas began to sound like a plea for help in the occupants' ears.

At least it was quiet inside the office. Solemn, even, in a way. Tina, Enju, and Rentaro were at their seats, meekly examining one another as the sweat poured down.

In a corner of the Tendo Civil Security Agency, lit diagonally by soft light from the setting sun, lounge chairs were positioned around a glass table. It was meant for conducting conversations with paying customers, although in practice it wasn't used for this purpose too often.

Kisara Tendo, wearing an apron tied over her school uniform, appeared through the *noren* curtain separating the lounge from the kitchen area, setting four plates on the glass table. The one placed in front of Rentaro emanated a sweet scent that found its way into his nostrils as the steam washed against his face. It was enough to make his stomach growl.

Settling down with her own plate, Kisara closed her eyes and put her hands together.

"All right, everyone. Ready to get started?"

Rentaro and Enju did the same, but just as they were about to tuck in, someone shouted "Wait a minute!" in a panic.

Tina looked around in abject bewilderment, then pointed at her plate.

"Um…what is *this*?"

Rentaro followed Tina's eyes down to the object placed on her lily-white plate. It was shaped like a somewhat elongated diamond, laid upon the plate in all its purple, tuberous glory.

"What is it? …Well, it's a potato, right? A sweet potato, to be exact. A perennial root vegetable from the family *Convolvulaceae*."

"Th-that's not really what I meant… I mean, is this *all*? This is all we have for dinner tonight?"

Kisara placed an index finger on her chin, having apparent trouble understanding Tina's complaint. "Hmmm," she muttered, before slapping a fist against her hand. "I got it! Just a minute, okay?"

Tina breathed a sigh of relief as Kisara ventured back into the kitchen. "Wow, President Tendo, you sure can be a prankster sometimes!"

Before long, Kisara cheerfully came back out, plinking a cup down in front of Tina.

"Here you go. A glass of tap water. All the seconds you want, too."

Tina's face stiffened for a moment.

"Uhhmm, President…? Is our agency really this short on money?"

"It's desperate."

"Wh-what's on the menu tomorrow?"

"Bean and bean-sprout soup. Also, plain udon noodles. I've got some bread crusts that the bakery gave me for free, too."

"What about the day after that?"

"Sautéed bean sprouts and bread crusts."

"And the next day?"

"Bread crusts."

Tina began to see a pattern emerge.

"Umm, and f-four days from now?"

Kisara, impressed that she even dared to ask, gave herself a confident thump on the chest and smiled warmly.

"Well, on the fourth day, I figure we'd change it up a little and go with *fried* bread crusts!"

"That's the same thing!" Tina shouted. "Just because they eat fried food all the time in the US doesn't mean *I* have to!"

This triggered a sudden mood swing on Kisara's part. She stood up and slapped her hands against the table.

"What do you want from me?! We've completed exactly zero cases *this* month, too! I was preparing beefsteaks for all of us tonight, but Satomi's such an idiot that we're out the entire bounty! And we even had *you* on site this time, Tina…!"

Rentaro scratched the back of his head. He was certainly not expecting the Katagiri Civil Security Agency to scavenge his (okay, their) kill like that. The end result was all too clear, however: Today, the civsec experts at the Tendo agency were going hungry.

"But why," asked Enju as she poked at her sweet potato with a finger, "are we always so penniless like this?"

"Yeah." Tina nodded, seeing the logic in this. "Where's our pay from the Third Kanto Battle, Kisara?"

The Tendo Civil Security Agency, after all, had at least three major jobs under its belt. The Kagetane Hiruko terror incident; foiling the attempt on the Seitenshi's life; and more or less snapping victory from the jaws of defeat during the Third Kanto Battle. Each should have generated a nontrivial payment on its own.

Kisara looked oddly startled for a moment. Then she turned her eyes upward, cheeks reddening. "Listen, Satomi," she mumbled. "I kept this under wraps until now, but about two months before the Hiruko case, our finances pretty much hit the limit and I couldn't pay the lease on the office any longer. So I, uh… I kind of borrowed some money."

"From where?" Rentaro asked, already dreading the potential answer. Kisara replied by bashfully pointing up at the ceiling. Their upstairs neighbors—Kofu Finance, the friendly neighborhood yakuza-funded loan shark.

"You might be too stupid to realize this," Kisara dolefully continued, "but when you take out a loan, there's something called 'compounding interest.' For example, let's say I borrowed a million yen, right? After ten days, they'd apply ten percent interest on it, so now I have to pay back 1.1 million instead. Then, ten days after that, they add on ten percent of that 1.1 million figure...so then it becomes 1.21 million."

That was all it took for Tina to put her hands to her face and start crying. Rentaro, for his part, closed his eyes tightly and silently apologized to her. *I'm sorry. I'm sorry, Tina. It's not your fault our president is so clueless.*

"What'd you use for collateral when you borrowed the money?"

"Y'organs."

"Buh?"

Kisara said it a little too quickly for Rentaro to pick up.

"I said...your organs, Satomi. Like, Abe up there said your lungs and corneas and stuff would go for a lot of money, so..."

"Wuh?"

Kisara, cheeks still flushed, put her hands on her hips. "Look, you're my employee, Satomi," she sulked. "I'm the president, and that means you're *mine*. Plus, you get to work for one of the cutest presidents out there. A cornea or spleen or two is more than a fair price for that!"

Rentaro stared at Kisara. There were no words.

—Did I just have this girl I like order me to hand over my internal organs?

Enju looked equally disgusted, but in another moment her eyes were back down upon her plate.

"So these potatoes..."

Kisara ran a hand up through her black hair. "Uh-huh," she intoned. "Kind of the Last Supper, if you know what I mean. Starting today, it's nothing but bean sprouts and bread crusts, day in, day out. By which I mean six days, because starting day seven, we're gonna have nothing but water to live on. I hope you enjoy all the luxury I'm giving you tonight."

The group listlessly stared at the sweet potatoes on each respective plate. A sudden quiet descended upon the office.

Enju silently raised a hand. "I have a suggestion on how we can split these," she said. "We should divide Kisara's potato into thirds and give one piece each to me, Tina, and Rentaro."

"Wh-why is that?"

"We three couldn't survive three days without food or water, but with all the nutrients you have stored in your breasts, Kisara, I'm sure you'd be all right for at least a year or so."

"Oh, a year without food or water, huh?" Now it was Kisara's turn to raise her voice. "I'm not a monster! Besides, Enju, you're always picking on me about my chest, but it's not like this is all wine and roses for me! They make my shoulders all sore, there are *never* any nice-looking bras my size, I keep getting prickly heat all over them..."

Sadly, the pain Kisara's gifts gave her was not shared with the others.

"Daaaaaahhhh!" Stricken by a sudden case of breast hysteria, Enju lunged over the table toward Kisara. "If you don't want them, let me take them from you! Give me back the boobs you sucked away from me!"

"Ow ow ow ow! Stop pulling at them, Enju! You're gonna rip them off!"

Tina shot Rentaro a nervous look. Rentaro shook his head at her and sighed. "The hunger's just getting us all worked up." Then he turned toward Kisara, an offhand premonition crossing his mind.

"Hey, um, we *are* kind of the 'saviors of Tokyo Area' and everything, aren't we? Shouldn't that earn us at least a little more regular work?"

Kisara, finally a safe distance away from Enju's ferocious attack, turned back toward him. "It is," she said, her breath ragged. "Someplace on the east coast of the United States wanted us to eliminate a great white shark Gastrea that's been appearing around the beach. Apparently it's been chewing up all the local shark fishermen with gusto, and the local oceanographers and police chiefs don't know what to do about it. How's that sound to you?"

"It sounds like something we better leave to an underwater specialist. What else?"

Kisara ripped a page from the memo pad next to the office's landline phone. "Here, I'll read it to you," she said. "'They're late with my food delivery again; do something about it.' 'I challenge Rentaro Satomi to a duel. Let's find out which of us is the *real* man!' 'Hey, President Tendo [heavy breathing], what color panties you wearing right now [groan]?' 'Get this cockroach out of my closet!' 'I want you to kill that good-for-nothing housewife next door for me.' ...That kind of thing."

A wave of hopelessness crashed over Rentaro. *What do people think civsec officers do all day, anyway?*

"Okay, well, do we have any other way to make money?"

"You could always work at the gay bar on the first floor, Satomi. They said they'd start you at 8,000 yen an hour."

"Why don't *you* work at the cabaret on the second floor, Kisara? They said they'd give *you* 10,000!"

"......"

Between the yakuza on the fourth floor, the den mother running the cabaret on the second, and the strapping lads behind the bar on the first, there was something about the Happy Building that kept its tenants either slaphappy or trigger-happy all the year through. Rentaro, given the choice, preferred not to deal with them.

"Still," Enju murmured, her face harboring serious contemplation. "We might not be wrapping up any jobs, but I heard the number of Gastrea sightings is creeping up."

Rentaro nodded at the observation. "Yeah. A little too much, if you ask me."

Whenever a Gastrea was sighted or caught on a security camera, an alert mail was automatically sent to all civsec officers within a ten-kilometer radius. From there, it was an all-out first-come, first-served Gastrea competition. Agencies may have occasionally worked with one another, but generally, whoever struck the killing blow first would get the entire bounty from the government.

That was how civsec agencies kept the books balanced—never receiving formal requests, just hoping the right Gastrea crept along at the right place and time—but the sheer number of incidents lately was getting crazy. The alerts would force Rentaro out of bed in the middle of the night, its shrill, piercing beep even going off during class before summer break began, making his teachers want to stab him.

None of these invaders had triggered a Pandemic yet, thanks to a citizenry well used to evacuation and a herd of civsecs always rushing to the scene in time, but the sheer numbers would put anyone on edge. And to someplace like Tendo Civil Security Agency, getting tossed this way and that by all these alerts and always missing out on the kill by the barest of margins, it was starting to become downright frustrating.

"Is there another Monolith problem, maybe?"

"No way."

Rentaro was quick to reject Kisara's question, but his voice trailing off showed that he wasn't too convinced himself. The previous Third Kanto Battle took place because of a defect in a Monolith, something thought to be impervious to damage. It was a completely avoidable, manmade disaster.

The only sure thing when it came to security was that there was no such thing as a sure thing. It hadn't even been a month since Tokyo Area paid a dear price for failing to realize that.

The eyes of the agency's employees wandered over to the window. On the other side, draped in a dark red, the line of Monoliths stood tall, their tops hidden by a line of clouds.

"This really doesn't taste good…"

Turning back, Rentaro found Tina chewing on the potato, her face puckered. Enju, driven by curiosity, took a bite herself, only to bunch up her face and stick her tongue out.

"Nnh! This isn't cooked all the way through."

"Um, really?" said a confused Kisara.

Enju sighed. "Kisara, you should really have Rentaro teach you how to cook sometime. For real."

The sheltered little rich girl shrugged despondently in response. After a moment, she dejectedly turned her eyes upward.

"Could you?"

"Uh, sure."

With another deep sigh, Kisara dragged her feet over to the reproduction of some Klimt masterpiece across from her ebony-colored desk. Slipping her hand behind it, she took out a thin envelope.

"All right," she said, burying a 10,000-yen note in his hand. "Here. My private stash, if you want to call it that. Go buy something with this. You can have Enju and Tina do the shopping."

The two girls' faces sparkled with joy.

"We'll try to keep it as cheap as possible!" Enju said with a wave as she took Tina out of the office.

The sound of them clanging down the stairs faded away, silence reigning once again. It was half past seven in the evening. The wretched-sounding drone and clicking of the evening cicadas filled up the emptiness, and across from the now deep purple sky, the last weak rays of sunshine were dimly lighting the room. Once the sunlight disappeared for good, a nearly full moon drifted into the heavens, the LED lights bordering the signs beyond the window began to systematically flicker into existence, and the Magata neighborhood found new life as a town of the night.

The moldy smell seeped into the room from somewhere.

"We're alone."

"We are." Rentaro stole a glance at the side of Kisara's face. "And?"

"Hmm?"

"Did you send the girls out shopping because you wanted to talk to me?"

"Well, sort of."

With practiced hands, Kisara untied the apron behind her back and shook her hair a bit. There was the sound of rustling clothes as the apron fell to her feet. She picked it up and, with the echo of her slip-on loafers, walked over and sat on her ebony work desk, a tad forlorn as she looked at Rentaro.

"Listen, Satomi… I've been offered an arranged marriage."

She looked at the surprised Rentaro, then back down at her feet as she began swinging her long, thin legs back and forth.

"It came to me through Shigaki. I told him I didn't want anything like that yet, but he's done a lot for me, so I couldn't just turn him down…"

Through Shigaki, huh…? Having that name brought up left even Rentaro in a weak position. Senichi Shigaki, once a butler at the Tendo residence, was probably approaching fifty-six years old this year. He had known Rentaro and Kisara since back when they lived in the Tendo manor. Even after he retired, he had helped them through all sorts of issues in their lives.

Most important, though, was that (on paper) he was the manager of the Tendo Civil Security Agency, not to mention Rentaro and Kisara's more-or-less legal guardian. They owed him a lot. She couldn't dismiss his offer out of hand.

"But why now?"

Kisara had long been disinherited from the Tendo family will. If she was still considered a Tendo woman, it wouldn't be unusual for her to be forced into a succession of arranged (or even forced) marriage proposals starting at sixteen—a sort of modern human sacrifice still prevalent in Japanese high society. But now that she was de facto not a Tendo, she could no longer effectively function as a tool for a strategic marriage.

What were Shigaki's aims, making a request like that? Kisara seemed to understand Rentaro's doubts, but merely shook her head in response. "I don't know. But you'd know the guy pretty well, Satomi."

"I would?"

Kisara took a piece of paper out from the desk and gave it to Rentaro. The moment he saw it, he felt a jolt of surprise.

"Atsuro Hitsuma…? …Why?"

The headshot, printed upon the fancy cotton paper used for the résumé-like introductory papers, stared blankly in response. He was somewhat oval-faced, wearing silver-framed eyeglasses and projecting an air of intellectual ease.

"We must have both been eleven, right? The last time we saw Hitsuma."

Sliding his eyes down, Rentaro saw that he was a police superintendent, working at Tokyo's metropolitan police department after passing the civil-servant exam. His whole family was in law enforcement, his father the commissioner of the entire force. A brilliant record, all written down in elegant block-style lettering.

He seemed like the embodiment of the perfect man—tall, handsome, highly educated, well paid. But before any of that…he used to be Kisara's fiancé, too.

"I thought the whole thing was broken off after you left the family, Kisara."

"I know. So did I. What could Shigaki be thinking at this point…?"

Rentaro could feel something spread out from his chest—something he couldn't describe, but wanted none of. He didn't want to hear anything else from her—for some reason, he was seized by an impulse to get up and walk out of the room immediately. But instead he silently handed the résumé back to Kisara, acting like it was nothing.

"So when're you gonna meet him?"

"…Tomorrow."

"Tomorrow?"

Which meant the proposal must've come a long time ago.

"So you've already agreed to meet, or…?"

Kisara twirled her hair around her finger as she averted her eyes. "I wasn't trying to hide it or anything. It was just kind of hard for me to say it…so I wound up dragging it out all the way to today."

Rentaro realized he had been unconsciously clenching his fists so hard that he could feel his nails against his skin. Kisara lifted her head.

"I want you to be there for me, Satomi. As my attendant."

"…What do you mean?"

"Hitsuma is going to have his mother and father as attendants, and Shigaki was going to act as both my manager and attendant, but I still need someone else. I don't really have anyone to ask besides you, so… Please. I know this is unusual, but would you mind accompanying me to the meeting?"

"……Fine by me."

"Really? Good."

The beauty in black breathed a sigh of relief, but still anxiously darted her eyes back toward Rentaro.

"What do you think, Satomi?"

"What…?"

"Are you, like, against it?"

Of course he was. Just imagining Kisara being held in the arms of another man made him feel sick to his stomach.

But Rentaro knew well enough by now. This was Kisara Tendo. A proper girl, from a proper family. The class system may have disappeared from modern Japanese society long ago, but among super-rich families like the Tendos, things hadn't changed much.

If she was a Tendo girl, it was only common sense that she would marry the scion of another suitably wealthy family. The idea of her running off with some stray dog instead was preposterous. Ever since it was founded, the Tendo family had never allowed a single exception to this ironclad rule.

Practically speaking, Kisara should never have even exchanged words with the mere adopted child she shared a home with—nor had any other personal connection, for the rest of either of their lives.

That was something the Tendo private tutor imprinted deep into Rentaro's mind from the moment he was taken in, almost to the point

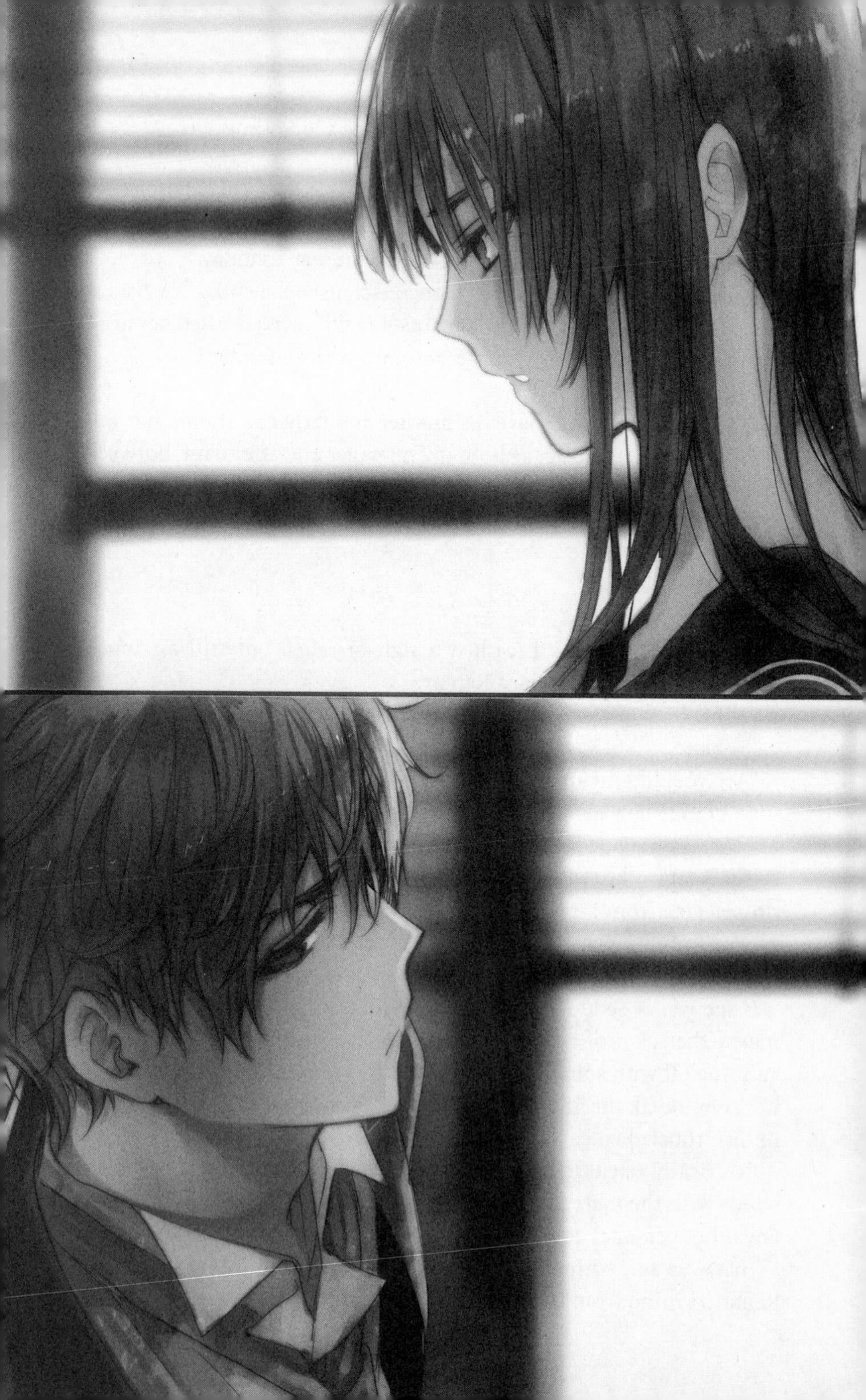

of brainwashing. "*Listen,*" she would say. "*Tendos aren't like regular people. Don't you dare catch yourself acting like you're one of them.*"

"...I think it'd be a good match. If it works out okay and you wind up being happy with it, I bet Enju and Tina would love that."

"You, too, Satomi?"

Light reflected from a passing car's high beams streaked across the room for an instant, bathing Rentaro's and Kisara's heads in white light. He looked up, straight at Kisara.

"Of course."

For some reason, the reply made Kisara lower her head, her face like a wounded animal. After a moment, she forced a smile, trying her best to bottle it up.

"Yeah...I guess so. It's not like we were ever exactly a pair or anything, besides. I'm acting pretty stupid, aren't I?"

She gave herself a light bop on the head and stuck out her tongue, determined to laugh it all away.

That was the last straw.

"Hey, I'm gonna go look for Enju and Tina. I'm kinda worried about them."

Rentaro turned around as he finished, going through the office door before he could hear whatever Kisara said in response.

As he quickly descended the staircase, trying his hardest to leave the Happy Building as fast as humanly possible, he felt a small jolt in his right shoulder. His mind was so occupied with Kisara that it took him a beat before he realized who he had bumped into.

"Hey! Hey, is that you, Rentaro?"

He looked up in surprise to find the face of a man, one who had only just begun to climb the building's stairs. Traces of happiness streaked across that face. He was young, maybe about Rentaro's age. His face was long, his brow broad, and his hair a shade between brown and orange. His pointed gaze gave him the look of a street thug, but something about his smile made him seem oddly charming when he flashed it.

Rentaro combed his memory—he looked familiar to him. The man before him began to overlap with the face of a boy from his memory. He let out a yelp.

"Wait, are you Suibara? Kihachi Suibara, year four, class five, seat ten?"

That was apparently the right answer. The man gave him a broad grin and stuffed his hands into his jeans. "Yuh-huh...Rentaro Satomi, year four, class five, seat nine..." Before he could finish saying it, Suibara's arms were around Rentaro. "Damn, it's been *years*!" he exclaimed. "Hope you've been doing good, you bastard!"

"Y-yeah, you, too."

Rentaro's vision lurched to and fro as this unexpected old friend jostled him in his arms. But instead of enjoying this almost too-perfect chance encounter, another sensation made the hairs on his neck stand on end.

He looked up at the roof of the building in front of him. "But, Suibara, what are you doing here? You haven't started cruising cabarets or gay bars at age sixteen or anything, right...?" He noticed the Rolex on Suibara's wrist as he spoke. "And I guess you aren't poor enough that you're borrowing money from the yakuza, either."

"Of *course* not, you dumbass," an astonished Suibara replied, eyes half-closed.

"So—"

Suibara thrust a thumb toward his face.

"You guessed it! I'm here to visit the Tendo Civil Security Agency. I'm a client, Rentaro."

—*A client?* This childhood friend that he hadn't spoken to in years was a *client*? Between this and Hitsuma's name coming up a moment ago, a lot of old friends were popping up in the oddest of places.

Suibara shrugged at the notably bewildered Rentaro. "Well, we ain't just gonna stand by the stairs here, are we? Show me where your company is!"

"Um..."

Rentaro hesitated. He had just half-forcibly ended a conversation with Kisara and all but sprinted out of the office. Something told him trudging back up wasn't a good idea right now.

He shook his head. *No. I gotta get this client back to our place. Why am I acting so guilty about this?*

Leading the way for Suibara, Rentaro stood before the Tendo office door. It was already dark out, but there was no sign of a light inside. Pushing the door open, he saw Kisara sitting in her office chair, staring forlornly out the window. Once she noticed them, she shot back to her feet and bounded up to them.

"Oh, good, Satomi," she gasped. "I was thinking about some stuff just now, and—!" She stopped abruptly, presumably noticing Suibara behind him.

Rentaro could barely stand the awkwardness of it all, but kept it off his face. "I got a client," he whispered.

Kisara, looking happy about something else up to now, froze. She hung her head back down, as if heartbroken.

"Oh..."

What the hell? Rentaro thought. *A few hours ago, you were practically pleading for a client to come in through the door.*

Suibara hurriedly intervened. "Um, I'm sorry, did I come at a bad time or something?"

Kisara shook her head before Rentaro could open his mouth. "No, not at all. Good evening. My name's Kisara Tendo, and I'm the president." With a shallow smile, she extended a hand. Suibara, a surprised look on his face, gingerly accepted.

"Uh, hello. I'm Kihachi Suibara."

"Come on in. It's kind of dirty, I know, but..." Kisara pushed a button on the remote she had stationed on the desk. Dazzling light poured from the ceiling, making Rentaro instinctively squint.

Pictures drawn by Enju and Tina were strewn around the room, and the would-be dinner of sweet potatoes and nothing else was still laid out on the table. Kisara's show of humility was clearly anything but a show as the full state of the office came into view.

"I'm sorry. I'll clean this up in a sec..."

"Oh! No, actually, about that..." Suibara paused a moment before continuing. "I'd prefer to talk to Rentaro alone about this job, actually. Sorry if that's weird..."

Rentaro and Kisara exchanged glances, and he silently signaled her to leave. The request seemed baffling to him, but he could hardly turn this guy down now. He gave an affirmative nod to Suibara, who nodded back in agreement.

"All right. I'll go look after Enju and Tina, then."

"Sure. Thanks."

Once he was sure Kisara was out of sight downstairs, Rentaro cleared the dishes and sat across the table from Suibara. The young man propped his arms on top of the backrest, clearly at ease.

"That's Kisara Tendo, huh? Man, you were head over heels for her back when we were all kids, weren't you? She's gotten *dang* pretty since then. That's the most beautiful girl I ever saw in my life, even."

Rentaro silently agreed. Between his encounters with people like Miori Shiba and the Seitenshi herself, he had run into a lot of women with sirenlike beauty. They had lived long enough together that it would occasionally slip his mind, but to Rentaro, the sight of Kisara side by side with Miori or standing alongside the Seitenshi was always such an embarrassment of riches for him that it'd often take his breath away. And now this beauty was going to discuss a marriage proposal with Atsuro Hitsuma tomorrow. Rentaro shook his head to clear his mind of the distractions plaguing it.

"So, what did you need?"

Suibara studied the office around him like a curious archaeologist. "Oh! So, hey, do you remember how it was when we first met?"

"Hmm? Yeah, I do…"

If he closed his eyes, he could instantly transport his mind back to the fourth year of elementary school. It was four years after Rentaro lost his right arm, his right leg, and his eye. Because he was still growing, he had to have his artificial limbs replaced frequently. The continual pain he experienced each day made him want to die at times.

The way he could hide his metal skin under an artificial human epidermis was a fairly recent invention in the grand scheme of things. In his younger years, during school and for every other hour of the day and night, Rentaro had to live with a pair of dull, black prosthetic limbs for all the world to see.

"Nobody wanted to come near me. They were all freaked out by this weird black arm and leg I had. But you weren't. I think the rest of the class shunned you, too, right? Because there was one of the Cursed Children in your family."

"Yeah. My little sister."

The story of Suibara and his sister ultimately fell down a tragic path. Once the child's presence was known to the general public, a lot of people naturally began to have a problem with that.

Their mother was the first family member to let it all break her down—the stones her neighbors lobbed through the windows, the filthy diatribes spray-painted on the fence. "*If only* she *wasn't here*," she'd whisper to herself over and over like a woman possessed—and, unfortunately, Suibara's father kept a pistol inside a locker at their home for self-defense. Everything was in place for a tragedy.

"We were together in our loneliness," Rentaro said in profound tones. "That's why we started hanging out and playing with each other."

"Yeah!" Suibara excitedly added. "You knew a ton about stuff like fish and bugs, and we'd go running around the hills and stuff. That was *so* much fun! It's like just being with you helped me learn all kinds of things, y'know? Like how to catch crayfish with a string, or how to mount an insect specimen."

His words were all it took to jog his memory. Soon they were sprung to life by the dozen, as if bursting out of a giant toy box. Back when he had no friends and couldn't even leave the house freely, Rentaro would hole up in the Tendo family library and spend the entire day poring over full-color insect field guides and plant references. After a while, there was no one who could even hope to challenge his knowledge.

"Yeah, and I learned how to trash talk from you, didn't I?"

Suibara beamed. "Yeah, I remember how you were all 'to-*mah*-to' when we first met."

Rentaro turned away, cheeks red with embarrassment.

"Ah, shut up. Kisara was really sad once you started rubbing off on me, y'know. She was like, 'Satomi's talking like this criminal now!'"

"Oh, don't give me that crap! Who's the guy who started imitating me in the first place?"

"Ah, eat shit and die."

"You first!"

Once their eyes met again, Rentaro and Suibara grinned at each other.

"Rentaro," Suibara said, leaning forward on his sofa deep in thought and lowering his eyes down to his clasped hands. "It probably wouldn't be fair if I didn't show this to you first."

The item he took out from a side pocket made Rentaro gasp. It was a black chunk of metal that made a *clink* when he put it on the glass table. He spotted a trigger attached to the dull matte-black frame. It was a sixth-generation Glock pistol, one where even the slide was made of a glass-fiber reinforced polymer to reduce the gun's weight.

Why? was the first question that came to mind. The general public still wasn't allowed to carry concealed weapons outside their homes. According to the laws of Japan in 2031, there were three types of people allowed to walk around armed in public: the police, members of the self-defense force, and—

Suibara placed something else from his pocket on the gun: a synthetic leather rail-pass holder. Seeing the civsec license inside, complete with ID photo, gave Rentaro the biggest shock of the evening.

"Suibara, you're a civsec?"

Suibara, grinning, tapped a few buttons on the cell phone in his pocket and showed it to him. The screen showed a photo of a girl, her hair done up in a bob cut, her averted eyes indicating she didn't enjoy having her picture taken very much.

"Whoa, did you...?"

Failing to notice Rentaro's astonishment, Suibara soldiered proudly on. "That's my Initiator. Her name's Hotaru Kouro, and, *man*, is she a cutie, am I right? I mean, my grandma used to say, 'You're so sweet, I could just eat you up,' but now I think I get what she was talking—"

"Stop."

Rentaro, his mind still a jumble, just barely managed to get the syllable out. Suibara's sister was one of the Cursed Children. It had wrecked the entire family. The idea of him teaming up with *another* one of them and working the civsec beat was hard for Rentaro to swallow. What's more, this job meant that he was all but completely dependent on his Initiator if he wanted to stay alive. It had to be a bitter pill.

"Is she...taking the place of your dead sister for you?"

The quiet question made Suibara peevishly turn his face away. "Nothing like that, no. What's the big deal?" Then, after a moment's pause, he placed an elbow on the table and rested his chin above it. "You wanna hear about this job for you, or what?"

Rentaro thought about that. A civsec hiring another civsec—subcontracting work, in other words—generally meant the client had a job that was too much work for him to handle alone. That often meant whoever he hired would get the short end of the stick paywise. But despite knowing that bit of conventional wisdom, something still told Rentaro there wasn't anything conventional at all about Suibara's job.

"Lay it on me."

"Now we're talking," Suibara replied. But what he had for Rentaro next was a complete reversal of his light, friendly tone.

"So, Rentaro, like... You were the last guinea pig for the Ground Self-Defense Force's enhanced-soldier project, right?"

This shock was enough to send Rentaro back to his feet.

Why did *he* know that? Maybe Suibara could surmise that Rentaro's artificial limbs were black because they were made out of Varanium, but there was no possible way he could've connected that with the so-called New Humanity Creation Project.

"Bingo, huh?" Suibara murmured as he glanced sidelong at the stunned, wide-eyed Rentaro. But there was something close to regret on his face, like he'd just realized he was right when he had wanted to be wrong.

"So look, Rentaro, I picked up on some *serious* shit earlier. Have you ever heard of the New World Creation Project or the Black Swan Project? Either of those names, at least?"

"New World... Black Swan Project? ...No."

The "New World" Creation Project? What's that? It sounded too close to the "New Humanity" Creation Project.

An ominous premonition started to build in Rentaro's spine.

"Okay," Suibara muttered in reply. Then he fell silent for a few moments, staring at the glass ashtray on the table. Rentaro waited patiently for him to go on.

"Well...I don't know how much you're aware of this, Rentaro, but among us civsec folk, you're the subject of a lotta rumors. You were raised by the Tendo family, and I've heard that you got personal connections with Lady Seitenshi." He paused, face turned upward. "So that's what I'm here for. I want you to get me connected with the Tendo Group or Lady Seitenshi. I don't care what it takes; I gotta get a person-to-person audience with either her or her aide, Kikunojo Tendo. We're talking serious crisis mode for all of Tokyo Area, you know what I mean?"

"Is that connected to the projects you just mentioned?"

"Yeah."

"There's no other middleman you can go through besides me?"

"No. If I try that, there's no telling where *they'll* hear about it."

"Are you trying to blow the whistle about something? 'Cause if you have any evidence you can give me, I can make sure it gets to her."

"...I'm sorry. My evidence got stolen."

"Stolen?"

Suibara nodded grimly.

"My place has been broken into a few times lately. A few things were stolen, including the evidence. The only option I got left is to appeal directly to the Tendo Group or Lady Seitenshi as a living witness. I mean, you're about the only guy left I can trust."

This was no longer a friendly chat between old friends. Rentaro rubbed his fingers against his chin.

He had no particular vendetta against Suibara, of course. He'd like to help make that request happen, as much as he was able. The problem was how. Not only was he no longer technically related to Kikunojo; they hadn't spoken a word to each other since their some-what...strained conversation after the Kagetane Hiruko case. He doubted Kikunojo wanted to see him much, and the feeling was abso-lutely mutual.

But the Seitenshi? He literally had her digits. *That* connection, at least, seemed plausible enough.

"Let me float up one condition. I want you to tell me beforehand what you'd say to Lady Seitenshi."

"Aw, c'mon, you don't trust me?"

"We're talking about the head of state, Suibara. I gotta be careful."

"...Yeah, I guess so, huh?"

Suibara seemed open to concessions. But then he looked around the office, his body language betraying his uneasiness.

"...Hey, this room ain't bugged or anything, is it?"

"Huh?"

"You know, bugged. Like, do you trust the guys who live above and below you?"

"Man, who knows?"

Rentaro's eyes followed his conversation partner's around the room. The floor and ceiling were surprisingly thin in this building. Sound had a way of traveling around. The walls were plain mortar, too, and it wasn't exactly a wide margin between this building and the adja-cent one.

In a rickety old dump like this, soundproofing would never be a priority. If someone had any sort of decent-grade listening device or parabolic microphone, Suibara's right to client confidentiality would be worth about as much as a sheet of toilet paper.

"Okay," Suibara said. "Not here, then. Tomorrow night… You know where they're building the new Magata City Hall, right? Let's meet there. But lemme make sure we're straight on one thing: Once I tell you, you're *in*, got it?"

The earnest truthfulness Rentaro saw in Suibara's eyes made him shudder.

After proposing an exorbitant sum of money for Rentaro's services, Suibara stood up from the sofa and prepared to leave. Rentaro stood up to see him off, and they chatted about assorted silly little things on the way downstairs.

It was completely dark outside, with women plying their trade and groups of drunken businessmen mingling on the congested city streets. The wind that beat against Rentaro's skin bore the lukewarm heat of an August night.

Right in front of them, Enju, Tina, and Kisara had returned, their arms laden with well-stuffed shopping bags. They were excitedly laughing and poking at one another as they meandered along, apparently enjoying their night out to the fullest as the streetlights lit them from behind.

Suibara squinted, as if looking at a bright light, then slapped Rentaro heartily on the back. "Rentaro, I'm pretty sure *they* think you're involved with me by now. Sorry I got you involved in this, but watch out, okay?"

"They?"

Suibara thrust both hands into his pockets and set off without another glance.

Watching him go, Rentaro realized that he still couldn't figure out how to parse this within himself—this old friend he just reunited with after so many years. He could practically see lines of depression emanate from Suibara's back. If this secret of his had to do with that, he would be fine with trying to get it out of him so that they could shoulder the burden equally.

Suibara tried to forget about his sister as soon as he could, way back when. Seeing him involved so deeply with the Cursed Children now was nothing less than astounding. Rentaro didn't know what changed his mind about it all, but the Initiator taking the place of his sister... How did *she* feel about it?

Either way, there were several terms Suibara bandied around that Rentaro could never let go unexamined. There was time until tomorrow night. He had some avenues he could research.

"Mm? Did our client leave?"

Looking down, Enju was right next to him, grinning from ear to ear as she held up the spoils of her big night out.

"Look! We picked up all kinds of meats and vegetables on the pre-closing sales. Tonight we're gonna have a *yakiniku* party with Kisara's secret stash!"

Turning his eye toward Kisara, Rentaro realized she was sizing him up at the same time. They turned their eyes elsewhere with near-perfect timing.

Straining to keep the awkwardness from showing up on his face, Rentaro flashed Enju a smile. "Sorry, Enju, but I'm not hungry. You three can eat by yourselves."

"Ehh?"

Enju's expression froze. Gradually, it began to grow anxious.

"Why...is that?"

"Oh, no reason. It's no big deal if a guy wants to eat by himself now and then, is it?"

With that, Rentaro turned around and walked off, making sure he didn't accidentally catch a glimpse of Kisara's facial expression as he did.

3

The hollow bamboo tube, its head heavy with water accumulated inside, had its tail end struck against a nearby boulder. It was a *shishi-odoshi*, a traditional Japanese contrivance meant for scaring birds away from gardens, and the sharp *clack* it made could be heard from the balcony above.

A beautiful sound, Kisara thought. Compared to that, the clamor from the equally traditional room she was sitting in, lined with tatami mats, was hard for her to stomach.

"...And so, while our child was quite the handful back during his more rebellious years, he ultimately decided to follow the same path his father did a generation ago. In fact, at the police academy he's head of the class—in the schoolroom, and out in the training grounds."

"Hey! You don't have to embarrass me like that."

"...Ha-ha-ha! Ah, how wonderful. Almost too good of a match for my Kisara here."

The middle-aged man at the head of the table, mouth wide open in a hearty laugh, was face-to-face with Tadashi Hitsuma, police commissioner, the scar across his face giving him a decidedly gangster look. By his side was his wife, sporting a pair of horn-rimmed glasses. She raised a hand to her mouth as she tittered in agreement:

"Oh, no, not at all," she said. "Your young Tendo is as beautiful as a porcelain doll! Why, our Atsuro told me it was love at first sight!"

There wasn't a girl on earth who really liked being called "beautiful" by a stranger, but considering how much of a farce this was, Kisara doubted even less that she could take the compliment at face value.

Kisara herself was currently ensconced inside Utoro, an impossibly fancy Japanese restaurant. Including her, there were six people seated around the table, participating in this *omiai*—an arranged-marriage meeting. Only about half of these six were active in the conversation, however. Rentaro, next to Kisara in his typical school uniform, sat there silently, his face inscrutable.

When she first brought up the engagement offer with Rentaro, Kisara honestly thought he'd explode in anger. That was why seeing him give such a blithe *okay* disappointed her—and enraged her. She was hoping Rentaro would stand up right now and do something to ruin the proceedings for her.

But why? She darted her eyes around the room as she pondered this, eventually settling on a mirror hung next to a wall scroll, the frame demonstrating the elegantly sculpted work of an artisan. She craned her neck to get a view of herself, only to find a Kisara done up in lipstick, blush, an elaborate hairpin, and a kimono, of all things. She was passing acquaintances with the daughter of Shiba Heavy Weapons' president, a lover of traditional Japanese clothing, and while she was reluctant to go near one at first, she had to admit—it suited her well, sitting here.

She adjusted her head in the mirror, wondering how she'd look at a forty-five-degree semi-profile. But as she did, she sensed someone's eye on her and turned around.

It was the bespectacled man sitting face-to-face with her, smiling warmly. It made her cheeks redden. She hurriedly returned to her original posture.

There was one other person in the audience left to describe. He was slender, even more so than in his picture; he hardly ever spoke at all; and he was more than a little handsome: Atsuro Hitsuma. He was seated in a formal kneeling position, the family crest clearly visible on his own traditional clothing. He had grown in the past five years, and it gave him a touch of masculinity that wasn't there before.

"Right," said his mother. "How about us old fuddy-duddies leave the room and let these two lovebirds talk to each other?" She stood up before anyone could respond.

"Oh, what, I gotta leave, too?"

"Of course you do, you fool," Senichi Shigaki said, pulling Rentaro up. "Come over here." The Hitsuma parents followed them, pulling the sliding screen open and leaving the room.

The only thing that remained was silence. Kisara emitted a light sigh as Hitsuma politely lowered his head.

"I apologize," he said. "My parents are getting carried away."

"It's been a long time, hasn't it, Mr. Hitsuma?"

"Yes. Five years, I suppose?"

Kisara had trouble figuring out how to interact with the man in front of her. She found it honestly bewildering.

"Um… So you got promoted to police superintendent?"

"Ha-ha! Yeah, the last time we met, I had just joined the force, hadn't I? I hardly knew right from left back then. Now, five years on… Well, really, I mean, look at *you*. You're a completely different person from five years ago. I still thought you were cute in a kidlike way back then, but now there's no doubt about it. You're beautiful."

"Oh, stop flattering me, Mr. Hitsuma!" She meant it, too. Kisara looked down, cheeks blushing. "But…why now, though? Out of the blue…?"

"What do you mean?" he replied, smiling graciously at Kisara. It made her feel a bit guilty as she went on.

"I mean that I feel bad for you, Mr. Hitsuma. I disowned the Tendo family by my own free will. That's why you received the cancellation notice that you did. So...and I'm sure you know this already, but...I don't think marrying me will help you make any inroads with the Tendo family. I'm fully separate from them now. They treat me pretty much like they've disinherited me. I still go by the name Tendo, but I don't feel that I'm a Tendo at all. Not one bit."

If Kisara had it her way, she'd have all the Tendo blood flowing within her drained from her body and replaced with someone else's. She opted against sharing that little tidbit out loud.

"Well, it's not that I made this request to Mr. Shigaki because I wanted to build a connection with the Tendo family."

"So why did you, then? Your dad's police commissioner; you're already a superintendent yourself... I'm sure you'd have no problem attracting attention."

"Is being taken with you at first sight a good enough reason?"

Kisara blushed and turned her face away at this unexpected attack.

"Oh, stop joking."

"I didn't mean it as a joke."

"That makes it even worse... You're embarrassing me."

She was willing to hear out Hitsuma's sweet nothings, but a darker voice was making itself known in her heart. There was a time when even Kisara believed in Cinderella. That dream she had, of some Prince Charming falling in love with her and saving her from disaster, disappeared from her life the day her parents were killed by being eaten alive. If there really was a prince or a wizard or whatever out there, she'd want him to resurrect her parents right this minute, not marry her.

Kisara urged herself to press on as she adjusted her posture. Then she decided to change strategies. She was getting sick of this whole arranged-marriage system—trying to make yourself out to be perfect while watching your partner like a hawk for any imperfections. It was time to buck the system.

"The whole reason I'm alive is so I can take revenge on the Tendos."

"I know."

"What?" Kisara heard the *shishi-odoshi* clack against the rock behind her.

"Of course. I'm fully aware of your circumstances, Ms. Tendo."

"And you went through with this proposal anyway?"

"Yes. In fact, I think I might just be able to help you on that particular matter."

"...Um, how so?"

Hitsuma briskly stood up from the table, a smile crossing his intellectual demeanor as he pointed outside.

"Would you like to go for a walk while we discuss it?"

Kisara nodded. It was the only thing she could do.

The pair left the room, walking around the perimeter of a gravel-floored garden. A small pond lay in the middle of it, with an arched, bright red footbridge decorated with ornate, knob-topped guardrails crossing it. Kisara sprinkled some dry food from the bridge, marveling at the dazzling colors of the Japanese koi fish that gathered to lap it up.

"So...?" Kisara began, not trying to sound too keen lest he was simply taking her for a ride.

"I...will omit the details for now, Ms. Tendo, but we in the Hitsuma family do not have exactly a cozy relationship with the Tendos either."

Kisara's eyebrows twitched. "That's playing with fire, you know," she said, eyes still focused on the koi she was feeding. "The Tendo clan is filled with financial giants. They train their kin from infancy to become full-fledged members of the political elite. Trying to resist them is like trying to resist the government itself. They would raze your family to the ground, just like all the other people who faded into darkness after opposing them."

"I imagine they would, yes, if we took a full-frontal approach. But even the most heavily guarded of fortresses can be conquered, if you just know which untended back door to strike at first. Someone like you, attempting to eradicate Kikunojo Tendo and his allies from the face of the earth, should know that all too well."

A koi leaped out of the water with a splash.

"...How much do you know?"

"Just what I've picked up through the grapevine."

Kisara turned around and looked at Hitsuma. "Well, I'm glad you're offering to help me, but this is my battle to wage. I'm not interested in having other people use me."

"But you may feel free to use me all you like. I will not use you at all."

This made Kisara's brows furrow. "You're starting to creep me out. What do you want from me? Just come out with it."

Hitsuma put a hand to his chin, as if pondering over something. "All right," he said. "Let me rephrase that, then. There *is* something I want from you." Then he suddenly wrapped his arm around Kisara's waist, holding her hand with his own. The presence of such a comely man at close range made Kisara's heart skip a beat.

"You've been making me go crazy, and it's thanks to your beauty. If I ever do anything to make you dislike me, then by all means, take up your sword. But if not…"

Hitsuma brought his face closer to hers. Kisara turned her red cheeks away.

"You've been reading too much Shakespeare."

"I mean it."

It was a surprise to her, this man's passion all but forcing her into his embrace. *Satomi would never do anything like this for me*, she thought.

Searching around in his pocket, Hitsuma took something out and placed it in Kisara's hand. Startled by the feel of cold metal, she looked down to find a disc-shaped object shining a golden hue in the reflected sunlight.

"What's this?"

"A pocket watch. Open it up."

Following his suggestion, Kisara lifted the watch's golden lid. Her mouth opened a little in surprise. The hour and minute hands were also done up in gold, and the fancy-looking clock face was lined with jewels, dazzling her with a flood of color.

"This is so nice. Is it for me?"

"I'd be glad if you took it. It won't go to waste that way."

She was about to say thanks, but swallowed the word after realizing something. "But," she said, "our old engagement was canceled."

"That doesn't matter. I love you."

"…If I had someone like you whispering about love into my ear, maybe I'd start looking for a pair of glass slippers before long."

"Would you like to try?"

Kisara watched as Hitsuma's lips advanced upon her. Then she closed her eyes.

*   *   *

Neither the beautiful white sand that extended out toward the right-hand side of the Japanese garden nor the sublime ephemerals of the rock garden's dry landscape were enough to brighten Rentaro's heart by now. He was walking down the wooden platform that lined the garden, in search of a bathroom as the anxiety began to well in his mind.

What is Kisara's problem, anyway? Getting all dolled up and putting on that nice kimono for his sake. She doesn't have to act all preoccupied about how she looks. Around me, it's been the exact same black school outfit, 365 days a year.

The gloominess in Rentaro's heart had, if anything, only been magnified by the five years that had passed since he last saw Hitsuma. He was, after all, the first real love interest in Kisara Tendo's life—and the worst part was that she probably didn't even realize it. He thought his shallow memories of that time would drift away over the years, but now that he saw Kisara dressed in her finest and discussing marriage like this, he wasn't so sure that would ever happen.

"Listen… Tendos aren't like regular people. Don't you dare catch yourself acting like you're one of them."

What do I want Kisara to do here? Do I…?

Just as he rounded a corner of the walkway, staring at the garden for lack of anything better to focus on, Rentaro stopped. Kisara and Hitsuma were talking on the arched bridge. He couldn't hear what they were saying from his vantage point, but if Rentaro's eyes weren't deceiving him, they looked like they were enjoying themselves.

"…!"

Then Hitsuma brought her close, his lips approaching her face. The two silhouettes overlapped.

Rentaro's body tensed up, as if struck by lightning. Sweat ran from every pore in his body. Then he turned around on the spot and swiftly walked out of the restaurant.

As Hitsuma's face dominated the entirety of her vision, Kisara closed her eyes. But, the moment before their lips met, Kisara brought her palm between them like a partitioning board, pushing him away with the other hand. ·

"...For now," she said, "let go of me." She was freed without complaint.

Kisara adjusted the neck of her kimono in order to focus attention away from her flushed cheeks.

"So is that how it is? You don't mind if I use anything of yours that I find useful, and in exchange for that, you want me?"

"You can feel free to see it that way, yes."

Kisara mulled this over silently as she pretended to adjust her wardrobe. No matter what she decided to do, her life was worth about as much as a pebble on the side of the road. All she had to do was make sure she kept it intact until the remaining four Tendos were slain. And being lucky enough to be born with this beauty, being able to use it as a bargaining chip for her aims—who could ask for anything more?

It's a matter of using, and being used. As simple a relationship as that. I might even find myself liking Hitsuma before long.

A prickly sensation ran across Kisara's chest.

...Wait a minute. Is this what love and romance is?

4

"So you saw Kisara get all kissy-kissy and that pissed you off so much that you ran away from her?"

Sumire Muroto, head of the Magata University forensics research lab, stared at Rentaro with a look of pure glee on her face.

"It's, it's not like *that*, or anything..."

"The way you look, you're not exactly convincing me otherwise."

Rentaro remembered that he was currently head down on the desk. He sheepishly sat back up and looked distractedly at the bare light bulb illuminating the basement room.

He liked visiting the forensics lab at times like these. It was his way of appealing for divine aid—or, in Sumire's case, demented aid. Someone older and more experienced was a treasure to have right now. Rentaro failed to sleep a wink the previous night. The whole thing with Suibara played a role in that, but to be wholly honest with himself, he was agonizing over Kisara's arranged marriage. He decided to give Sumire the whole story because he was certain she'd have just the right piece of advice to cut through this crisis. Right now, he was being disappointed.

"Well, forget it. Just give it up. The fact that a prime piece of land like Kisara hasn't been snapped up yet is a miracle in itself. She just found the right buyer, is all."

Rentaro grimaced. "Jeez, Doctor... I thought you were rooting for the two of us."

"What, are you kidding me? I'm just trying to stir the pot a little, 'cause if I didn't, nothing would change until you both had one foot in the grave. In fact, if things start working out between you two, I'd start sabotaging it for fun."

"Awful. Just absolutely awful."

"Though actually, I was *really* hoping you'd finally let your hormones get the best of you and just push her down. Think about the headlines you'd make once the police caught you!"

"Why would the *police* get involved?"

"You think you'll ever bag Kisara any other way?"

Rentaro snorted in disgust as Sumire pulled up a chair facing him, waving a hand in front of his eyes.

"Just knock it off, okay? Knock it off. I know you're thinking about some hanky-panky with Kisara and maybe marriage in the future, but why do you think marriage is such a good thing anyway? Lemme give you a little lecture on how men and women work. Men, you know...they have to put up with women nagging them to no end until it drives them insane. They give up on their dreams, and they have to resist the urge to stare at every big-titted bimbo they see on the way home from work. And women, too—they have to deal with men's crazed fetishes; they have to cook and dress in a way that pleases them; they give up their entire bodies to them! It's just a constant string of sacrifices for them both. Men, at the core, really hate women, and women, at the core, really hate men."

"So why do people get married, then?"

"'We all need the eggs,' as Woody Allen put it."

"What's that mean?"

"Eesh. Look, Rentaro, could you at least *try* to make an effort to think a little? People in ancient times thought that brains were used for nothing but creating the snot out of your nose, but you're not using *your* brain for too much apart from that, are you? Your whole existence is a tragedy. I'm a nihilist, remember? Just take the nihilism out of my advice if you don't like it."

"What'd even be left?"

"Men, at the core, love women, and women, at their core, love men. Don't tell me you don't even get *that*."

Rentaro froze, as if bewitched. It was impossible to tell where the jokes ended and real talk began with Sumire. She stood up and turned her back to him, no doubt off to whip up another batch of coffee. Rentaro stared at the back of her oversize lab coat and resolved to bring up another topic close to his heart.

"Doctor, have you ever heard of something called the Black Swan Project?"

"No, I haven't," Sumire said as she filled a kettle with water and pushed the ON button within her induction cooker. "However," she added, "if they named it 'Black Swan,' it might have something to do with the black swan theory."

"The black swan theory?"

Sumire measured out a suitable amount of instant coffee from the can. "Swans, you know," she began, "are supposed to be all white in color, but then they found a population of black swans in Australia. It turned the world of ornithology upside down back in the day. The entire world ran on this assumption that swans were supposed to be white, so nobody was ever able to predict that black swans would ever be a thing, too.

"So the 'black swan theory' is where you build long-term predictions while bound by your current state of comprehension, but thereby fail to account for unpredictable events even after they happen. It can cause all sorts of damage if you're not careful. There's no such thing as absolutes in this world—life's full of uncertainties. Making predictions as if these uncertainties are ironclad facts always costs you in the long run.

"You could kind of see this theory as a warning to the human species, and how their minds work. If you've had ten years straight of bountiful harvests, you'd never imagine that a flood would ravage your farmland tomorrow, right? Or maybe crises that theoretically shouldn't occur for millennia keep taking place every few decades, or an unexpectedly huge earthquake causes a meltdown at a nuclear power plant, or—"

"—Or a pack of virus-infected parasites appears and tries to destroy the human race?"

Sumire grinned. "That's exactly it. Glad to see you're quick on the pickup, at least."

Rentaro turned his eyes toward his hands. The "Black Swan Project"—something about the name disturbed him. He was already starting to regret what he'd said before. Perhaps the situation Suibara fell into was a lot more dangerous than he thought. Perhaps he should've forced the whole story out of him at the office.

He checked the clock. There was still a fair amount of time until their meet up.

"There's something else, too, Doctor. The 'New World Creation Project'—does that ring any bells?"

Sumire swung around, surprised. Judging by the reaction, Rentaro knew he hit the nail on the head. The eerie resemblance between "New World Creation Project" and "New Humanity Creation Project" was something that stuck out in his mind from the moment Suibara uttered the term.

The kettle began to emit a shrill whistle, the lid clattering around on the top.

"Where did you hear that name?"

"A client relayed it to me."

"How much do you know about it?"

"Pretty much nothing. That's why I'm asking you, Doctor."

Suibara had been acting far too jumpy. He had been paranoid about bugging devices and wanted to talk at a separate location. It seemed fair to think that these "New World" and "Black Swan" projects were something dicey enough to put the fear of God in him.

Sumire considered this for a few moments, a thoughtful hand on her chin.

"I think I told you why the New Humanity Creation Project was disbanded."

"Yeah…um, because it cost too much money and stuff."

"Right. The natural-born Children we use cost nothing, but even building one of you took vast sums of money."

Sumire picked up two heat-resistant beakers and filled both to the brim with coffee, staring up and down Rentaro's body as she did.

"You're a ten-billion-yen kid, Rentaro."

Yeah, that'd sure torpedo the project, all right. If it took that much to produce just one soldier, setting up some kind of mass-production system would've been all but impossible.

"But if it weren't for the Children showing up," Sumire continued, "the New Humanity Creation Project was prepared to move on to the next phase. In other words, the New *World* Creation Project. You can basically think of the New World project as the final, complete version of the New Humanity one."

"Complete version…?"

"Right. People like you and Tina and Kagetane Hiruko are walking high-tech marvels—superfibers, replacement organs, metal skin, you name it. The New World Creation Project would've taken that one more step. The aim was to replace at least half the human body with machines. The idea was to eventually work up to replacing the entire body, except for the brain."

"Wait a minute," Rentaro interjected. "You said that the success rate for New Humanity surgeries was pretty low as it was. If you guys tried to replace even more of the body at once…"

Sumire sat back down, looking a bit remorseful as she squinted at the light bulb. "Well," she replied, "there was a nonzero chance of it working. And if there's a nonzero chance, a scientist is always gonna take a crack at it."

"…But you're a doctor first, aren't you? Not a scientist."

"*I* am, yes. But the poison you and I call 'curiosity' works its magic at astonishing speed with people like us. It kills a lot more than just the cat, you know."

Sumire slid one of the beakers Rentaro's way. He picked it up with both hands and stared at the murky black liquid inside, a faint warmth spreading across his palms.

"But what're you talking about, though? The New World Creation Project never took place, then? I heard that name right from the mouth of my client…"

"Yeah, I'm awfully curious about that myself. I was the woman in charge of the New Humanity project, but I never heard anything about the New World one starting up. But...hmm. Maybe it's got to do with *those* murders?"

"Which ones?"

Sumire sat in silent thought for a moment before continuing. "Well," she said, "a man was killed at the New National Theater a bit ago. Kenji Houbara, age thirty-five. An opera aficionado. He was stabbed during a performance. At the same exact time, someone went into the home of Saya Takamura, age twenty-eight, and murdered her with what's believed to be a shotgun. And at the same time as *that*, Giichi Ebihara, age fifty-three, was shot to death by a sniper while on a high-speed train."

"Three murders on the same day...?"

"Yeah. But that's not the point. The point is that all three victims had something in common." Sumire took a sip of coffee, her tone suddenly growing dark and heavy. "Kenji Houbara and Saya Takamura were both surviving soldiers enhanced by the New Humanity Creation Project."

"What?!"

Sumire crossed her legs and tilted her glass again as she glanced at her dumbfounded guest.

"They were both my patients. Let me tell you, I was shocked. I knew them both really well. I was hoping you wouldn't have to know about that—two ex–New Humanity soldiers, hunted down like that... But this was premeditated murder. Both of them saw action in the Gastrea War, unlike you, and they both retired to civilian life after the war because they were sick of fighting."

Rentaro had heard from Sumire earlier that a lot of enhanced soldiers, finding themselves with no place to go, wound up becoming civsec officers like him. Apparently there were exceptions, though. Sumire put her hand back on her chin and stared off into the distance.

"If they wanted peaceful lives for themselves, I welcomed that with open arms. But it looks like there was a snake tempting them. This guy."

Sumire picked up a sheaf of papers from her cluttered desk and tossed it over. An autopsy report, apparently. The first page had Giichi Ebihara's name and profile printed on it.

"Who's he?"

"Someone high up in Public Security."

"Public Security" referred to the Public Security Force, the department that protected the national government from things like radical extremism and international terrorism. Most of their investigative techniques were classified, but word on the street indicated it was akin to a secret police or spy organization.

"Why Public Security?"

"It looks like this Ebihara guy made secret contacts with these two war retirees. He had them do some kind of secret-agent stuff, apparently. I say 'apparently' because now that he's dead, I can't establish what kind of relationship they had. He's the only one who would've known that. I only learned about this because Ebihara's secretary saw him conduct a secret meeting with Houbara in their building. He said that he heard the term 'New World Creation Project' in their conversation, not that he knew what that meant at the time."

"And now all three of them are dead. Which means…?"

"They all knew something they shouldn't have. What, I couldn't say."

Silence descended upon the basement. The humid air lapped against Rentaro's neck as Sumire extended a pale, veiny hand toward another file on her desk.

"By the way, Satomi, have the police visited Tina yet?"

"No…why?"

"Well, I got all curious about these murders, so I had Miori give me some information. There were no witnesses to Kenji Houbara's stabbing at the theater and they couldn't find any fingerprints on the knife, but apparently there was a faintly sweet scent left on the weapon. Saya Takamura was murdered with anti-personnel rounds fired by a twelve-gauge shotgun. No witnesses there, either. As for the train murder, the bullet that killed Ebihara was a powerful type of sniper bullet known as Lapua Magnum. I don't know all that much about guns, but the train would've been running at high speed at the time—200 kilometers an hour or so. Despite that, the sniper made a clean kill through the train window and right through his head. Can you believe that?"

Now Rentaro knew why Tina's name came up.

"Wait a minute, Doctor! Tina's not a murderer!"

"Well, I'd like to believe that, too. But if you whittle down the suspects to the kind of people with superhuman skills like that, Tina's bound to show up on the list sooner or later."

No way. There's no way Tina could do anything like that.

"Lady Seitenshi pulled a lot of strings to keep Tina's punishment down to just probation, but remember, she tried and failed to assassinate our leader. If she racks up any more charges, it's gonna be the firing squad for her."

"...But—all right—even if we assume there's some kind of superhuman hit man group out there, that doesn't necessarily mean they're from the New World Creation Project. If they were, though…like, could I even beat them, being an older type?"

Among Kagetane, Tina, and Aldebaran, Rentaro had a lot of high-profile kills under his belt by now. But he never thought his powers ever gave him an inherent advantage. If anything, he was amazed he always managed to eke out a victory at the very end each time.

Sumire sighed dejectedly, apparently knowing what Rentaro was getting at. "I don't know if you have the wrong idea or something, but there's still a lot of potential for improvement in your artificial limbs."

Rentaro paused for a moment, having trouble parsing this statement. "R-really?" he said, all but pressing Sumire for an answer. She confidently lifted her hands in the air.

"Really really. You're in the top class of the soldiers I created, and when I say that, I'm talking about your potential, too. You're doing a great job using your limbs and your eye, but I can't say you're performing up to the specs I envisioned at first. That eye, for example."

Rentaro instinctively brought a finger to his artificial left eye.

"There's a limiter circuit in your eye that ensures its processing speed doesn't go above a certain level."

"Wh-why's that?"

"Because you'd *see too much.* It probably feels like time's slowing down for you as your eye calculates the enemy's range and future position, but it can still go a lot further than that. We transplanted a version of your eye without a limiter into several patients, but none of them ever came back."

"Came back…?"

"The moment their eye was unlocked, their brain scans started going haywire, then flatlined to zero. I have no idea what they saw, and I couldn't really use it if I didn't know what was going on, so we were forced to stick a limiter on it. It's a pity. I mean, every day of our lives, we use things that we can't fully observe—operate a car engine, write data to hard drives, that sort of thing. But when bio-ethics get involved, the bosses get all picky about every little thing."

"Well, yeah. If you ignore stuff like that, that's criminal neglect, isn't it?"

"Neglect, huh…? I see. So I'm a criminal to you, then?"

"You're pretty much as gray area as you can be without going full black."

Sumire offered an offended snort. "It's all in the way you put it, isn't it? Though I'll admit, the limiter was probably the right answer. Lowering the processing speed does a great job reducing the burden on the user's brain. But there's one term I want you to remember: terminal horizon."

"Terminal horizon?"

"Right. Your eye's processing speeds up in tandem with your emotions, such as anger or sadness. When you have it activated, I'm sure it feels like time slows down for you, but it's not like time itself is slowing. Your brain is just operating at faster speed as it works with the powerful computer in your eye, so time feels slower by comparison. But eventually you hit a wall, and that wall's one two-thousandths of a second—in other words, a second of real time slows down to what feels like two thousand to you. That's the terminal horizon. All the patients who crossed that never came back. Their brains were completely fried."

Rentaro was shocked. Even in the fight against Kagetane Hiruko—when he was sure his eye ran quicker than it ever did before—he'd peg the slowdown to around fifty virtual seconds for every real one. Maybe it maxed out at a hundred on limited occasions, but even that was iffy.

Two thousand, though? That far ahead?

But Rentaro also understood that, if anything, this was good news for him. If he didn't want to see himself lagging behind the rest of the Tendo Civil Security Agency's employee roll, trying to come as close to this terminal horizon as possible would never be a bad thing for him. Even if he still couldn't handle a sniper rifle as deftly as he wanted, it would be a killer advantage.

"But let's get back on topic," Sumire said as she recrossed her legs. "I know you have to maintain confidentiality with your client, and I don't need to know his name, either. But you better make sure this guy's safety is a priority for you, as much as you can. If your client has the same info the other three victims had, he could be in serious trouble."

That settled it. Rentaro stood up, figuring he'd better go to Suibara's meet-up site immediately.

"One more thing." Sumire shot a sharp look at Rentaro. "We still haven't come to terms with something else. What are you gonna do with Kisara?"

Rentaro froze to the ground.

"I'm not gonna do anything."

"Nothing? So you'll just sit there and gnash your teeth while she goes off with another guy?"

Rentaro left his stool, looking down at Sumire. "Doctor...I talked to you before about the thing between Kazumitsu and Kisara, didn't I?"

"Yeah..."

During the Third Kanto Battle, Kisara Tendo killed Kazumitsu Tendo, her adoptive brother. In the cruelest of manners, no less.

"I...I mean, I like Kisara. I'd be willing to do just about anything for her. But after that experience, I think I realized something. She's let her hatred for the Tendo family dominate her."

For a period, after her parents were eaten by a Gastrea before her eyes, Kisara lost both her speech and any reason to keep living. One day, though, she just got out of bed, begged Sukekiyo Tendo to teach her, and began learning swordsmanship at an astonishing pace.

The one thing driving her heart and having her try to keep living was the desire to plunge the people who ruined her life into the deepest pit in hell.

"Things were pretty fun for the first year or so the Tendo Civil Security Agency was running, so I thought she was forgetting about it. But I was wrong."

"Don't you understand? Justice isn't good enough. Justice can't oppose evil. But absolute evil—evil that goes beyond evil—can. I have that power."

Rentaro gritted his teeth, head hung low.

"Nothing I said reached her..."

As he spoke, his thoughts gradually coalesced together. Now he was starting to see what kind of attitude he needed to approach Hitsuma and Kisara's arranged marriage with.

"Ever since the Tendos took me in ten years ago, I've owed so much to Kisara. I could never pay her back in a million years. I'd do anything to make her happy. I've made up my mind, Doctor. I want Kisara to realize something. That life's worth living for more than just revenge. And if I can make that happen..."

Then Rentaro realized something. The decision he had just made in his heart meant a final good-bye to all the emotions he had accumulated for Kisara over the past ten years.

Sumire looked dubious. "You're gonna stand down because you're putting Kisara's happiness first? Do you know what that means, Rentaro? If you really just want Kisara to be happy, you're gonna have to keep killing off your own feelings. There's no way to half-ass that. Do you swear you'll do that?"

Rentaro closed his eyes. Behind his eyelids, he could see the beautiful Kisara, a graceful hand near her lips.

"I swear, Doctor."

"Even if this proposal goes well and Kisara gets married, has children, gets happy—even then, she still might not forget about her revenge. You can always rebuild a broken body, but a broken heart's beyond all help. You can't do a thing with it. And if it's too late for Kisara, that's gonna be up to you to manage. Can you do that?"

Rentaro stood up and turned his back to Sumire.

"I'm leaving, Doctor. I'm meeting with my client in a bit."

He half-walked, half-fled from Sumire, but his feet were heavy as they pounded on the stairs.

I can do anything for Kisara's sake. Anything...

Realizing that his breathing was growing rapid and out of rhythm, Rentaro instinctively put his hands to his hips. He wanted to grab his pistol's grip with both hands, clasping his fingers around it in a macabre prayer as he tried to calm himself.

But his hands caught air instead. The familiar weight hanging from his side was gone. In a panic, he felt around with both hands. Nothing. Rentaro's XD gun was gone.

He couldn't believe it was possible, but there was no sign of the gun in any of his pockets. *Did I drop it somewhere? It's been hectic all day since the morning, so I wasn't really paying attention, but...*

Suddenly, his conversation with Suibara shot back to his mind.

"...I'm sorry. My evidence got stolen."

"Stolen?"

"My place has been broken into a few times lately. A few things were stolen, including the evidence. The only option I got left is to appeal directly to the Tendo Group or Lady Seitenshi as a living witness. I mean, you're about the only guy left I can trust."

And he'd said *this*, too, hadn't he?:

"Rentaro, I'm pretty sure they think you're involved with me by now. Sorry I got you involved in this, but watch out, okay?"

He shook his head. *This is ridiculous.* There was no way Suibara's enemies could just reach out to him like that in less than twenty-four hours. And even if these supposed "enemies" were behind this, why would they bother stealing *Rentaro's* gun?

It was almost time to meet up. Rentaro shook off the premonitions making themselves known in his mind and hurriedly walked to the designated building.

5

The new Magata City Hall building was still under construction, its bare concrete walls lit dimly by the pale moonlight, which itself fell through a mass of scaffolding and temporary platforms to create an evocative piece of shadow art.

In this landscape stood Suibara, scuffing at the floor with his hands in his pockets. He was a good hour early for the planned meeting because he was fresh from a little quarrel with his Initiator back home.

He began to wonder if meeting in a more crowded public place would've been a better idea, but quickly shook it off. There was no way they could have a relaxed conversation someplace where there was no telling who might be listening in.

Just a little bit longer, Suibara forced himself to think. *If I get this out to the public through Rentaro, it'll all be over. Then I can finally sleep in peace again. Everything's going exactly as I want it. Just a little bit—*

Suibara turned around, hearing heavy footsteps behind him that echoed across the darkness. His shoes were the first things to appear, the moonlight streaming in diagonally through a crevice, illuminating the man from the bottom up.

Checking his cell phone, Suibara realized he still had forty minutes to go. He grinned to himself. *Man, he's here already? What's with all the hurry?* The idea of Rentaro being as impatient as he was gladdened him as he walked up.

"Yo, Renta—"

The roar and light of the muzzle flash was perfectly synchronized with the impact he felt on his side. The force made his cell phone fly out of his hand and into parts unknown.

"Uh?"

He didn't know what had happened at first. An empty shell casing clinked on the floor, and right after that, his side felt burning hot, as if someone took a branding iron to it.

Hesitantly looking downward, he saw the blood that seeped through his shirt in the abdominal area.

"Ah…nnh…!"

The moment he realized he was shot, Suibara experienced an intense pain across his entire body.

No. This isn't Rentaro.

The figure fired two more shots as it walked forward, striking Suibara in the thigh and stomach. He crumpled to the floor.

He couldn't breathe. And as a second wave of pain crested over him, he felt something rise up from his stomach and vomited a large volume of blood.

Now chills ran across his body. Not wanting to die without knowing what happened, he bent his body like an inchworm, stretching it out, trying to get even another millimeter away from his assailant.

But the awkward attempt at escape ended in an instant. Something thumped against the back of his head. He could tell by instinct that it was the barrel of a gun.

An array of happy memories began to flicker across Suibara's brain. Tears fell in a waterfall. His breathing pitched; he reached out into the air to grab at the greatest memory of all—the memory of a certain girl.

"Hotaru…!"

*   *   *

There was a gunshot, and the building was bathed in light for an instant. The sound of the empty cartridge clinking against the floor, and the seemingly incessant echo of the explosion, stayed in the attacker's ears for a long time to come.

A warm wind blew through, shaking the nearby rows of trees.

The moment he arrived at the Magata City Hall construction site, Rentaro stopped, sensing something was wrong as he looked up at the building. There was a crisp, clear August moon above the unadorned walls. He still had around twenty minutes until the meet-up time, and as he ascended the stairs, he wondered if he had shown up too early.

He shook his head and continued climbing to the fourth floor, remembering Sumire's parting words. They'd agreed to meet here, but it was still dark, vast, and empty. He turned on his smartphone's flashlight and called out to the void.

"Hey, Sui—"

He didn't make it to the *bara* part before the smell of blood wafted into his nostrils. He swallowed nervously, motionless for a moment until his brain could catch up, then brought his smartphone above his head to light up the darkness.

It took only a few moments for him to notice the man in a pool of blood, collapsed behind a column.

"Suibara!"

Rentaro flew like an arrow to the site, desperation already consuming him. Suibara was lying facedown, having been shot four times: in the side, the thigh, his right breast, and the back of the head, which must have been the killing blow. He was dead—this man who, just yesterday, was breathing, smiling, talking assorted random nonsense with him.

Then Rentaro spotted something that put him in even more disquieting spirits.

"What the hell...?"

On Suibara's exposed back was a gun, presumably the murder weapon. Hesitantly, Rentaro reached out to it. A voice in his heart was urging him to stop: *This is a crime scene now. You're about to tamper with a crime scene.*

The warm night air brushed past his skin, and a cold bead of sweat ran down his cheek. Driving the appeals to reason out of his mind, he picked up the gun.

The slide was four inches, the left side engraved with a notice that it was a .40-caliber weapon. It all looked too familiar to him.

In fact, it was clearly a Springfield XD pistol. The slide was the same length as the one he used. It was the same-caliber model. And there was no doubt at all this gun was just used to commit a murder. A closer look at the nicks and scratches on the frame and slide, the results of years of heavy use, confirmed it for good—this was the gun that saw Rentaro through his battles against Kagetane Hiruko, Tina Sprout, and Aldebaran.

The gun he thought he lost was right here all along. At the scene of Suibara's murder. Why?

Then, right at that moment, two beams of light flooded the room. Rentaro covered his face against the brightness.

"Police! Don't move!"

Squinting, Rentaro could open his eyes just enough to spot the police uniforms. A cold shiver ran up his spine.

"No! Wait a minute!"

"Drop the gun now!"

With a loud boom, a warning shot gouged its way through the floor beneath him. It made Rentaro realize he had a steely death grip on the gun that just killed Suibara. He let go of it at once.

One of the light beams approached, and before Rentaro knew it, he was tackled, his arm screaming in pain as it was twisted behind his back. The concrete floor advanced upon him, and he groaned as the impact hit him face-first.

There was the sound of metal against metal, and then he felt something uncomfortable around his wrists. Gritting his teeth, he turned himself around, only to find his hands connected together by a pair of dully shining handcuffs.

"Secured!"

Rentaro shut his eyes tight.

This was a trap!

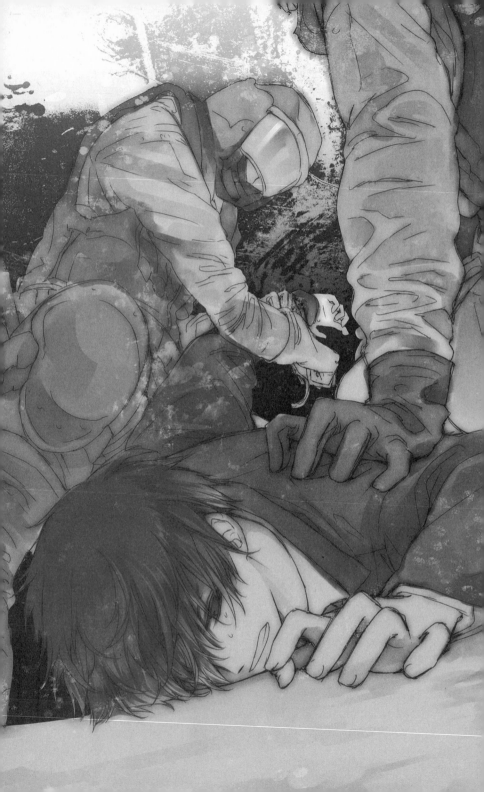

6

Rentaro slammed his fist on the steel desk as hard as he could.

"God damn it, I'm telling you I didn't *do* it!"

"Quit lying to us! Who else would there be?"

"Someone framed me!"

"The victim was killed with your gun. The rifle in our database was a perfect match with yours. We got all the evidence we need. Trying to deny it all's just gonna give you a longer sentence."

This was getting nowhere. Rentaro crossed his legs and plopped himself back down on his stool. The cramped interrogation room he was brought into dripped with tension. The dull, dark-gray walls were complemented by a set of tiny stools. It was the size of a shoebox, but it was certainly tidy—there was no other furniture or decoration.

After two hours of pointless prodding and coercing, Rentaro was starting to get sick of it all. Enju must have noticed he wasn't coming home by now. Hopefully, she wasn't worrying herself sick.

Why did this have to happen to me? *I need to get home ASAP.* The frustration of being accused of a crime he didn't commit brought him to the point where he wanted to beat some sense into the officers.

The door opened, and the detective interrogating him stretched up to see who it was. A thick, wrinkled face peered through the doorway. To Rentaro, it was like a helping hand pulling him up from hell.

"Inspector Tadashima!"

It was Shigetoku Tadashima, an inspector in the violent-crimes department. They had conferred with each other during any number of Gastrea attacks. Finally, a kindred soul! Rentaro was sure he'd testify that he'd never commit a crime like this.

But, at the next moment, he realized exactly how over-optimistic he was.

"So, you're Rentaro Satomi?"

"What?"

His eyes looked like they were chiseled into his square-jawed face. A glare from him was enough to make even nonoffenders involuntarily shiver. That's when Rentaro realized it. Tadashima wasn't here to talk with Rentaro Satomi, his acquaintance in the civsec industry. He was here to question Rentaro Satomi, murder suspect. Expecting a warm welcome from him now would be as useless as crying and pleading for clemency on the guillotine stand.

Tadashima traded places with the younger detective in the room, sitting face-to-face with Rentaro. The detective questioning him before now stood behind him, pacing back and forth along the wall—a classic intimidation tactic.

Then Tadashima leaned over the steel desk. It creaked under him.

"How about we start by you telling me what you were doing the night of the murder? From the start."

"I've already told you guys a thousand times."

"You didn't tell me."

Rentaro stopped himself from lashing out at his arrogance. This was another conventional police tactic—have the suspect give his story time and time again, searching for any contradictions that appear along the way. He kept himself cool as a cucumber as he gave Tadashima the basic outline.

"So I understand the pistol belongs to you?"

"I told you, someone stole it from me. I reached for it, and it was gone."

"If it was gone when you reached for it, why are you so sure it was stolen? You didn't think that you dropped it somewhere?"

He broke into a greasy sweat. This wasn't good.

"That… I said it was stolen because it wound up getting used to commit a crime. I didn't think it was stolen at the time."

"Misplacing a gun is a pretty serious issue. Why didn't you immediately inform the police about it?"

"Well, like I said, I didn't think it was stolen. I figured it'd turn up if I searched the office or my home."

"When did you notice it was missing?"

"Um…a little bit before I was gonna meet Suibara."

"Hmm. Just before meeting the victim, huh? Kind of a convenient time to remember that."

The doubt and suspicion was clear in Tadashima's eyes. *Ah, shit.* If Rentaro had a time machine, he would've used it right now to warn his past self to report it to the police first.

"Listen, Inspector Tadashima, when Suibara called upon the Tendo

Civil Security Agency, he was already fearing for his life. Why would *I* be the one killing him?"

"Who would know about that?"

"What do you mean?"

Tadashima opened his notebook, licked his thumb, and flipped through a few pages.

"Before I came here, I asked a few basic questions to the people in the Tendo Agency."

Rentaro thought his heart was going to stop. So Kisara, Tina, and Enju all knew he'd been arrested.

"Your boss testified that the victim, Kihachi Suibara, visited you to discuss a job. Thing is, though, she didn't hear what the job was about."

"He only wanted to discuss it with me. It was a trust issue."

"All right, so who would know about that?"

"We were the only two people in the office. Suibara told me to get everyone else out of there—"

"—So nobody besides you knows what the job was about?"

"…What are you getting at?"

Tadashima's eyes settled on his notebook. He began flipping through pages again.

"Well, I have some testimony here from your Initiator. She said you were clearly acting strange when she got back from her shopping. She offered to eat dinner together with you, but you declined and disappeared somewhere, apparently."

"That…!" Rentaro raised his voice at first, but fell silent for a moment, unable to figure out what to say.

"What is it? Go ahead."

"That's a different thing…"

"You're using your right to remain silent about it?"

"No! My boss got an offer for an arranged marriage, so…you know, it was hurting me, sharing the same space as her."

Tadashima's face indicated this wasn't the reply he expected.

"So you're in love with your boss?"

Rentaro blushed and stared at the floor. He could hear snickering from behind.

"Stop trying to dodge the question."

"What do you mean by that?" Rentaro turned around and glared at the detective behind him. "Keep your eyes on me," a low voice rumbled from in front. He followed the order, as Tadashima placed his elbows on the desk and clasped his fingers together.

"All right, so this is what we're saying here. Basically, we don't think Kihachi Suibara had any job for you at all."

"What?"

"The victim was demanding money from you. Blackmail. I don't know what he had on you, but you knew each other since childhood, so I'm sure he could dig up something. You saved Tokyo Area's hide in the Third Kanto Battle and the Kagetane Hiruko terror attacks, so Suibara figured he'd try extorting whatever money he could from you. He threatened you, and that freaked you out so much that you didn't feel like eating dinner together with your coworkers. Am I right?

"Then, once you decided to kill him, you lured Suibara to the site of your choice, you pulled the trigger, the police got a report of gunshots, and there you were. Kind of a silly thing to commit murder for, isn't it?"

"That's bullshit, man!"

Where did all that come from? There wasn't a shred of truth to it... But there was, too. He was the only person to hear the nature of Suibara's request. And he really did leave afterward, because he couldn't bear to face Kisara. He never dreamed the events of that evening would lead to *this* kind of misunderstanding. The sweat continued to run down his cheeks.

"...Look, Inspector. I fought in the Third Kanto Battle. I fended off Kagetane Hiruko. Do you really think I'd kill someone over something like that?"

Rentaro was ready to turn to prayer at this point. If he lost Tadashima, the only person he could turn to now, his fate was all but sealed.

But the inspector just gave him an indifferent head shake. "I don't know that. That's why I'm here questioning you right now. Evil people do evil things. They get arrested for it. I've seen dozens of so-called 'nice guys' in here after something possessed them to go bad."

Rentaro weakly shook his head.

"I didn't do it."

"So you're denying the charge?"

"Of course I am! I'm not gonna own up to something I didn't do. Get me a lawyer. You gotta have a lawyer on duty, right?"

Tadashima gave Rentaro a tiny sigh, staring straight through his suspect with cold eyes.

"Rentaro Satomi, I'm officially placing you in police custody. I'm gonna request an extension from the judge tomorrow, too, so I hope you're ready to spend a little while in jail."

7

"Well, I guess luck's not been on your side lately, huh, Rentaro?"

Sumire Muroto sat on one side of the reinforced-glass barrier, picking at her hair distractedly as she griped at the prisoner on the other side.

"I swear, every time I get involved with you, I wind up being forced out of the basement over and over again. I hate it. I had to expose myself to the sun at full blast on the way here. I thought I was gonna turn into a pile of ashes, ha-ha-ha."

Even by Sumire standards, the laugh sounded terribly contrived.

"They wearing you out in there?"

Rentaro gave her a shrug. "I'm doing pretty good, actually. Three hots and a cot, and all that. Plus, I can nap all I want."

Sumire looked surprised for a moment, then curled her lips upward. "That's the spirit, my boy," she said. "If you could keep your spirits up long enough to escape, that'd save me a lot of trouble."

A cough emanated from behind Rentaro as the prison guard chose that moment to make his presence known. Sumire replied with a calm shrug.

The two of them were in the visitation room. A week had passed since Rentaro was placed under custody.

"Y'know, I figured if you ever got yourself arrested, it'd be once you finally succumbed to your raging hormones and started licking little girls' rear ends in the park. But murder, though, huh? For better or for worse, you've really surpassed my expectations."

"I didn't kill anybody."

"They must've let you talk to an attorney by now. How's that going?"

"It's going nowhere. I'm a shoo-in to get prosecuted, and he said I don't stand much chance of winning."

"Must've been a shock, huh?"

"Not really," Rentaro lied. Somewhere in his heart, he still believed in himself. He didn't kill anyone, so someone would understand soon enough. Justice would be served. But it turned out that he didn't need much time for that hope to transform itself into hopelessness. There were the intense interrogation sessions, the extension of his custody period, the cuffs and belly chain they made him move around in like a hardened criminal, the being forced by detectives and assistant prosecutors to recite what he did on that evening dozens of times. His miserable pleas of "I didn't do it" were cut off by apathetic inquisitors telling him to "just answer the questions you're asked," shouting down the voice of innocence.

The idea that some assassin group rubbed Suibara out was greeted with open derision. On more than one occasion, the desperation made him want to confess to everything and put the matter to rest finally.

"I bet we could improve your chances if I represented you in court, but I guess I'd need to go through all this stupid paperwork and licensing and so on first."

"Uh, you're a doctor."

"Nothing in the law books saying a doctor can't be a lawyer, is there?"

"Well, no, but…"

"Besides, I've read all the statutes already. All of them. Pretty heady reading. It took me thirty whole minutes to memorize them all."

"What did you think of it?"

"It's a remarkable guide to all the greedy desires of mankind. There's a lot of them. And by the way," Sumire said as she looked at Rentaro's chest, "I heard that Enju's been paying you regular visits."

She was staring at a poorly made patchwork rabbit sewn into the loose hoodie he was wearing. He touched it, noting the quilted fabric. A gift from Enju.

The school uniform he had on during his arrest was confiscated from him—he could've hung himself with the belt, or swallowed the buttons on it to die of suffocation or blockage or something. He really should've had his cybernetic limbs taken from him, too, but the artificial skin covering them meant he didn't have to worry about that unless he blabbed about it.

Enju had been his only other visitor. Neither Tina nor Kisara showed their face once.

"How's Tina doing, Doctor?"

Sumire shook her head. "She hasn't gotten back from the police yet."

Tina was detained not long after Rentaro's arrest. Just as Sumire feared, Tina was the only person they could find capable of shooting a target traveling on a 200-kilometer-per-hour train. According to Enju, she wasn't charged with anything, but the police hauled her in as a material witness and she hadn't been sighted at the office since. Her inability to provide an alibi for the day of the murder was another black mark on her credibility.

"If this keeps up, they'll probably make you out to be the mastermind behind Giichi Ebihara's murder, with Tina serving as your hit man."

"That's insane!"

As Rentaro spat out the words, Sumire, distracted, leaned over and calmly placed her elbows on the table in front of her, putting her chin on her crossed arms.

"It is. It's really insane. But whenever something absurd and non-sensical happens, they always try to rationalize it as much as possible. You were at the scene of the crime, and you were standing there with the murder weapon in your hand. Meanwhile, a sniper killed their target under next-to-impossible conditions, and they can only find one person realistically capable of doing that. Only the scales of justice know what the verdict will be, and all that, but it's pretty easy for me to imagine the jurors' faces listening to that story."

"……"

"But enough good news, huh? Lemme give you the bad news. Once you're found guilty in a court of law, the regulations say that your civsec license's gonna be revoked. I guess they don't want convicted felons carrying those licenses around. Who knew, huh? But the worst part of that is, once you're stripped of your right to perform civsec duties, Enju's gonna be turned over to the IISO—the International Initiator Supervision Organization."

"They're…?"

"You're allowed to live with a ten-year-old girl you're not related to because your civsec license gives you that right. If you lose that, Enju's gonna be put in a pretty rough situation."

"She can just retire from the Initiator business, then."

She should have the right, Rentaro reasoned. Initiators in Tokyo Area were fielded from a pool of volunteers and scouts. But Sumire shook her head. "I don't think that's gonna work. If Enju quits that gig, her supply of anti-corrosion drugs from the IISO will dry right up. In her current state, that's gonna be fatal."

"Shiiiiit." Rentaro slammed his fist against the table. "We're all screwed, aren't we?"

The prison guard rolled his eyes at them as Sumire stood up.

"Well, just think about it, all right, Rentaro? It's do-or-die time."

Then she left the room.

What should I do? Rentaro internally asked himself. But no clear answer came to mind. As long as he was locked in here, it wouldn't be easy for him to do much of anything. His last hope was that they'd decline to prosecute due to lack of evidence.

Calming his frayed nerves, Rentaro put his hands against each other, as if in prayer. *I won't get prosecuted. I mean, I didn't kill anyone.* Even after the guard motioned him to stand up, he stayed right in place, silent.

Two days later, Rentaro Satomi was officially indicted by the assistant prosecutor and went from being a suspect to the accused.

8

Days of dejection followed the filing of the prosecution papers.

When he was first told about it, Rentaro grew so angry at all its unfairness that the guard escorting him had to hold him down. What followed after that was a profound emptiness.

He hadn't been able to see Tina since his arrest and detainment, but based on what he heard, the situation wasn't too favorable for her either. Normally, the ten-year-old Tina Sprout would be offered at least some protections in the juvenile courts, but the prosecutor was apparently bound and determined to throw her to the gallows, using the excuse that she was not strictly a human being in order to try her as an adult and get her on the stand in court.

The despair in Rentaro's mind weighed on him intensely. Wasn't the law supposed to be the final line of defense the weak could turn to? Had human civilization decayed to the point where witch hunts like these were allowed to happen? Or was it that the hearts of the people themselves had decayed?

Enju, at least, came to visit him almost every day. She'd lean close to him, almost pressing her face against the partition, and give him all sorts of trite pleasantries—"It's gonna be all right," "You haven't done anything bad at all, Rentaro," "Once you get out, I'll let you cop a feel free of charge," that sort of thing.

Rentaro, for his part, gave what he thought were suitable replies— "Thanks," "Of course not," "I'll pass on that." Still, he was deeply in gratitude for her. Without her encouragement, the punishing despair he was facing would cause irreversible damage to his psyche. If it weren't for the shatterproof glass in the way, he'd embrace her in a shower of kisses. Then, realizing he was getting this worked up over a ten-year-old girl, he felt an odd sense of embarrassment.

Today, once again, Rentaro was seated on his visitation-room chair. The person sitting across from him, however, was neither Sumire nor Enju.

For a while, Rentaro stayed silent, not knowing how he should break the ice. To the girl in the black school uniform, it must have been the same way. The clock on the wall robotically ticked off three minutes of their valuable visitation time before the girl opened her mouth.

"I'm sorry," she said. "I had wanted to show up earlier than this..."

"It's all right, Kisara. I don't mind."

Enju had given him enough advance warning that he had managed to keep himself calm at the sight of her.

He had no way of knowing this at the jail, but Rentaro's arrest and Tina's volunteering herself to police questioning had drawn the attention of the mainstream media—a frenzy that fell squarely on Kisara's shoulders to handle. He respected how wild and audacious she could be, but he also knew that this was still just a sixteen-year-old girl.

Worse, Tina's and Rentaro's absence meant that the Tendo Civil Security Agency now boasted a roster of exactly zero pairs. Enju mentioned that they'd had to turn down the paltry number of jobs they'd been offered in the meantime due to that—and, to help prop her up mentally, Kisara had met up with Hitsuma several times, her potential marriage partner now serving as her closest confidant.

"So what're you gonna do about the marriage, Kisara?" Rentaro gently asked.

Kisara put a bright face forward. "Well, Hitsuma's a really good person. He's with the police, so we've been able to talk about your case a lot, Satomi…" Then she stopped for a moment, head hung low. "But, Satomi, you want to ask me a lot more than that, don't you?"

"Like?"

"Like, why I haven't come to see you until now?"

"Not really," Rentaro bluntly replied. "You were busy, weren't you?" But the accusation startled him internally. He did want to know. It was driving him nuts. No matter how busy she was, she didn't have a single moment to stop by? Did Hitsuma have something to do with that? …It sounded so pathetic to him, asking about trivial nonsense like that. What remained of Rentaro's pride kept him from doing it.

"You know, Satomi, I've been thinking about a lot of stuff. I thought that I probably shouldn't see you until I was ready to give a concrete answer…but I think I have that now."

Kisara raised her head up, adjusting her posture as she looked at Rentaro.

"Satomi, I'm willing to do anything for you. I'll hire the best attorneys I can find. You don't have to worry about the money. I'm going to make sure Tina wins her case, too, and then all four of us can go back to running the Tendo Civil Security Agency. I know it took a little too long, but that's my answer."

Rentaro looked at Kisara, speechless, emotions welling up in his chest.

Where would Kisara, who once tried to make her employees live off nothing but sweet potatoes, get that kind of money? She must have been talking about taking all her assets—her stocks, her savings, the deposit paid toward her tuition at Miwa Girls Academy—but, no, that still wouldn't be enough. And if he wound up losing his case, that would be the final straw for their agency. She'd be so in the red, she would never be allowed to run a business again. And yet, that was the decision she made.

Rentaro felt ashamed of himself. He was obsessing so much over Hitsuma and Kisara's relationship that he completely lost sight of what was important. The ugly jealousy that ruled over him melted away into nothing. Love replaced it. He wanted to smash through the partition and bring Kisara close to his heart right this minute.

But a voice in the back of his head stopped him.

"Do you know what that means, Rentaro? If you really just want Kisara to be happy, you're gonna have to keep killing off your own feelings. There's no way to half-ass that. Do you swear you'll do that?"

The forensics department head asked him that in Magata University Hospital's basement. How did he reply, again?

It was clear enough from what Kisara had told him that he was important to her.

Rentaro closed his eyes and slowly opened them again.

I won't hope for anything more.

"Kisara, I'm glad you feel that way, but I don't need that."

"Wh-why not?"

Rentaro stared at his knees, gauging the shocked Kisara from the corner of his eye. "How about you calm down a bit?" he asked dryly. "I've sat here and let you talk, and what I see is that you've been running around with all your might, trying to be a hero. And that's your right and all, but I don't want your help."

"What's with that…?"

Kisara, eyes wide open, was at a loss for words.

"What's with it is that I don't *need* it. Besides, you're about to go through with your marriage anyway, aren't you?" He loosened his voice, taking on an admonishing tone. "Well, now's a good time to start transitioning, isn't it? Now that I'm like this, I can't watch over you anymore, Kisara. You can have Hitsuma protect you from now on."

Happiness would never materialize for Kisara Tendo as long as Rentaro Satomi was by her side. That was his steadfast conclusion. To Kisara, Rentaro's existence was just a painful reminder of her parents, the ones she lost in the most traumatic fashion imaginable. All he was doing was holding her back, in bondage, and if that's how it was: Their only choice was to separate. That was the only and final way for Kisara to forget about revenge and find happiness.

If it was possible, Rentaro wanted to be the source of happiness in her life. He wanted to teach her everything that could make a woman happy. He thought perhaps he was the one who could send her to dizzying heights of ecstasy. But he wasn't, and it grievously troubled him.

Kisara stared at the aloof Rentaro, ruefully pointing her chin at him.

"What is your *problem* today? I mean, Hitsuma's a nice guy, okay? He treats me like I'm important, unlike some people in my life. He's got money, unlike some people in my life. He's tall, unlike some people in my life. And he wants to marry me, too, okay? Maybe you don't know this, Satomi, but *I* actually have a social life with the opposite sex. Hmph!"

"Oh? Well, that's great."

"What do you *mean*, that's great?" For some reason, Kisara demonstrated an extreme dislike for Rentaro's blunt reaction. "Look, Satomi, are you *looking* for them to find you guilty, or what? You didn't kill him, did you? You're acting weird!"

Kisara blushed and turned her head away, rubbing her thighs together nervously.

"You know that my chronic diabetes prevents me from fighting for extended lengths of time. That…that's why I want you to keep protecting me, Satomi. Because in the end, I'm just another weak little girl."

Rentaro wordlessly shook his head. "Please, Kisara. I don't want you to come here anymore."

"Why not? Why are you saying that? Do you hate me or something?"

Rentaro stared straight into Kisara's eyes.

Thanks, Kisara. I've been so grateful to you, ever since the Tendo family took me in ten years ago. The Gastrea that killed your parents took an arm and a leg from me, too, but the fact I managed to keep you safe is something I'm kind of proud of.

I really like you, Kisara.

"Please don't come back. I don't want to see your face again. That's all there is to it."

With a clatter, Kisara stood up off her chair, covering her mouth with both hands. Tears were welling out of each eye, running down her cheeks.

"What is…? What *are* you?"

No matter how much she wiped at them, the tears incessantly came down. She must not have been expecting this display herself, saying "What?" and acting terribly confused. Then she quickly turned around and tried to rush out of the visitation room.

This is how it should be, Rentaro said to himself. *Hitsuma will make her happy.* He watched Kisara as she reached for the doorknob, as if that was the punishment he was facing this whole time.

Just as her figure was about to disappear behind the door, Rentaro had a flashback to Tina, Enju, Kisara, and himself around the dining table, laughing with one another. Something he would never have back again. The tears rushed into his eyes.

Don't go, Kisara.

"Help—"

Rentaro closed his eyes and put both hands over his mouth, struggling with everything he had to keep the rest of the words from coming out. He didn't have to worry. The door closed shut with a heavy bang, and then only a cold silence remained.

Tears dripped down from the end of his downward-facing nose, spreading across the thighs of his pants. He sobbed, his voice cracking, at the pain of losing something he could never replace.

The image of the Tendo Civil Security Agency breaking apart in midair quietly spread across his mind.

9

"Why…?"

For the nth time today, Rentaro's mouth opened a crack and whispered the word as he took in the view of the Seitenshi's palace, in District 1 of Tokyo Area.

Why am I here?

Looking back, he should have suspected something from the moment he woke up, when he was ordered to put on his school uniform instead of the hoodie Enju gave him. That same prison guard effectively banned belts and buttons from his life when he was first sent to jail.

Even when he noticed that the minivan he shared with a driver and two escorts was taking a different route from the usual one to the public prosecutor's office, he didn't pay it any special mind apart from finding it a bit odd.

The view out the window was dull, dark, and bereft of any color.

Since his first and last meeting with Kisara, Rentaro had grown indifferent to nearly all external stimuli, spending more and more of his time lost in thought. Diligently, he tried to collect all the fun, happy memories he had and examine them all one more time. The problem was, recollecting his time in the Tendo Civil Security Agency seemed all too short to him.

"Keep your head forward. Lady Seitenshi is seeing you."

His unfocused thoughts jumbled with one another as his consciousness returned to reality. They didn't come fully together until he finally understood what he heard.

"Lady Seitenshi?"

Upon following his escort's directions, a key was thrust into his handcuffs, freeing his hands. He was relieved from the chain wrapped around his waist like a dog's leash, and then he was led forward, guards in front of and behind him.

The palace guards, standing like statues of Adonis in front of the entrance, saluted the procession as they passed. They must have received advance word.

After a few minutes' wait in the reception room, lined with dozens of trophies and an unnervingly realistic hawk sculpture, the group was led to a large hall meant for special events. The high ceiling arched above them; the well-polished floor formed a mosaic beneath their feet. Rows of marble columns lined the space. Every piece of décor was done up to enormous proportions, making Rentaro feel like he had stumbled into the home of a giant.

Everything inside the palace was refined and splendorous. Nothing like the gray walls of the interrogation room, or the jail cell he was in. That, at least, brightened Rentaro's spirits a little.

"Here," a guard said, "take this." It was, oddly enough, the same civsec officer's license that was confiscated from him at the time of his arrest.

"Why this? What's happening here?"

The guard did not respond. Instead, he just nudged his back, making him stand in front of a large door. With a low rumble, it opened from the other side, letting a warm beam of light enter the room. Proceeding in, then up a steep, winding stairway, they found the Seitenshi at the top, just as she left her throne and was on her way down. The two guards around Rentaro straightened their backs as tightly as they could.

The Seitenshi made a sweeping motion with her hands. The guards sandwiching Rentaro on both sides gave each other worried looks.

"Lady Seitenshi, it's too dangerous for you to be alone!"

"I don't care. Stand aside, please."

They disappeared behind the door with extreme reluctance. Only Rentaro and the Seitenshi remained in the gigantic space.

"It's been far too long, hasn't it?" The Seitenshi smiled a sad smile.

"Well, yeah. You're the head of state, and I'm a failure of a civsec officer. You wouldn't be meeting up with me unless you had some kind of business."

"Yes. In which case, I suppose this is a good thing. A civil security officer out of a job means the world must truly be at peace."

"Yeah, sure." Rentaro rubbed a shoulder as the Seitenshi gave him a graceful laugh. The tension palpably melted between them.

"So what do you want?" he asked.

The Seitenshi put both hands together in front of her dress skirt. "Mr. Satomi, are you aware of which way public opinion is going on your case?"

"Can't say I am. They don't allow any media in jail."

"People were beginning to soften their stance against civil security agencies, after they made such a heroic effort guarding Tokyo Area through the entirety of the Third Kanto Battle. Your on-the-scene arrest for murder, sadly, put an end to that."

"...You think I killed him, too?"

The Seitenshi shook her head. "I don't know that, and I am in no position to determine that."

"But you rule this whole area."

"I am the head of the political apparatus, yes, but that does not extend into the realm of judiciary power. I do, however, have the power to appoint people to certain positions. I've done that for you before, and I've also helped you get your rank promoted no less than three times. Along those lines, the attention I've demonstrated for you has also made me the target of criticism."

Rentaro, realizing the conversation was drifting into hostile waters, broke into a cold sweat. *Why was I invited to the palace today, anyway?* It still made no sense to him.

"Today, Satomi, I'm afraid I need to tell you some bad news." The Seitenshi paused deliberately, raising her face to eye level. "As of today, your civil security agency Promoter license has been revoked."

"Wha...?!"

Revoked? If that happens...

"Do you remember, Satomi?" the Seitenshi continued, indifferent to Rentaro's obvious consternation as she continued. "When you protected me from that sniper, I remember telling you this: 'I will have to ask you to work continuously from now on. For me, and for our country.' It is a shame I have to renege on my word in so short a time."

"Wait a minute! If you confiscate my license, the IISO's gonna take Enju away. You can't take Enju from me, too!"

The Seitenshi turned her face away from Rentaro, a dejected look on her face as she kept her eyes away from view.

"It has already been decided."

Rentaro's fists began to shake. He took the license from its plastic cover and, with shaky hands, placed it in the Seitenshi's hand. Then he turned his back to his ruler, just as she opened her mouth to speak, and briskly left the chamber.

The fifty-million-yen paintings that lined the corridors, as well as the brass vases with arabesque patterns sculpted upon them, were nothing that could move the Seitenshi's heart any longer.

As she trudged down the hallways from the meeting chamber to her personal room, she came across a man in a white formal *hakama* gown, his white hair and beard a seeming mismatch for the firm, muscular body he possessed. It was Kikunojo Tendo, the Seitenshi's aide and a major powerbroker in the world of politics.

"I admire your hard work, my lady."

"Kikunojo...do you think that was the best thing?"

"But of course. Our story is this: Before he was arrested, he requested to be removed from the roster of civsec officers and returned his license to the authorities. That way, the civsec industry can retain its good name, and damage to your administration for appointing him will be kept to a minimum."

"But...we are drowning out the voices of those pleading his innocence!"

"It is my priority, my lady, to do whatever it takes to protect you."

"But that is not *my* way."

"Lady Seitenshi, you... I am afraid you have to choose. If the lifeboats are already full of people, you must have the resolve to let those who couldn't find space on them die. That is a must in order to keep the boat itself viable."

"If I jump off the boat, I could rescue one more person."

"Are you saying you would let a starving person cannibalize you, then? That is very self-sacrificial, my lady, but it has no role in politics, and it is the political system that you are charged with directing."

"But what do *you* think of Satomi, Kikunojo? He was once your adopted son, and when you were chosen as a Living National Treasure of Japan, I understand you designated Satomi to be your apprentice, though not a blood member of the Tendo family. Your opinion of him couldn't have been entirely negative; at least, not at the time. But how can you be so coldhearted to him now?"

"...Ever since he abandoned our family with Kisara, he has been neither my kin nor anything else to me. If this is the end for him, I can only call it his just deserts."

"How could you...?" The Seitenshi stared at the floor and bit her lip. Unable to withstand it any longer, she flew into Kikunojo's breast and clung to him. "I can't help but notice," she whispered softly. "Wherever Satomi goes, there I am, watching from behind. Whenever I speak with him, I feel my heart beating faster. I...I *yearn* for him."

Kikunojo's chest twitched with rage.

"What...?!"

"It pains me. My public persona demands that I must be harsh, but as a living, breathing person, I wish I could use all my political influence to help him out of his plight. My heart, and my body, are being pulled in two different directions. I feel like I'm going to be ripped apart."

"......"

"It pains me. Kikunojo, what am I supposed to do...? What...?"

Kikunojo placed a hand on the Seitenshi's back and silently stroked it up and down.

10

Touji Watagasa put his hands on the Elgrand minivan's steering wheel, placed his foot on the accelerator, and turned his eyes toward the windshield, even though his mind was still focused on the eerie silence unfolding behind him.

It was night. The unpaved private road lit by his headlights made for a bumpy, uncomfortable ride, the car lurching to and fro whenever it ran over an odd tree root sticking out. The tall trees jutting out from both sides depressed him, and—unusually for him—he began to regret trying to take a shortcut.

Touji's main work for today involved picking up the prisoner Rentaro Satomi from lockup and driving him to the Seitenshi's palace. Now he was making the return trip, taking him back to jail. He was on standby inside the van while they spoke, and thus had no idea what had transpired in the palace, but judging by how much gloomier the atmosphere was in the car leaving than going, it must've been something bad.

He looked behind him in the rearview mirror. Rentaro Satomi, slumped down between his two guard escorts, looked like he just had the life sucked out of him. He already looked pretty rough when he picked him up, but now he was even worse—a gruesome sight to see, even. He couldn't help but feel sorry for him.

Touji would readily admit that he had a visceral disgust for the Cursed Children, these Gastrea Virus carriers strutting around like there was nothing wrong with them. But he also understood well enough that he was still alive right now thanks to their efforts in the Third Kanto Battle. It was complicated—and it didn't help that he lost the lottery for a shelter spot during that fight, forced to stay with his family and curse his bad luck.

The joy he felt when Aldebaran fell was difficult to put into words. Seeing this Promoter in such a miserable state right now made Touji wish he could do something to help. But what, though, exactly?

The question made his mind hit a wall. Even if he did something as reckless as help him escape, the sense of satisfaction that would give him wouldn't be worth the lengthy prison term he'd receive afterward. He had a family to support.

Touji chided himself. No, he didn't have what it took to be a hero. All he could keep safe was a small sphere of people around him. And that was good enough for him. Sometimes it was better to listen to the timid little voice of his conscience.

This was the kind of hero who could stand up and devote all his courage to the preservation of Tokyo Area. Now, though, he was yesterday's news. The rules of the world could change with just a snap of the fingers, it seemed.

Thinking about all this caused Touji to lose his concentration. It made him notice just a moment too late that something was jumping in front of the minivan.

He didn't see what it was at first, but once the headlights thrust their way through the darkness, a girl with chestnut hair cut in a bob danced between the beams.

There she stood, in the middle of the road, arms open wide—it was already too late by the time Touji realized this. An instant later, no doubt, the bumper would be smashing into the small figure's body. A chill ran down his spine, and before he could think about it, his foot had slammed the brake to the floor as he pulled the wheel to one side.

There was a screamlike screech as the wheel locked itself. The car veered into the woods. They had just barely dodged the girl, but the tires fell into a rut on the side of the road, and the van was lifted into the air like someone had tipped it up.

Just when Touji realized he'd made a poor decision, the bloodcurdling feeling of weightlessness struck his body as his vision slanted to the side. Only a few seconds ago, he'd been picturing himself pulling into the jail's parking lot, just like he had done a million times before. There was no way he could have predicted the intense pain that would invite itself into his life a moment later.

The results were similarly disastrous for Rentaro in the backseat. He felt his rear end rise up, then he yelped in pain as his vision lurched and his body was battered around the interior. The noise of the crash drowned out all his shouting.

The next thing he knew, Rentaro was lying facedown, his face buried in something soft. The droning sound of the car's stuck horn just barely kept him conscious. He heard something dripping, and a disquieting scent sickened him. He felt something pricking under his eyelids. Something must have struck his throat, because even groaning was painful for him. It was hard to breathe in whatever confined space he was in.

His consciousness still hazy, he opened his heavy eyes, only to find one of his escorts right in front of him, blood dripping from his head. He was approaching his golden years, loose wrinkles on his cheeks.

Then Rentaro realized the van had flipped over, and he was staring at the ceiling. Why was that? It was too dark to figure out how the car had fared, but all of the guards in the car were completely silent. The thought that they were possibly dead made him anxious.

I gotta get outside, first of all.

But— *Oh, wait, I'm still cuffed.* Groaning in frustration, he started kicking at the side door. It took about three good kicks before the door blew open. He crawled his way out, experiencing the crisp, warm night air of summer.

Just as he'd thought, the minivan had flipped on its roof, an impressive layer of burned tire rubber on the road behind them. He had no idea what led to this.

Then he noticed a black liquid seeping out of the car. It jogged his memory. The smell that caught his attention in the vehicle was gasoline. The engine was still sparking. The whole thing could blow soon.

Even with his hands cuffed, Rentaro managed to pull the two guards in the rear out to safety. It was just when he was trying to pull out the unconscious driver that a spark finally lit up the fuel. A wave of heat and flame pushed upon him, making him shut his eyes. He just barely got him out in time.

Rentaro sized up his body. Miraculously, apart from a few scratches and bruises, he was not seriously hurt. He turned back toward the minivan, now engulfed in flames.

Really, though, why—?

"Are you Rentaro Satomi?"

A startled Rentaro turned toward the voice, only to find a girl dancing on the other side of the undulating curtain of flame. She was short, child-size, and while he couldn't discern her face, the legs jutting out from her hot pants indicated she was definitely female. Did she just stand by idly while he was trying to rescue the guards?

"Why did you help them?" she asked.

"Who're you?"

"That doesn't matter to you."

"Did you make this van flip over?" he demanded.

"You're the one who killed Kihachi, right?"

"Kihachi? You mean Suibara? No. It wasn't me."

The moment he denied it, he felt a wave of rage emanate from the figure. She took a step forward, trampling the earth with her foot.

"So why were you arrested for it?"

"I..."

For a moment, Rentaro flashed back to an image of himself at the crime scene, XD gun in his hand.

The girl picked up on his lack of an immediate response. She pointed her arms forward toward Rentaro. There was a small-size revolver in her hands.

"Don't think bad of me for this. I'm never going to be at peace with myself if I don't."

Her trigger finger moved without hesitation, setting off the percussion hammer and slowly spinning the magazine around with a metallic sound. Rentaro's body froze at the expected blast to come.

But, for whatever reason, the shot didn't arrive. The contradiction taking place before the girl—this guy who killed Suibara rescuing three guards from a burning vehicle—perplexed her. And just before she could pull the trigger that little bit more, the sound of a wailing police siren plunged between the two of them. There was no doubting it.

The girl groaned to herself and quickly executed a flip that propelled her into the woods. The leap sent her form flying all the way up to the top of the tree canopy. Her jumping skill was clearly something beyond any ordinary human's ability.

Oh, great, she's an Initiator, Rentaro thought to himself as he watched her bound away. The voice didn't sound familiar to him, and he couldn't make out her face. But if this was an Initiator on a first-name basis with "Kihachi," who was also out for revenge, that narrowed it down pretty quickly.

Rentaro scoped out his surroundings. There were three unconscious guards and one burning minivan. It wouldn't be easy to explain this, but his only choice, he supposed, was to be honest.

Suddenly, he noticed a small key that fell out from one of the guards' pockets.

It was for a pair of handcuffs.

His heart thudded loudly in his ears. As if on cue, the police siren began to grow louder as it approached.

Right now, right at this minute, he could get away. But if he fled now, in the worst case, he might wind up copping the blame for this accident. As of right now, he was merely indicted for murder, not condemned. It'd take time to plead his case in court. If he wasn't going to scream his innocence to the high hills to the end, why did he go through all this up to now?

But, he asked himself, *is that really the case?* A trial was all about sizing up the available evidence and using it to decide between guilty or not guilty. Had they discovered any sort of evidence so far that'd clear his name? Judging by the highly loaded questioning he had been subjected to so far, it seemed beyond a reasonable doubt that the "presumed innocent" clause would be worth about as much as the paper it was printed on.

Many times now, Rentaro had been forced to put on that belly chain and shuffle between jail and courtroom. They'd be much quicker with Tina. She'd be found guilty before she walked in the room, and—with her role in the attempt on the Seitenshi's life brought into consideration—she would be immediately condemned to death.

Thanks to the astonishing regenerative powers of an Initiator, the government was aware that the usual method of hanging would only serve to make execution a needlessly painful process. An injected cocktail of barbiturates and muscle relaxants wouldn't work, either—the Gastrea Virus would immediately take action to neutralize the poison.

So, by process of elimination, Tina would be sentenced to death by firing squad. Her legs would shake as she was dragged to the execution stand, a sack placed over her head as she was tied to a pole. There was no way the fragile psyche of a ten-year-old could withstand the sheer terror of this situation, so she would sob, crying about how she didn't want to die. But no one would be willing to listen.

Varanium bullets would be the ammunition of choice, naturally. The firing squad would line up in a row, waiting for their captain to give the signal to fire at once. As per tradition, one of the squad's rifles was equipped with blanks, but none of the team knew which one. This gave the squad members plausible deniability for their actions, believing in the possibility that *they* hadn't killed her as they went home and enjoyed a hearty meal with their families. But Tina would still be dead.

With her employee list now empty, Kisara would have little choice but to shut down the Tendo Civil Security Agency. She would marry Hitsuma, live her life, and—despite the handicaps her diabetes presented—successfully give birth to a child.

Over time, her memories would fade. Of Tina, whom she treated as her own sister; of Enju, whose boundless energy put her at her wit's end on so many occasions; even of Rentaro—she would forget about them all, and never take another look back.

With the loss of her partner, Enju would be picked up by the IISO, which would then assign her another Promoter to work with. Her new partner would be far from ideal. He would refuse to give Enju so much as a decent meal, and he would regularly abuse her. The girls' healing abilities were the result of a metabolism that worked several times as quickly as regular people's, so being left to starve meant her wounds would stop healing correctly.

Without her corrosion-suppression drugs being administered, Enju's internal corruption rate would surpass 50 percent, making her experience pain like her guts were being turned inside out, and eventually she'd transform into a Gastrea. The total cost of an Initiator with the overwhelming strength of Enju going Gastrea would be nightmarish, both monetarily and in terms of human lives.

And how ironic would it be, that the group charged with hunting her down would be other civsec officers—the only group that Enju took pride in ever belonging to...

Rentaro, his breathing shallow, returned to reality. Was the sick prediction of the future he just envisioned really nothing more than paranoia in action? What made him think the future would turn out any other way, once he was found guilty? He looked down upon his palms. His wrists, black and blue from the handcuffs, stung at him. He shook his fists.

I didn't kill Suibara. Why do I have to put up with all this absurd insanity? Whoever framed me is probably cackling to himself right now, thinking everything's gone to plan. He *never got taken to court.*

Rentaro's vision grew hazy as the insides of his eyes became warm. It was frustrating, so frustrating that he couldn't stand it. He wanted to get it back. Everything from his normal life. Everything that was taken from him. The same Tendo Civil Security Agency he once knew, with Tina and Kisara and Enju.

More than anything, he wanted to hunt down the real murderer and burn him with the brimstone of rage. His pride and his reputation, so cruelly ripped from him and trampled upon, demanded nothing less.

The siren grew stronger, bashing against his earlobes. It clearly wouldn't be long before police officers would be swarming down the road. The time that remained forced Rentaro to make a decision.

After a moment, Rentaro's body stopped shaking. He turned his face up and gave a cold stare to the dazzling neon city beyond the woods.

Several minutes later, once police arrived on the scene, they found a flipped and burning Elgrand, three unconscious but breathing guards, and an empty and abandoned pair of handcuffs.

Rentaro Satomi was nowhere to be found.

11

"What...?!"

The Seitenshi couldn't help but say it out loud.

"Satomi...escaped...?"

"Yes, my lady," the saluting palace official replied. "We believe he staged a deliberate attack on his transport back from the palace in order to escape. The three guards on the van haven't regained consciousness, so we don't know the details yet, but..."

She could hardly believe her ears as she palpably felt the blood drain from her face. How could this be? Did taking his license in order to keep him safe wind up driving him to desperation?

What was I supposed to do, then?

The Seitenshi, as the political leader of Tokyo Area, loved all her subjects equally. She was not allowed to see anyone as more special than anyone else.

She noticed a heavy hand on her shoulder.

"Lady Seitenshi, please get ahold of yourself."

It was Kikunojo.

"With all due respect, my lady, he fled his fate because he is spiritually weak. It is your task to do what must be done."

The Seitenshi closed her eyes, refocusing her attention on her situation. Her pulse slowed. "Are the police in pursuit of him?" she said, somehow managing to remain calm.

The palace official stood bolt upright. "Yes, my lady," he bellowed. "We believe they will arrest him before long."

"Then—"

"—Would you mind leaving that business to me?"

"And you are...?"

The Seitenshi looked up at the interrupting voice. The tapping of thick boots rapped across the chamber as a man walked in from the darkness on the other side of the corridor.

He was perhaps just a little under sixty, his medium-length crew cut partially interrupted by a diagonal scar that ran across his scalp. His eyes were deeply sunken into his head, the excessive white between the iris and the eyelids giving the impression of someone prone to anger.

It was a familiar face.

"Ah, Commissioner Hitsuma," said Kikunojo, standing to the side of his leader.

Commissioner Tadashi Hitsuma walked up to the Seitenshi, giving her a respectful salute.

"I apologize; I couldn't help but overhear the conversation. Forgive my lack of communication, Lady Seitenshi."

"It is good to see you, Commissioner. But what brings you here?"

"I called for him," Kikunojo responded, giving a glance at the Seitenshi before continuing. "Since your former bodyguard conspired against you, I have been your sole protector, a situation that cannot go unaddressed for much longer. I asked the authorities if they would be willing to assign a security-police unit to you."

"And judging by what I hear, the escape was entirely a failure on the part of the police," Hitsuma continued. "But do not worry, Lady Seitenshi. We will capture this cowardly fugitive as soon as humanly possible...and I know the ideal person for the job."

"The ideal person?"

"Yes. My grandson. He may still be green, yes, but he is a well-put-together lad. I am sure he will hook this would-be escapee in very short order."

The car door slammed shut as some of the lukewarm night air found its way inside, the smell of raw earth reaching his nostrils.

The scene around the burning minivan was crawling with media, swarming out from God knows where and lighting up the night with their flashbulbs. Even without them, the flashing lights from the police cars and ambulances nearby would have provided more than enough ambient light, further punctuated by the reflective police tape around the scene.

Pushing his way through the reporters, Shigetoku Tadashima ducked under the tape. "Chief," a familiar voice called out. Turning toward it, he saw Yoshikawa, a younger detective with a look of regret on his face. "Oh, I mean, Inspector..."

"Where's the scene?" Tadashima asked, ignoring him.

"This way," Yoshikawa replied, taking him to the burned-out husk of the minivan.

He sized up the upside-down minivan, its ceiling crushed by the impact, and peered at the brake marks left on the road.

"What do we know?"

"This minivan was transporting the suspect back to jail when a girl ran in front of the car. The driver swerved and flipped the vehicle. The two guards in the rear are in the hospital with broken bones. The driver got out of it better, though. He's awake and alert, and we're questioning him now."

"A girl? Did that civsec's Initiator come to help him?"

"Doesn't look like it, actually. Rentaro Satomi was being transported from Lady Seitenshi's palace, where apparently he voluntarily resigned his post. He surrendered his license on the spot. At about the same time, a person from the IISO visited Tendo Civil Security Agency and met with his former Initiator, Aihara…um…"

"—Enju."

"Right, yeah, Enju Aihara. He apparently seized her, and *that* reportedly wasn't so voluntary. Either way, though, she's got an alibi."

"Okay. So who was it?"

Tadashima sighed. He remembered how drained and pathetic Rentaro looked when he told him that Enju was captured by the enemy during the whole Seitenshi sniper crisis. The type of Promoter who really cared for his Initiator, in other words. If he gave up his license, then was told he'll never see his Initiator again, that might just drive him to do something rash.

Fanning himself, Tadashima sat on a nearby fallen tree trunk and looked up at the starry sky. "Pfft," he said. "I didn't think we were really gonna indict him."

"You're still saying that, Inspector? You think he's innocent or something?"

"Nah, I mean… He's the hero of the Third Kanto Battle, you know. I just figured someone up high would've stepped in to cover all this up by now."

"You know Lady Seitenshi hates doing that, though. She likes keeping things clean like that. Bet she's been crying her eyes out the whole time, though."

The conversation trailed off. Tadashima tapped a pack of cigarettes from his breast pocket, taking a smoke out and lighting it.

"You think he's really the guy, though?" Yoshikawa muttered to the side.

Tadashima took a deep drag and exhaled the smoke into the air. "Who knows?" He stood up from the tree trunk, watching the officers scurry to and fro around the scene. Just as he took in a lungful of air to bellow his orders, he heard someone say, "Are you the man in charge here?"

There, among the flashing lights, the police tape, and the seemingly endless flashbulbs, was a slender young man walking right up to him.

His posture was straight, his silver-framed glasses matching with his business suit. He was unfamiliar to Tadashima.

"Atsuro Hitsuma, sir," he said as he saluted. "Superintendent at the department. Are you in charge of the scene?"

Realizing he was outranked, Tadashima hurriedly dropped his cigarette, put it out with his heel, and saluted.

"Y-yes, sir. Inspector Shigetoku Tadashima with the Magata department."

There was something almost cartoonlike about the scene—the wide, barrel-chested Tadashima and Hitsuma, barely a wisp of a man, saluting each other. Tadashima couldn't help but feel a little cowed.

"Oh, great, a career-track grunt," Yoshikawa groaned forlornly from behind. Tadashima elbowed him to shut him up.

"I apologize, Inspector, but I'm taking over the investigation."

"Sir, this crime took place in our jurisdiction. Besides, why would a police superintendent go hands-on with a sorry scene like this? I really think we're in a better position to handle it."

He tried his best to remain polite around his superior, but the irritation behind his words remained clear. But the pale, wispy man remained composed, using his middle finger to adjust his glasses.

"Inspector Tadashima, I'm afraid I can't allow that. This is a much bigger situation than what you're picturing. We've decided to form a special investigation team for this case. They'll be based in the metropolitan police HQ instead of the Magata department, and it's being led by the commissioner. Starting now, the Magata department will be taking their orders from us, and us alone."

"It's going up to commissioner level?" asked Tadashima, clearly taken aback.

Hitsuma shrugged. "Well, this was caused by ground-level police error. We want to get it squared away as soon as possible."

"God damn..."

What the hell is going on here? Tadashima wanted to scream. It had to be one hell of a major case if they were forming a team to handle it. It wasn't something they'd deploy just to catch a single fugitive.

"Inspector, how long has it been since the suspect fled the scene?"

"I'm told it was about an hour ago."

"All right. He shouldn't be far, then." The light glinted off Hitsuma's

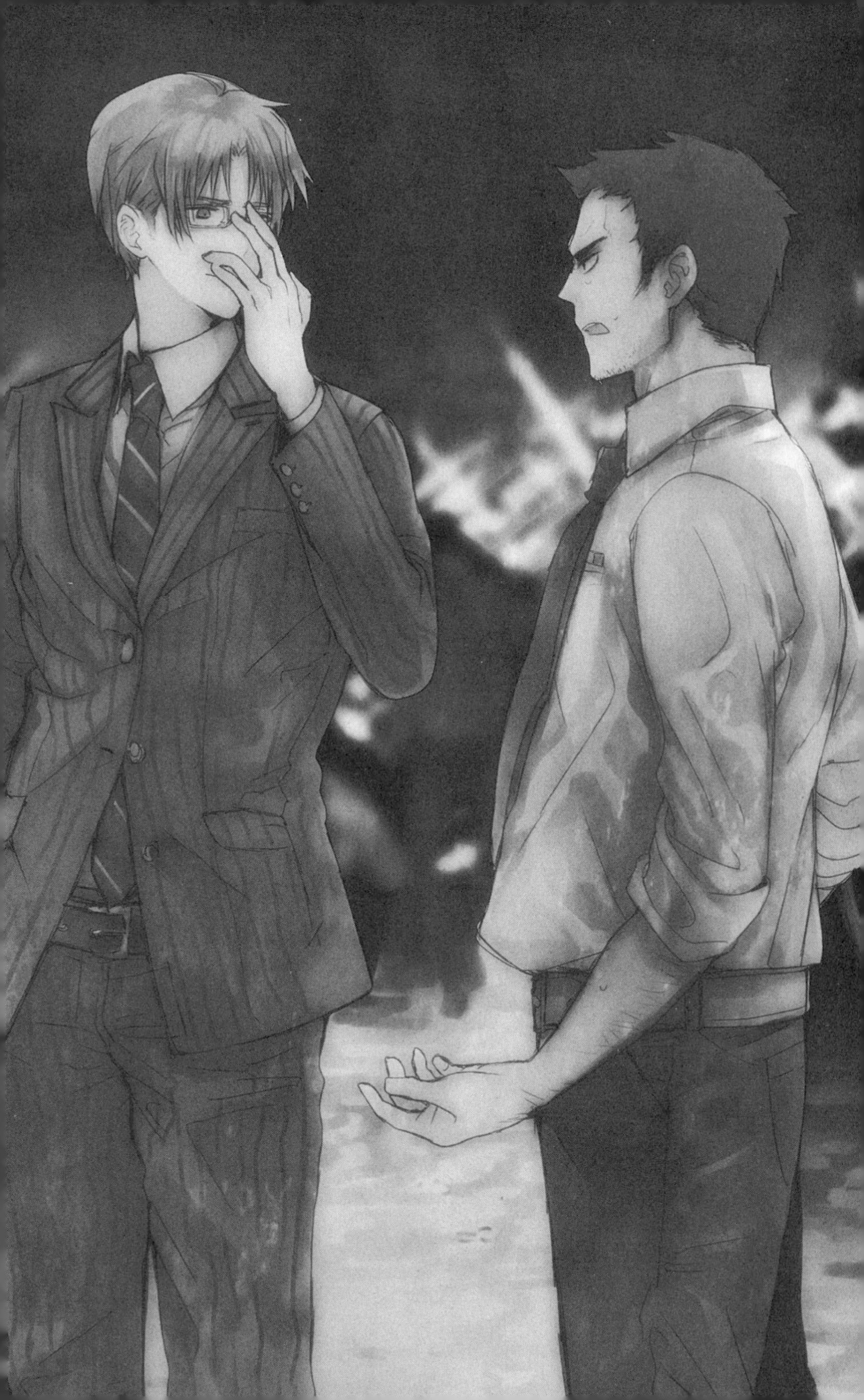

frames. "Could you tell me what you know about Rentaro Satomi? I read his profile on the way here—height 174 centimeters; weight 61 kilos; first-level black belt in a combat style called Tendo Martial Arts. That's not what I want to ask about. I understand that you knew him personally, Inspector. What kind of person was this Rentaro Satomi, would you say?"

"Well, he might act all happy-go-lucky and clueless, but he's a natural at his job. And if I may speak freely, Superintendent, I really don't think you have a chance at catching him."

Hitsuma stared blankly at Tadashima, then gave him a forced smile. "Oh?" he said. "You seem to be quite a fan of his, Inspector."

Tadashima's spine shivered as Hitsuma clapped his hands to attract the attention of the nearby investigators.

"All right, everyone, I want us to establish a perimeter at a 25-kilometer radius around the area before we let the fugitive get away from us. The escapee's name is Rentaro Satomi; average size, average build. He's a student and former Promoter at a civilian security agency. I'll get photos out to everyone. Repeat: Rentaro Satomi, fugitive at large."

He clapped one more time, signaling them to start their work. The investigators, presumably his own underlings, sprang into action and dispersed.

Tadashima dolefully stared at Hitsuma's back. "So, Superintendent, what are you gonna do next?" he asked.

"Rentaro Satomi doesn't have that much of a social life. It'll be pretty easy to figure out who he'll try to contact first. In fact, I know the person myself, so I'll handle that on a personal basis. Don't worry, Inspector. I have a feeling you'll be proven wrong. We're going to solve this case by the end of the night."

12

A heavy silence flooded the Tendo Civil Security Agency, the sole tenant on the third floor of the Happy Building. Kisara Tendo, in her usual black school uniform, sat at her wide ebony desk without saying a word.

The clock ticking away the seconds sounded abnormally hollow to her ears. In her mind, she pictured the second hand beating against a fully inflated balloon, ready to burst at any minute. Instinctively, it felt like once the hand inevitably popped the balloon, it would all be over for her.

It hadn't been long since someone claiming to be an IISO agent appeared at her door, taking the reluctant Enju and all but dragging her out of the office. He said Rentaro had voluntarily surrendered his civsec license to the Seitenshi, which officially made Enju IISO property.

That was just too ridiculous to be true. Kisara had a front-row seat to Rentaro's behavior around Enju, and if anything, she thought he was a little *too* attached to her. Even if they knew they were doomed to be pulled apart, there's no way he'd so readily toss out his civsec license like that.

Something else must have happened at the palace.

But another voice in her mind wondered about that.

"Please don't come back. I don't want to see your face again. That's all there is to it."

Why did he have to be so curt with her? Kisara still couldn't figure that out, but if that was the moment when Rentaro changed his whole outlook on life, then maybe he really *would* abandon hope for Enju and obediently hand over the license.

She felt her heart throb. It made her sick to her stomach. Enju was gone, Tina was gone, and Rentaro was gone. Why bother running this firm, then…?

Just then, her cell phone rang. She used the third movement of Rachmaninoff's Piano Concerto No. 3 as her ringtone. Reluctantly, she picked it up.

"Kisara, it's me; you gotta help me."

"Satomi?" She jumped out of her seat. Looking at the screen, she saw the call came from a public phone.

"Wait, what…what happened to you?!"

She could hear the hesitancy in his voice from the other side of the call.

"—I don't have time to explain. Things have changed. I need you to help me."

"Things have changed? What…?"

"*Listen. First floor café lounge, Magata Plaza Hotel, eight thirty. Can you do that? I'll tell you everything there.*"

Kisara glanced at the wall clock. That was only half an hour from now.

Rentaro grunted. She could hear police sirens faintly over the connection.

"*'Kay, see you there, Kisara.*"

"Whoa, wait a—"

The sound of him hanging up seemed to linger in the air for a few seconds. She had no idea what she just experienced. Rentaro couldn't have been released, on bail or otherwise. His custody period was extended because the prosecutor convinced the court that he might try tampering with evidence. That he contacted her from the outside meant he was out on his own initiative. Kisara couldn't think of too many legal ways he could've done that.

"Oh, no…"

"Sorry, but I can't let you go anywhere."

Turning around at the unexpected voice, Kisara was shocked to find a handsome, bespectacled man leaning against the wall by the entrance.

"Mr. Hitsuma! Why are you here?"

"That was a call from Satomi, wasn't it?"

"N-no."

The harried denial made Hitsuma mournfully shake his head. "I don't know if you heard yet, but he flipped over the transport vehicle he was in and escaped with a girl we believe is his accomplice."

"His accomplice? …Who?"

"I don't know. We're investigating."

Hitsuma spread his arms as he approached Kisara, the smell of his pomade flying into her nostrils. "Ms. Tendo," he said, "as someone in the business of Gastrea extermination, I'm sure you know how important the initial hours of the investigation are in solving a crime. Unfortunately, he's already gone past a certain point. If you know where he is, would you mind telling me? I still have authority over this, so I can be gentle with him."

"But you…"

Hitsuma's arms were extending out, attempting to embrace her shaking body. Kisara took a step back and pushed Hitsuma's chest away. He looked at her quizzically, like a hurt puppy.

"Do you like him?"

"No...I don't. He's an idiot, he's useless as an employee, he's chronically poor, he treats Miori like she's some kind of goddess, he pays zero attention to me, he never calls unless I call him first..."

Kisara ran out of things to say. She turned away from Hitsuma, head hung low, then felt a gentle hand on her shoulder.

"If he was innocent and wanted to earn justice for himself, he could've proved his innocence in a court of law. He might *be* innocent, for all I know. Maybe it was a false arrest. Maybe the police messed up the investigation.

"But even if they did, I can't really approve of him crashing a police vehicle and sending three innocent men to the hospital. Ms. Tendo, if you really want what's best for Satomi right now, you know what you should do, right? Tokyo Area's not that big of a place. He can't run from us forever. Sooner or later, we'll find him. But *you're* the only one who can keep him from adding any more charges to his record."

"*Please don't come back. I don't want to see your face again. That's all there is to it.*" Kisara shook her head from shoulder to shoulder. "I just don't know. I don't know what Satomi's thinking, I don't... I don't know anything. I did before, but now, I just don't."

Before she knew it, Kisara felt a hand raising her chin, dragging her face toward Hitsuma's friendly grin.

"Well, you can just leave the rest to me. I promise I won't treat him badly. Where is he?"

Kisara hesitated. Hitsuma decided to keep pushing.

"You don't want to see it all end with an officer shooting him down, do you?"

"N-no," a startled Kisara said.

"Okay. So you know what you should do, right, Ms. Tendo? Just think about what's the best thing you can do for Satomi right now. Take your time."

After excusing himself from the Tendo Civil Security Agency office, Hitsuma went down the stairs and stood in front of the building. The blissfully unconcerned face from before was a thing of the past. He was close to losing his temper, ready to kick the first thing that came into sight—an empty can, a small dog, anything.

Hitsuma took out his cell phone and tapped a number in his call history. He didn't have to wait long.

"Hey, how's the reception on the bug you put in Kisara Tendo's cell phone?"

"Loud and clear. But I'm sure Rentaro Satomi's moved on from his previous call location. She promised she'd meet him at the café on the first floor of the Magata Plaza Hotel. We'll have some people there."

"Pfft."

"Something wrong, sir?"

"Kisara Tendo... She didn't disclose anything to me."

"Are you doubting our technology, sir?" The man on the other end of the line didn't understand what he meant. "Whether she cooperated with you or not, we've got all the intel we need—"

"—No. Not that. I was testing her. I wanted to see whether she'd testify against Rentaro Satomi or not. But she kept mum. Right up to the end."

"It's nothing that's compromising our mission, sir."

"No...it's not." Hitsuma shook his head, trying to put his mind back on track. "Do we know where the memory card is yet? What about Hotaru Kouro's whereabouts?"

"Nothing on either front yet."

"This is getting messier than I thought it'd be."

He had a mountain of issues to deal with. The only way to deal with them was to tackle them head-on, one by one. *Let's start with Rentaro Satomi.*

"I'll tell the police about this later. We got thirty minutes."

"What are the higher-ups telling you?"

"Feh. My father told me that Lady Seitenshi ordered him not to be killed. Maybe the rumors about her having some kind of special feelings for the guy were true after all."

"Well, that sure makes me jealous. What are you planning to do, then? I'm assuming you don't want him *un*hurt."

Hitsuma snickered to himself. "Don't be stupid, Nest. We have no idea how much Suibara told him. I don't care anymore. Rub him out. We're using Dark Stalker for this job."

13

The Magata Plaza Hotel was even more gaudy and ostentatious than what he was picturing. The lounge café, an open-air setup underneath the lobby's vaulted ceiling, was separated from the rest of the world by a series of connected glass pieces, all in assorted geometric shapes.

A combination of recessed lights and a chandelier filled the space with warm orange light, the atmosphere tied together with the calm melodies of classical music.

A waiter made his way between the tables, each covered with a prim white tablecloth. Occasionally one would see men in expensive-looking business attire or pastel-colored Oxford shirts, entertaining their lady friends with impassioned discussions about what the Varanium industry would be like in ten years or whatnot.

Although it was theoretically open to the public, the café's customers all seemed to be overnight guests. *Perhaps this was a bad time after all*, Rentaro thought, as he began to regret the uncharacteristic location he selected. The sight of a nervous-looking young man in a dirt-stained school uniform fidgeting by himself at one of these tables was bound to stand out a fair bit.

His mind was a frazzled mess, and not merely because of the cups of coffee he drank just to give his hands something to do. Looking at the clock on the wall, there were less than ten minutes until the appointed hour. He doubted the police could have targeted this hotel before the end of the evening, but looking back, opting for such a public place was hasty thinking on his part.

Rentaro was isolated, helpless. The police could figure out where someone like that would attempt to spend the night. He could rough it outdoors for a night or two, but sooner or later, he'd want a roof over his head again. Once he did, the first place they'd scope out would be hotels like these.

When the time hit twenty-five minutes after eight, Rentaro decided to ditch the café. He was too worried that something might've happened to Kisara.

"Are you eating alone?"

Rentaro's face darted up at the voice. A smiling young man was peering down at him. He was about the same size as Rentaro and couldn't have been much older. The navy-blue stand-up collar on his uniform looked familiar to him. It was from Nukagari High School in District 9, not far from where he lived. The smile seemed friendly enough. For someone like Rentaro, whose facial setup made it seem like he was faking every smile no matter how hard he tried, the warmth behind this one almost made him envious.

The mystery kid shook a deck of cards in front of his face.

"Care for some blackjack, maybe?"

"Uh, no, I…"

Before Rentaro could piece together a coherent response, the boy sat down across from him and dealt him two cards from the deck, turning one of them faceup—the king of clubs. *Well*, Rentaro thought, *guess I missed my timing. Better just play a game with him, then shoo him away.* He very reluctantly turned the other card. It was an ace of diamonds—and since an ace counts as eleven as long as the total doesn't exceed twenty-one, this meant his total was twenty-one, a natural blackjack. The boy's own cards totaled sixteen, so Rentaro won with absolutely no effort on his part.

The boy grinned and opened his palms wide. "Congratulations!" he said. "You're just like what the rumors say, Rentaro Satomi. Guess you really *do* have the luck of the heavens on your side, huh?"

Rentaro's shoulders twitched.

"Why do you know my name?"

The boy put the used cards into a separate pile and began setting up a second game. "If you're looking for Kisara Tendo, she's not coming," he said indifferently.

Rentaro instinctively began to lift himself from his seat. "And *you* are…?"

The boy ignored the question, eyes on the game as he pointed at the deck—his signal for another hand. This irked Rentaro, but he still sat back down, figuring he wasn't going to start swinging at him here in public. Picking up the corners of his facedown cards, he saw he had an eighteen—nothing worth taking a further risk on. Then his opponent revealed his cards. Another eighteen. A push.

The boy placed his elbows on the table and crossed his arms together, fixing his gaze on Rentaro.

"We went through all the trouble of taking care of Suibara and the Public Security guys and pinning the blame on you, but you're just so stubborn, aren't you? You keep running on us, so our entire blueprint's about to fall apart. That's pretty grave news for us. We've already decided on our script—Suibara tried to blackmail you, you killed him out of desperation. It's a little too late for rewrites."

"So are you—?"

"—The New World Creation Project. Nice to meet some of the old alumni. I was built to surpass you."

It was like someone hit the side of his head with a hammer.

"That's crazy..."

If Rentaro was pursuing a case that already cost the lives of Suibara and a Public Security officer, he was prepared to deal with not just the police, but other, more nefarious organizations. He didn't know who was involved with it—he had only a hazy idea of its structure, really—but he was convinced it was far more dangerous than anything the police could do to him.

What he wasn't expecting was for this assassin group to track him down less than two hours after his escape. He would've laughed it off at the time, but here it was, all laid out in front of him. The sight of this perfectly composed kid sharing a table with him was an utter shock. He fell silent for a moment. The boy picked up the slack.

"My code name is Dark Stalker, but my real one is Yuga Mitsugi. You can call me whichever one you like more. Glad to get to know you. I've been assigned to your execution."

"That's bullshit! The New World Creation Project never got off the ground!"

"So what does that make me, then?" Yuga said, the spite becoming clear in his voice. "Some kind of ghost? Satomi, we need you as a sacrifice. Tina Sprout's going to be executed. Kisara Tendo's going to be trained to destroy the Tendo family. Enju Aihara's actually got her next Promoter assigned to her already. He's a bad seed. A buddy killer. Worse than you'd ever imagine. And once you're found guilty, the whole picture's complete."

So everything from the very start…

"I've been told to ask you this, so I will," Yuga blithely continued as Rentaro gritted his teeth in anger. "Where is the memory card Suibara gave you?"

Rentaro stopped himself from asking *What's that?* just in time. He had no memory of Suibara giving him anything like that. But his instincts told him that if his foes had the wrong idea, he needed to find a way to exploit it.

"If I give it to you, what'll you do?"

"That'll be your best way to assure this meeting ends as amicably as possible. It'll give you the right to shut up and get back in your cage. You'll get to keep your life."

"That's a load of crap, and you know it."

Yuga laughed derisively at his conversation partner. "So that's the end of negotiations?"

"We never started negotiating in the first place."

"Well, I suppose that means I'll have to kill you and strip it from you instead. Which is really stupid of you, you know that? I gave you a chance at survival and everything."

Invisible sparks flew between them. They could have exploded at any time. Rentaro quelled his emotions and analyzed his enemy's war power. Yuga, calmly seated in front of him, was average in size and height. His physique wasn't much different from his own. His capabilities, though, were a complete unknown. If he was really part of the enhanced-soldier project, at least part of him had to be cybernetic.

If Sumire was correct, in fact, these were the guys who killed Kenji Houbara and Saya Takamura—the New Humanity Creation Project specimens who were completed ahead of Rentaro. People with real experience in the Gastrea War.

Losing this battle would mean New Humanity would be forced to completely submit to New World. For the sake of the dead, at least, he couldn't afford to lose.

He made a tight fist beneath the table.

"Well, should we get started? Where did you—?"

Seizing the first move, he swung his leg and kicked the table upward.

The guests around them nervously shouted. Yuga's surprised expression was soon masked by the table's circular shape as it knocked itself over. Standing up, Rentaro planted his left foot on the ground, lowered his hips, and kicked the middle of the table with his right leg. From Yuga's perspective, not only did the table block his field of vision—the obstacle was advancing upon him. There was no way he could dodge it.

—That conviction was why the sight of Yuga easily leaping high over the table and advancing upon his vision was something Rentaro failed to instantly react to.

Realizing he was about to unleash a flying kick, Rentaro promptly wrapped the tablecloth on the floor around his toes and kicked it up, sending it flying. The white cloth billowed in the air, catching Yuga's body. The moment he used every bit of his agility to crouch down, Yuga's kick scraped just past his ear.

Rentaro had only a moment to shake the sweat off before he adjusted his stance toward the cloth-covered, mummylike Yuga.

Tendo Martial Arts Second Style, Number 16—

"How about…*this*!"

—Inzen Kokutenfu.

The roundhouse kick, delivered with all his might, slapped home against the side of the struggling Yuga's head. He was sent into the air, crashing into an adjacent table. Plates of dinner meals flipped into the air, and the shrill sound of shattering porcelain rang through the lounge. The guests' shouts were escalating into a panic.

He felt he had something good going. But, in the next moment, it was Rentaro yelping in surprise.

Yuga wasn't down. He had carved a pair of large gouges in the carpet as the kick drew him back, but he wasn't knocked down—he had blocked it. No forward vision at all, and he blocked it. Unless he was tapping directly into Rentaro's mind, that shouldn't have been possible.

His adversary finally tore the tablecloth off his body. The moment Rentaro saw his face beneath, his eyes opened wide enough to nearly tear his eyelids off.

A pair of geometric shapes were laid over his irises, both rapidly spinning.

"That...that's crazy..."

Both *his eyes are cybernetic? That's like saying he's—*

"Oof. Guess you noticed, huh? Didn't I tell you I was built to surpass you?" Yuga, the very picture of calm composure, pointed a finger at his right eye. "This is the 21-Form Enhanced, an improved version of the 21-Form Varanium Artificial Eye. Compared to what you got, all of this model's specs received major upgrades."

"The 21-Form Enhanced...?"

Who did *that?*

The 21-Form Varanium Artificial Eye, developed by Sumire, was just one reason why she was hailed as one of the Four Sages. Your typical member of the scientific community, as he understood it, wouldn't be able to decipher even its basic workings.

As he stood there in a state of near-total desperation, he heard someone say, "Um, excuse me, sir..." from behind Yuga's back. He was a muscular hotel employee clad in a black suit, clearly a bouncer or something of the sort, and now he was placing a hand on Yuga's shoulder in a belated attempt to restore order.

"I can't have you brawling in here, guys; you're interfering with other—"

With a sharp *blam*, the man spouted a fountain of blood as he arced through the air, flipped over and unconscious the moment he hit the floor. The backward punch Yuga unleashed without even turning around smashed cleanly against his chin.

"Aaaaaaaaaaahhhh!"

There was a series of ear-piercing screams as the hotel guests, their panic unleashed by the sheer bizarreness of the situation, began to swarm toward the revolving door at the hotel's entrance like an avalanche. Amid the echoing screams and shouts, only Rentaro and Yuga remained quiet, a distance away from each other as opponent sized up opponent.

Yuga reached down to his waist and took something out. It was no coincidence, perhaps, that it was almost exactly where Rentaro liked to keep his gun.

In Yuga's hand now was a Browning automatic revolver, high-powered. Yuga raised it up, cocked it, and pointed the barrel forward, his squinting eyes focused on his prey. Rentaro could feel the murderous rage already. The shrill drone of the alarm drifted away as his mind immersed itself in the situation. He swallowed hard, his heart beating like a drum.

Ignoring for the moment the question of why he even had cybernetic eyes, Rentaro decided to consider his position. His own artificial eye was built for gunners' work—to help him predict the path of a bullet, from the barrel to the target. But if his foe had the same capability, how effective would that remain? There were fewer than ten meters between them, but to him, it may as well have been a yawning chasm.

Quietly, Rentaro closed his eyes.

Don't get scared.

Along with his keen, natural eye, his artificial one began its high-speed calculations. He could feel a burning pain behind his eyelid as it began to heat up. As Rentaro's vision began to go into a bizarre sort of slow motion with the overclocking of his eye, Yuga's finger tapped against the trigger and slowly began to squeeze. For a single-action weapon, it had a uniquely long and sticky stroke, a trademark of high-powered revolvers. With his focus turned up to maximum, Rentaro could even hear the trigger spring creak as it was being compressed.

Soon, the bar attached to the trigger did its work on the sear, the hammer swinging its way forward, the firing pin inside the breechblock striking the bottom of the cartridge.

Then, with an explosive flash, the bullet spiraled its way out of the barrel with 339 foot-pounds of muzzle energy, plowing its way straight toward him.

Rentaro calculated his escape route and started moving.

The sight of hotel bystanders screaming and crawling out the hotel door in a panic was quickly noticed by Inspector Tadashima, whose crew of officers was secretly staking out the building from the outside.

"Superintendent!"

Hitsuma, accepting the radio call from his director's van, replied an "All right" and nodded to the man beside him. "Inspector, the commissioner just gave the order to deploy a Special Assault Team."

"An SAT?! Do we really need to go that far?"

Hitsuma brought in a blue-uniformed special-forces captain. They saluted each other.

"Captain, I need you to bring your guys in. Take the fugitive dead or alive; just get the situation under control ASAP."

"B-but, Superintendent Hitsuma, Lady Seitenshi said to not hurt the fugitive as much as possible…"

"I think we've got some wires crossed, Captain. I want you to shoot the fugitive down. You have my backup on that."

Just then, a single gunshot rumbled its way across the hotel, as Rentaro Satomi and an unknown teenage boy began to wage battle in the middle of the lounge.

"What in the…?" Tadashima groaned.

The battle proceeded in bizarre fashion. The mystery kid would fire off a succession of shots, and Rentaro would step to the side or back to dodge them all. Not only that, but whenever there was an opening, he'd edge that much closer to his opponent. By the fifth shot, he was at point-blank range, the point where fists would decide the path of the fight.

Rentaro unleashed three punches from his arms. All of them would have ended the match right there, if they landed in the right place. The kid deflected them, retaliating with a high kick of his own. Rentaro bent his chin back to dodge it as he unleashed a horizontal chop designed to smash against his opponent's throat.

It was a dizzying array of attacks, dodges, and further counters, like an elaborate martial-arts demonstration. The number of strikes offered by each fighter in the space of a single second made any side observer's head swim. They appeared to be looking at each other, but in a way, they were both looking somewhere much farther off. When he realized they were simultaneously dodging attacks while piecing together a strategy for their next ten strikes, Tadashima's entire body shuddered.

This wasn't the sort of battle any human being could tag into.

What in the hell is going on?

Tadashima slipped a hand inside of his suit and tightened his grip on the revolver in his holster. He was going in after the first SAT assault.

Not that Tadashima could have known, but there was no way a battle whose participants could conduct the entire thought process—

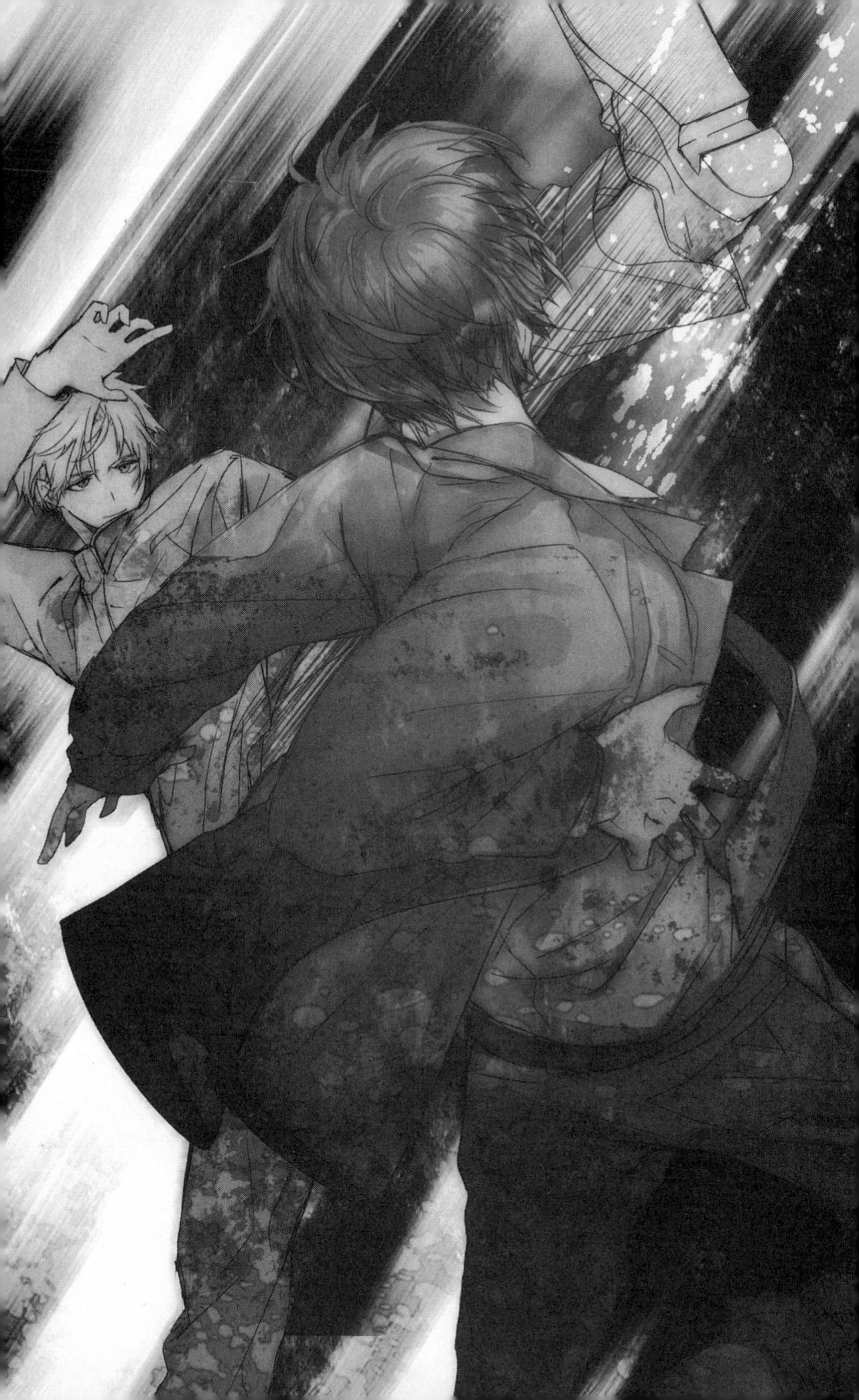

observation, comprehension, action—behind each move in a hundredth of a second could ever be stopped by a team of regular people, whose comparatively paltry muscle-reflex time never had a chance of reaching below 0.20 seconds.

The core processors behind each of their cybernetic eyes calculated furiously, straining near their maximum output to find a hole to exploit.

But, gradually, the battle began to demonstrate a certain one-sidedness.

"Gah!"

Taking a kick that made it feel like he was about to be reunited with the contents of his stomach, Rentaro found himself falling over a nearby upturned table. A flurry of glass shards rained upon him.

"We're working with different specs here, okay? Different specs."

Ahead of him, he could hazily see Yuga, calm and content as he opened his arms to him. Rentaro gritted his teeth as he stood up, readying himself for battle on unsteady legs. Yuga, observing his actions in detail, snorted.

"I know, Satomi. You've applied force to your right hamstring, your right femoral bicep muscle, and the ulnar extensor and ulnar flexor muscles on your left wrist. You're planning to feint with a left and strike me with a mid-level kick, aren't you? That's gonna be a poor move, though. Once we exchange blows for the thirty-seventh time, I'm going to smash your skull bone to pieces. Checkmate."

Startled, Rentaro tossed his accumulated tactical analysis into his mental garbage can and began to conceive a new strategy.

"Oh, are you changing gears now? That's gonna be even worse. If you lunge at me to try to pin me down, I'll break your jaw in ten moves or less. Checkmate."

"No..."

The short circuit taking place in his brain made it impossible for Rentaro to even formulate a plan. He found himself edging back in fear.

Yuga lowered his stance, a self-assured smile on his face. The moment he did, a team of blue-suited assault troops streamed through the entrance and windows behind Yuga, charging for both of them.

The SAT? Why?

This was going too fast. The alarm bell only just started ringing a second ago.

The situation was beyond Rentaro's comprehension, but he could tell they weren't exactly here to rescue him. He had to get out of there. Now.

At that moment, a move flashed across his brain like lightning. A move that could completely turn the tables.

So how about this?

Tearing through the skin on his right leg, he revealed his artificial limb, the black chrome shining brilliantly in the light. The striker hit the cartridge hidden inside his leg, the ejector kicking it away.

"Raaaaaaaaahhhhhhhh!"

Leaving his body to the power of inertia, Rentaro kicked. His foot was aimed at the floor beneath the carpet. His Super-Varanium toes tore through the fabric, pulverizing both the marble beneath it and the bare concrete beneath that as it blew all the debris forward.

The results were akin to a directional anti-personnel mine, one with a lethal, unavoidable payload of shrapnel.

The rock and marble, now crushed into several hundreds, several thousands of shards, unerringly advanced upon the SAT troops and Yuga. Even one of them striking anyone's head would cause a sure concussion—and if not, a few dozen of those striking Yuga's armorless frame could very likely result in multiple bone fractures.

But, amazingly, Yuga covered up his face and plunged right into the storm of shrapnel. An innumerable amount of fragments pounded against his entire body. Blood flew. His clothes were ripped to pieces. But he still made it through the shockwave.

By the time he realized Yuga was at his chest, the heel of his palm right against his breast, it was all too late. The blood drained from Rentaro's face as he witnessed the twisted look of joy on his opponent's.

"I admire your performance, Satomi. Good-bye."

He twisted his palm. A paralyzing pain took Rentaro, as if the torsion was applied directly to his internal organs. Picturing the cold hand of death clasping itself around his heart, he quickly spun his body, kicked at the floor, and flew back, avoiding lethal injury. Something heavy smashed into his back, knocking the air out of his lungs.

The next thing he knew, Rentaro had flown into an elevator car, panting for breath. Yuga was positioned for a follow-up strike. Reflexively, Rentaro jabbed his finger against the DOOR CLOSE button and the one for the top floor. The door closed so slowly, he wanted to scream—and Yuga was advancing on him the whole time.

Just as Rentaro thought his adversary disappeared behind the heavy doors, Yuga let out a shuddering kick to prevent his escape. With the sickening sound of twisting, crushing metal, the door began to dent inward.

The entire elevator car shook, bits of wall tile falling off and plinking against the floor. It took Rentaro some time to realize this disaster was engineered entirely by a single kick.

Still, after a moment or two of thought, the cable hoist installed at the top of the shaft apparently decided to haul the elevator up. The elevator rose with a slow, listless, but nevertheless constant force.

Rentaro gritted his teeth at the grinding pain as he rolled up the long-sleeve shirt he was wearing. The mark Yuga's palm had left on his chest was a sickeningly deep shade of blue. What kind of strike could damage the human body so profoundly? All he knew was that Yuga meant that last move to be his finisher. If it had hit him full bore, he'd be dead right now.

That was the New World Creation Project.

"Damn it…!" He sighed deeply as he stared at the ceiling, languid.

Despite losing his prey, Yuga—eyes staring at the elevator's floor indicator to see where Rentaro would escape—felt perfectly refreshed in his heart. The edges of his lips curled upward.

"The game begins, Satomi. Just try to escape this hotel alive."

"Halt!"

Suddenly, a rather impolite voice flew at him from behind.

"Put the gun down and put your hands on your head!"

He narrowed his eyes, annoyed at the interlopers ruining the mood. As he expected, a large force had their eyes and guns pointed at him.

They were clad in blue, which nicely framed their black bulletproof vests and the visored helmets on their heads. The front line wielded handguns and riot shields, the troops behind them armed with submachine guns. It was the SAT.

Yuga very reluctantly put his left hand above his head, the right one pointing at a pocket in his light jacket. Receiving a nod of permission, he slowly, deliberately took out a card holder and threw it on the ground.

An SAT team member gingerly picked it up, fixing his gaze upon it. It contained a civil security license.

Yuga was not a Promoter, nor did he have an Initiator partner. It was a fake, given by his "employer" to make it easier for him to walk around armed in public, but the special-forces team would never have a chance to confirm that.

"Oh, what, you're a civsec? What're you doing here?"

"I heard about him escaping on the news. I spotted him on the street, and as a fellow civsec, I felt it was my duty to do something about this. Guess he got away, though."

The SAT member tossed the case back at Yuga and waved him away. "All right, you can go. We'll take over the scene."

Yuga shrugged and walked toward the entrance. Just as he did, two detectives came through the revolving door. One was clearly Hitsuma—tall and handsome, even from afar—but who was that worn-out old guy next to him?

Hitsuma clapped his hands to get the SAT troops' attention. "All right, hurry up and cut off the elevator's main and backup power. Once we trap Rentaro Satomi in there, you guys take the stairs up. I have another team coming down from the roof; we'll close in on him from both sides. Do not let the fugitive get away."

With a single order, the hall filled with noise as the SAT crew divided into two groups, one running for the emergency stairwell. As he passed by Hitsuma, Yuga took advantage of the loud footsteps to whisper into his ear.

"I'm ambushing Satomi from another point."

"Don't make this harder for me, Dark Stalker. Not even I can cover for you forever."

"I know, Mr. Hitsuma."

The whole interaction took place without so much as their eyes meeting. Once Yuga emerged out the revolving door, he found a small herd of police cars, their lights bouncing off every surface in the area around the hotel. A hot, sticky wind blew against his face, but it still felt weirdly refreshing to him as he looked up at the Magata Plaza Hotel, looming large in the night sky.

They had already allowed him to escape once. If Rentaro made it out of the hotel, the police's reputation would be at stake. There was no doubt they'd pull out every stop to hunt him down.

From this point forward, Yuga's adversary would be the SAT.

Rentaro slapped his cheeks to mentally refresh himself. He couldn't sit in this car forever.

Before long, the elevators would shut off. They'd operate a circuit breaker or two, he figured, to make sure only his elevator would stop in place. This meant the car would turn into a giant metal tomb. He'd just have to sit there and wait for his arrest.

But how am I gonna get out of this hotel…?

Looking at the floor indicator, he found the hotel spanned a total of thirty-two floors. He pushed the *20* button, nearest to where he was now, and in a few moments, the door opened with a chipper *beep*.

Then the light in the elevator shut off, darkening his vision. Just as the door was about to close, it stopped cold for good. Rentaro had no time to be startled—he knew immediately what had happened. A bead of cold sweat ran down his back.

The lights were still on in the corridor he stepped into—recessed lights, illuminating the beige wallpaper. Towels, nightgowns, and other detritus lined the floors. Perhaps unnerved by the sudden alarms, most of the guests on this floor left their doors wide open, fleeing the scene with whatever they could grab. In other words, most of them were long gone. He couldn't sense anyone nearby.

Keeping his guard up, Rentaro crept up to a twentieth-floor window and carefully looked down. The police had already arrived, and the flashing lights of their cars silently revealed the multilayered perimeter they built around the hotel, ringed by yellow police tape. Beyond that, a crowd of reporters and onlookers teemed. There wasn't enough room for so much as an ant to slip through.

Suddenly hearing a rotor from afar, he squinted at the sky, spotting a helicopter restlessly spinning its searchlight around. Rentaro edged away from the window as the ray of light swept past it.

There was no way he could stay on this floor for long. The police already knew the elevator was stopped on floor twenty. But going down was out of the question...which meant his only option was to go up. Rentaro knew all too well that things were only getting worse for him.

Pushing open a metal door beneath a green emergency-exit sign with a little running man on it, he felt a chill wind against his face. In stark contrast to the magnificent interior décor, the rustic emergency stairway was lined with exposed pipes as it spiraled up and down.

Hearing subdued footsteps from below, Rentaro looked over the guardrail to find SAT troopers in riot gear, their faces covered by visors, about seven floors below him. He met eyes with one of them. In a panic, he pulled his face away from the guardrail, in tandem with the trooper pointing his gun upward and pulling the trigger.

With a blast muffled by a silencer, a hail of bullets clanged against the rail, making Rentaro snap his head back. Sweating, he crouched down low as he sped off. One way or the other, his only path was upward.

But, after a few floors, he heard a clatter of equally subdued footsteps from above. His spine froze in terror. They must have climbed out from the helicopter.

Realizing he was the victim of a pincer attack and feeling the desperation settle in, Rentaro looked at the metal plate in the stairwell. Floor 26. Opening the metal door, he rolled into the hallway, fairly wide and lined with beige wallpaper, recessed lighting, and familiar-looking doors on both sides. The same as the twentieth floor. Several doors were open, left unattended by panicking evacuees, some leaving their shoes and even their wallets on the floor as they stumbled away.

He had to stand his ground here.

Rentaro thought about barricading himself in an empty room, but the voice of reason stopped him. He was dealing with professionals at resolving standoffs and disarming terrorist groups. What chance would he have?

He ducked into the nearest room, went up to the bathroom mirror, and took an elbow to it. With a dry cracking sound, it shattered. He chose a suitable piece, left the room, dove left at a T intersection, plastered himself against the wall, and pointed the mirror fragment at the hallway he had just left, pulling his wrist back as he adjusted the angle.

As he guessed, he heard the faint creak of the emergency-exit door, stirring up the otherwise-stagnant air of the empty hotel.

Here they come. Six of them, with riot shields, in the mirror-image world. Surprisingly, even though they were in heavy headgear, protectors, and combat boots, he could no longer hear them move. Their intense wariness indicated that they were sure of his position.

Quietly, Rentaro wiped a sweaty palm on his pants.

The troopers' headgear protected their eyes from things like flash grenades. Their submachine guns were a half-and-half mix of Heckler & Koch and Shiba Heavy Weapons, both deadly accurate. Luckily, they hadn't noticed him yet.

Since he was still in the clothes he wore to the Seitenshi's palace, Rentaro had neither his wallet nor any sort of gun. He'd have to tackle them empty-handed. An all-or-nothing bull rush at them might allow him time to finish off one or two, but no more than that before someone shot him. But if he stayed still, they'd spot his position, roll a Flash Bang down the hall, and that'd be it. Those things were serious business—between the sound, the light, and the pressure wave from the explosion, they were the perfect weapon for indoor combat zones.

The shockwave, in particular, was powerful enough to break cell phones, wristwatches, and other precision devices. Having one blow up at point-blank range could even cause bone fractures and ruptured eardrums—nothing you could avoid just by closing your eyes and sticking your fingers in your ears.

Rentaro's pulse quickened, the hairs on his nape sticking out.

What do I do? What do I do? Even as he thought about that, the SAT were following what they learned in training, tackling each doorway in pairs to eliminate blind spots before entering and clearing out the hotel rooms. It was shocking how silent they were.

Something bounced off Rentaro's foot as he began to walk. Looking down, he realized it was a Magata Plaza Hotel–branded box of matches. A guest must have dropped it in the frenzied confusion earlier.

A flash of intuition struck Rentaro's mind, and looking straight up, he found exactly what he was looking for. Resolved to his plan, he nodded to himself and performed a move he never thought he'd do in his life.

Suddenly, one of the hallway doors opened, revealing a confused-looking woman wandering out. He thought she might've been a straggler who missed the evaluation, but one look, and he knew it. Those empty eyes told Rentaro she was struggling under some sort of illness.

A surprised SAT trooper pulled his gun on her.

"Whoa, wai—"

Before Rentaro could stop him, an empty-sounding blast ripped across the hall as an unfortunate shot bounded its way toward the woman. She fell to her knees, then to the floor. Rentaro sped out to get near her, only to be pushed back by a steel wave of bullets, pulverizing the wall behind him and creating a cloud of dust that got in his eyes.

They got my position, too.

He had no time to think. He dove into a nearby room, took a chair out of it, then stood on it as he struck a match against the flint. A warm flame kindled itself in his hands. He thrust it toward the edge of the ceiling.

It was aimed squarely at the fire alarm system. The heat-detection sensor picked up on the flame from the match, immediately ordering the adjacent sprinkler to activate.

An intense rain sprang up across the floor.

Listening to the SAT team fall into confusion and making sure their fire had stopped, Rentaro looked down the corridor. The scene was exactly what he envisioned. The SAT troopers, their sight robbed by the sprays of water, were a disorganized mess, trying their best to remove their helmets.

This was his chance.

Leaping out from the wall, Rentaro activated his gunpowder-activated artificial leg, firing off a single burst. Thrusters spat out exhaust from the back of his foot.

"Haaaaaaaaaaaaaaah!!"

His body zoomed at superspeed down the hall, so quickly that he felt like his body would fall apart. Then he smashed right into the SAT men in front of him. Even through their visors, he could tell he had the element of surprise on his side. Keeping the thrust going, he used his pivot leg to give himself rotational force, unleashing a roundhouse kick. It slammed into one of the polycarbonate shields, smashing it along with a trooper's visor as he was sent flying through the air backward.

The point man—lagging behind because of the potential for friendly fire—along with two troopers desperately trying to rip their helmets off, were struck in the face by a pair of fists launched from Rentaro's body. Without skipping a beat, he searched for his next target. The heel of his palm applied to another trooper's chin rattled both the SAT member's visor and his brain. He finished another with a chop to the throat before his opponent even knew what happened.

One could only guess what the final survivor was thinking, watching his comrades get picked off in less than a second. After an instant of thought, he threw off his submachine gun and tried to take out his backup revolver. It goes without saying that this move was ill-advised. Handguns had little power when one was within closed-fist range of a target. After that point, it all came down to how gifted a martial artist one was.

Rentaro lunged at his chest, grappling at him as he placed a hand above his holster to keep him from drawing. His other hand was placed palm-down on the plating in his bulletproof vest.

"Tendo Martial Arts First Style, Number 12—"

A bolt of terror flashed across the man's eyes. But it was all too late.

"—*Senkuu Renen!*"

With a heavy *thump*, the very air shook across the floor. The trooper's body bounced off the floor, eyes lolling upward. The force applied to him at such tight quarters was enough to finish him, no matter how thick the plating on his vest was; that was an ironclad rule in close-quarters combat. This was the unchanging credo that gave Tendo Martial Arts such all-powerful strength.

Amid the torrential rain from the sprinkler, Rentaro quietly took the Infinite Stance, calming his heart just as the five SAT troopers he had faced fell to the floor all at once, flopping over the one Rentaro had defeated first with his roundhouse.

The fight was over. The rain falling around him was warm to the touch, weighing down his school uniform. Sensing the water droplets falling from his hair, his chin, his nose, Rentaro adjusted his breathing for a moment as he remained in his stance. Then, returning to reality, he crouched down next to the woman one of them shot.

"Hey. Hey, hang in there."

She was shot once in the abdominal area with a 9-mm bullet. It was still lodged in her body.

The woman groggily opened her eyes. "I...I couldn't sleep... I...I took some...pills..."

Rentaro heard that being forced awake after taking a strong relaxant resulted in intense feelings of anger and the inability to walk steadily. Whatever her illness was, her medicine knocked her out so cold that she couldn't even respond to that alarm in time. He fetched a towel from a nearby room and pressed it against the open wound to stop the blood. It went bright red in the blink of an eye. The sprinkler water was chilling her body as well. This was nothing first aid could solve for her. And he had no time left to lose.

Giving himself a nod, Rentaro walked over to an SAT trooper—the one who fired the fateful shot at her. Kicking the submachine gun away, he grabbed his knife and gun, holster and all. Making sure he was wholly unarmed, Rentaro crouched down and slapped his cheek.

With a groan, he opened his eyes, trying to hazily focus on Rentaro in front of him. A professional to the core, he didn't make a noise once he realized the situation, and instead glared at Rentaro.

"You've got nowhere to run. Stop filling up your rap sheet."

Rentaro aimed his gun at him. "Shut up," he threatened. "That ammo you fired hit an innocent woman. She needs surgery to remove the bullet right now. Can you carry her down to the lobby? Just nod if it's yes."

The man looked overwhelmed for a moment, but quickly returned to his usual grave countenance. Still pointing the gun at him, Rentaro made the man pick the woman up and saw him off to the stairwell. Before they left, he grabbed the woman's hand.

"Stay calm, okay, lady? They're gonna save you."

The woman gave him an unfocused look. "You...," she said, unsteadily. "You're...a killer... Why'd you...help...?"

"......"

Then the woman extended a hand to him.

"I...ah... Thank—"

"Don't talk. Just think about staying alive." Rentaro gave the man a nudge. He looked back a couple times, clearly wanting to say something, before descending the stairwell. Carrying a person down from the twenty-sixth floor was hard work, but a trained SAT trooper could probably deal with it.

Rentaro watched him go down, thinking to himself.

The HQ might be panicking about the lack of contact from their SAT group, but once they realized how it doesn't affect their position all that much, they'd just send in another team. There was no guarantee he'd win next time. And there might be other stragglers like that woman. If he broke down a door or two, grabbed some quivering hotel guest, and took him hostage, that might prevent the cops from making the first move.

"...Don't be stupid."

Rentaro immediately shook his head. He made it this far because he wanted to prove his innocence and find the real killer. Committing more crimes for non-self-defense reasons would be putting the cart before the horse.

He took a glance at the floor above him. He knew this great escape had every chance of ending soon, but there was nothing else he could do. He just had to struggle for as long as he could.

Not bothering to stop at the top floor, he continued climbing the stairs, through an AUTHORIZED PERSONNEL ONLY sign and right up to the door leading to the roof. He shook the knob. It didn't budge. Locked. Activating his artificial arm, he swung a fist right into the middle of it, sending it off its hinges and into the outdoor air.

Stepping onto the roof, he noticed the clouds zipping by at high speed in the night air. The sky was so much closer now; the wind lapping between the high-rise buildings made the sopping-wet Rentaro feel unpleasantly cold.

Running to the edge of the building, Rentaro observed the police lights flash on and off below him. The sound of the helicopter rotors was, thankfully, far away.

Spotting a building in front of him taller than the Plaza Hotel, Rentaro found himself seized by an odd sense of déjà vu. Then he remembered something. His battle against Tina Sprout, the Seitenshi sniper, amid the derelict buildings of the Outer Districts. In order to get under her position, he had used his leg thrusters to launch a series of rapid bursts to leap from building to building. It wasn't pretty, but it worked.

Could that work here, too?

Rentaro took another glance down. The authorities had surrounded the hotel building, but nowhere else. The adjacent building was free.

Eyeballing it, he estimated the distance between *here* and *there* to be around twenty meters. A wide river flowed between the two buildings. He had made it across a much larger distance, he figured, in the Tina battle. Just do it the same way as before, and it would be a shoo-in.

Can I do this? Can I?

Rentaro brought a palm up to his face. It was shaking slightly. He'd be lying if he said he wasn't scared, but knowing this wasn't the first time he had faced a deadly leap like this pushed him over the brink.

Walking back from the guardrail, he went all the way to the other side, giving himself ample space to build up a head of steam. He pictured the successful traverse in his mind. One little error in his timing, and he'd be falling straight down to his death. The hotel, if his memory served him, was 147 meters tall—not exactly the duplex down the street. Mess this up, and not only would they have to peel him off the sidewalk; he'd have plenty of time to picture the whole scene on the way down, too.

He stretched out his fingers, forming them into fists and opening them up again to calm the nerves. The sweat came right back to his palms. He inhaled, then exhaled.

Staring at the space in front of him, he started running. Slowly at first, not more than a jog. Then gradually building up speed, then at full blast, making sure not to get his feet tangled.

The guardrail was in sight. He stepped over it, then flung himself into the air. After a moment spent gliding, he felt an odd type of weightlessness as the wind carried him into its current. Simultaneously, he set off a cartridge in his leg. With a bang, he felt acceleration hit him like a wall as it propelled him forward.

Barely managing to squint ahead, he saw thin air spread in front of him. The angle, and the timing of the thruster blast, were perfect. Now he just needed to maintain a steady rhythm of cartridge blasts to keep him—

Suddenly, he felt a shock rip through the side of his stomach.

"—Uh?"

He'd been so sure of his success just moments ago, he couldn't immediately identify the plume of blood fanning out from his side at first.

From that point forward, the world went into a bizarre sort of slow motion. Rentaro's body flailed in the air, head pointed straight down. Then he saw it.

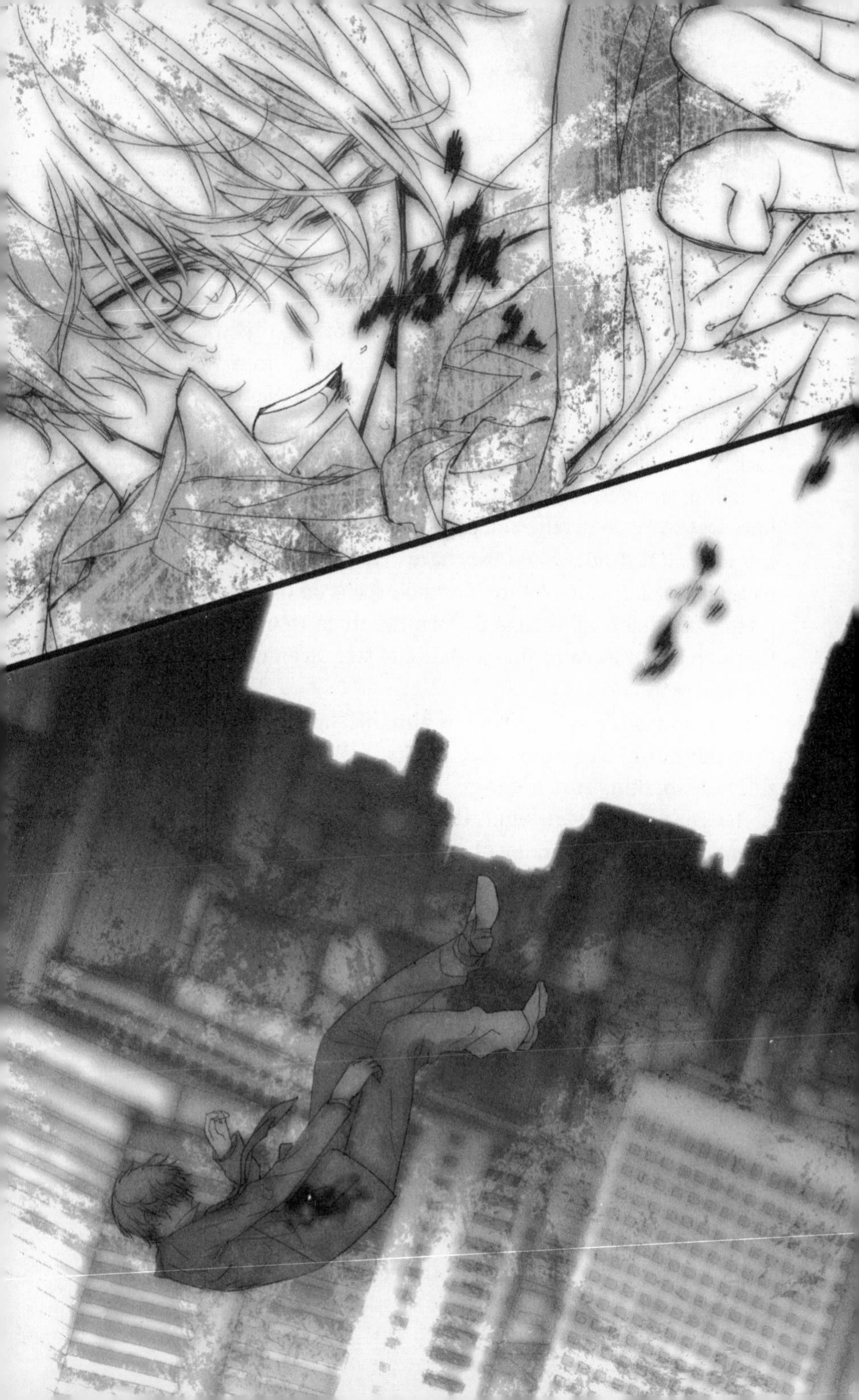

There was a gunshot wound on his side. A sniper hit him, in midair, at blazing speed.

The rangefinder almost reflexively activated in his eye, spotting a figure 200 meters off in the distance, on top of a roof with a gigantic light-up billboard on it.

"N...no..."

Feeling gravity do its work on his body, Rentaro was swallowed up in the perpetual darkness.

The smell of hot smoke wisped out from his gun, searing his nostrils.

"Checkmate."

Yuga, assuming a kneeling posture on the roof, lifted his head up from the night scope mounted on top of his DSR sniper rifle. He turned the handle as he pulled it forward. An empty cartridge flew to the ground.

Standing up, Yuga watched Rentaro fall for a few moments as he took out his cell phone.

"Dark Stalker to Nest. Mission complete. Target silenced. Awaiting further orders."

"You're sure you got him?"

"He fell in the river, so I can't be sure, but falling in water from the height he did is just like impacting concrete. He must've broken every bone in his body. My condolences to his family."

14

"No...!"

The Seitenshi rose from her throne in horror, both hands covering her lips.

The police commissioner in the crew cut, hands clasped behind his back, sadly shook his head.

"They were apparently forced to neutralize him after he put up heavy resistance. There was nothing we could do."

The shock was similar at the Tendo Civil Security Agency.

"You, you're kidding me..."

Kisara, rearing away, was blocked by her desk from going farther. Hitsuma quickly acted to hold her before her legs gave out.

"I'm deeply sorry, Ms. Tendo. I told my men multiple times to take Satomi alive if they could, but apparently there were some crossed wires in our command chain."

Kisara shook violently as she embraced Hitsuma.

"What am I gonna do...? I... What am I gonna do? Enju, Tina, Satomi... They're all gone."

There was something moving about the sight—such a firm, resolute woman, looking so pitifully small now. Hitsuma turned her head away from the desk, then lightly blew into her ear. It practically made her leap out of his arms.

"Now you're all alone," he sweetly whispered. "I want to be here. To help you forget about your loneliness... Will you marry me, Kisara?"

They both had their respective chins on each other's shoulders so he couldn't gauge her face, but through the shaking, he could feel one firm, palpable nod on his body.

Now this girl is mine.

Resisting the urge to shout out in joy, he turned his face downward.

Her hair was as jet-black as a raven, her skin almost a sickly white, her neck thin. Her collarbone was flushed with pink, no doubt from her emotional agitation. Her breasts, like fruit, pushed up by her black school uniform, were ripe and ready for the picking, practically dripping with sweetness radiating off her body. It was like a work of art.

Just as he was reaching toward one of them, hoping for perhaps a small taste, the cell phone in his breast pocket rang. He nodded at Kisara, almost groaning in frustration in the process, and answered it.

"This is Nest. Dark Stalker says he needs to talk to you about Rentaro Satomi. It's urgent."

It was now one o'clock in the morning.

Police officers swarmed to the riverside where Rentaro fell, Yuga Mitsugi among the crowd. He stared at the river with his hands in his pockets, motionless.

Is this it? he wondered to himself.

Rentaro Satomi... He considered the life of his adversary: the savior of Tokyo Area. Part of the civsec pair whose names were on the lips of people worldwide. The slayer of Kagetane Hiruko, Rank 134. Slayer of the Zodiac Scorpion. Slayer of Tina Sprout, Rank 98. Slayer of Aldebaran, the immortal Gastrea.

If this was any normal civsec, he would've been 100 percent dead in these circumstances. But *was* he?

A bespectacled young man sidled up to him.

"What is it?"

"Mr. Hitsuma," he said as he stared at the black water, "can you get divers on the scene right away?"

Hitsuma eyed him doubtfully, wondering what inspired this.

"There's no point doing that until sunrise."

"It'll give me some peace of mind, at least. It'll be too late by then anyway."

Hitsuma's eyebrows arched downward. "You think Rentaro Satomi is alive? You *said* you defeated him."

"I'm saying that we need to prepare for anything. Common sense doesn't apply to him."

"That's high praise, coming from you."

"You haven't fought him, Mr. Hitsuma. You wouldn't understand. My specs were defined so I'd be able to suppress Rentaro Satomi. When we did the calculations before the mission, there was supposed to be a 0.02 percent chance of Satomi even landing a blow on me. But even though I deflected it, Satomi landed the *first strike*. A kick. When we unleashed our eyes, he managed to graze me three times because I couldn't calculate his moves fast enough. In the end, I was hit by a rain of shrapnel I had no chance of dodging. Satomi was starting to get accustomed to my moves."

"……"

"Wouldn't that make you sleep better, too, Mr. Hitsuma, if we found an arm or his head or something?"

"Look, are you threatening me?"

Yuga shrugged and raised his hands in surrender.

"No, no, no. I'm just making a suggestion. Just get those divers in here, all right? As long as we don't find a body, I think it'll be smarter for all of us if we treat him as alive."

BLACK BULLET 5

CHAPTER 02

THE NEW WORLD CREATION PROJECT

1

He could hear droplets of water going *plink-plink* into a puddle at regular intervals. Some insects were faintly droning a fair distance away.

He could smell rusted metal. The air batting against his skin was humid, and he felt something hard and solid on his back and hips that made him wonder where they put him down.

How long had he been asleep? He needed to get up. He had important things to do. Something really important...

Trying to move his body, he realized that he almost couldn't move his arms at all. Whenever he tried, all that resulted was some kind of jingling metal sound. His arms hurt.

Was he tied up somewhere?

—*Where am I?*

Finally, he came to the core question. His eyelids felt like they were made of iron, but he struggled through it, blinking several times until he could finally start to make out the environment around him.

The first thing he saw was a wall lined with light blue tiles. He was sitting on tile as well. He couldn't move his hands. Something was hanging between his arms, keeping them aloft. He twitched his neck upward to look. Both of his wrists were cuffed, binding him to an orange, rusted metal pipe. It appeared Rentaro had been resting his back on the side of a bathtub.

Yes. That was the case: He was handcuffed to a pipe in a bathtub. It wasn't a large bathroom, just big enough for the tub in question, and he couldn't even stretch his legs all the way out. He guessed he was in someone's private residence.

After a few more moments, he finally realized his predicament. He was being held. Beyond that, he knew nothing. Who was keeping him in here, and for what reason?

His mind was still hazy, but he felt he had a grip on at least two things. One, he was alive. Two, he probably wasn't taken in by the police. If that were the case, he would've awoken on a hospital bed or something.

Looking down at his abdomen, he found several layers of bandages wrapped underneath his open shirt. It was basic, but he was receiving *some* treatment, at least.

The bathroom was dark and partitioned by a sliding door. It was bright on the other side of the opaque glass, but he could only discern faint outlines beyond it.

Forcing his body to shift position, he felt an intense pain shoot out from his side and course across his body.

"Is…anybody there…?" he called out haltingly. Then he repeated it a few times. At the third repetition, he heard heavy tramping as a shadowy figure came up to the glass and slid the door open.

"You're awake?"

The first thing he noticed was her legs—too thin to be called supple. Looking up, he realized her thighs and arms looked just as thin, like easily snappable twigs. She had on short denim pants, a pink tank top, and an American Apparel jacket. Her cold eyes and bob-cut chestnut hair danced around in the air, a quiet anger burning behind her gaze. She was a girl as frigid as ice.

"Do you know who I am?"

Rentaro slowly nodded, trying to will his pounding head into kindling his memory for him.

I think her name was—

"Hotaru Kouro…right? Suibara's Initiator."

Hotaru slowly returned the nod.

"And do you know why I'm confining you in here?"

Rentaro took another look around the cramped bathroom.

"More or less."

His memory served him up to the point when he was shot out of the air by a sniper and smashed into the river's surface. Given that he wasn't six feet under, he supposed that meant he was dragged out of the water at some point.

That, and he had an idea of what this girl who saved him wanted.

At that exact moment, the barrel of a gun darker than death dominated his sight. An automatic revolver, pointed right between his eyes.

"Got anything you want to say?"

"You're the girl who flipped that van over, aren't you?"

"Mm-hmm," the girl murmured without hesitation, staring icicles at him.

"Why did you do that?"

"To get revenge for Kihachi. Is there any other reason?"

"You look pretty calm, considering."

"Do you have any idea how long you were out? Three days. Three days is long enough for anyone to calm down a little."

"Why didn't you kill me before now?"

"I wanted to see you confess your sins," Hotaru replied, eyebrows wholly motionless as Rentaro glared up at her.

"I didn't kill Suibara, man."

"Don't give me that shit."

The words were quiet, but Hotaru's irises were a blazing shade of red. The gun's hammer was cocked, her hand virtually crushing the grip. Silent rage enveloped her tiny frame.

"Don't you care about your life at all?"

"I mean it. Seriously, I didn't kill him—"

Then he took a teeth-shattering blow to his lower jaw, and the next thing he knew, he was looking at the ceiling tile. It broke a molar or two—he was gritting his teeth at the time. The metallic taste of blood filled his mouth. It took some time for him to realize Hotaru landed a straight kick on him.

"Gnh... Ahghh!"

He fixed his gaze on Hotaru as he spat out the tooth fragments. A ribbon of saliva mixed with blood hung down from the side of his mouth before falling. Hotaru watched from above like an executioner.

"I don't think I heard you."

"I already told you, I didn't—"

The next kick was to the wound on his side.

"Grhh...nnh!"

She kept her foot on the opening, making him experience enough pain to make his brain explode.

Hotaru refocused her gun's aim on Rentaro's head.

"All right—I'm not into tormenting people like this, so this is your last chance. If you admit to your crime and beg for mercy, I'll turn you over to the police instead of killing you. But if you lie to me, the next time your head hits the floor, it'll have a hole right in the middle of it. Think it over before you decide—do you need to live, or do you need to die?"

Rentaro, still staring at Hotaru, nodded silently.

"Okay. Here goes: Do you feel any guilt at all about killing Kihachi? He said you were one of his best friends, and *you* caught him in that dirty little trap and killed him. Are you even a little sorry for that? Answer me."

What a witch hunt this was. All she wanted was for Rentaro to confess to it. She didn't believe he was even a little bit innocent.

But, perhaps because of that, the girl's words were completely unadorned. They came from the heart. If Rentaro screamed his innocence, she was absolutely going to pull the trigger.

The voice of logic in his mind shouted at him to admit to it for now. He could make up for it later. *This girl's just like the cops.* Why would he ever hesitate to deceive her?

His conclusion made, he gave Hotaru a defiant, resolute look. "Please believe me," he said, elucidating every syllable. "I didn't do it. Really."

The gunshot blared across the bathroom. Rentaro's body spasmed. With a *tink*, the empty cartridge bounced off the tile a few times before the silence returned.

White smoke wafted out from the gun barrel.

Gingerly turning his head to the side, Rentaro found a bullet lodged in the bathtub, millimeters from his nose.

Hotaru turned away from him as she took out a cell phone and dialed a number.

"Oh, hello," she said after a moment, "is this the police?" She turned back to Rentaro for just a moment before continuing. "I came across the wanted fugitive Rentaro Satomi, so I placed him under citizen's arrest... Right. No, this isn't a prank. It's true."

After relaying her name and address, Hotaru ended the call and looked back at Rentaro. "They thought I was kidding," she stated, "but they're still coming. They said I wasn't far from the nearest station, so it won't even be five minutes."

Hotaru leaned in, putting her eye level on the same height as her quarry.

"I'll listen to what you have to say. But only until the police arrive. Once they do, that's it. You're going with them."

"Why didn't you kill me?"

"Because you're not worth it anymore. Have fun getting strung up by the court."

"Whoa, what did the police tell you?"

"They said you lured Kihachi over to you and killed him for money."

Rentaro attempted a scornful laugh, but gurgled out a cough instead. He gazed at Hotaru as he spat out a mixture of phlegm and blood.

"The story they told *me* was, Suibara was blackmailing me for money and I killed him to shut him up."

"...That's a lie. There's no way Kihachi would do that."

"Of course not. He didn't do that at all, and I didn't blackmail him, either. So there, you see? Right from the start, our stories are contradicting each other. I think we've got enemies in the police, too. Don't you think there's something weird about all this? Nothing striking you as odd?"

"...You got four minutes."

"There's something I do need to apologize to you about. It's that I couldn't keep Suibara safe. He was a nervous wreck by the time he came to my office. I was fully willing to listen to his story so we could share the burden, but he was too freaked out to tell me. And I didn't pursue it. I misjudged the situation, and for that, I am truly sorry."

Hotaru kept her eyes away from him, twisting her eyebrows low as she anguished for her Promoter.

"Stop it."

"Look, in a court of law, you're supposed to listen to both sides of the story and then the jury or a judge or whatever makes the decision, right? You've already heard the police's side. Now I want you to hear mine, but I can't wrap that up in the course of five minutes. I want you to give me a chance."

"A chance?"

Hotaru found herself leaning forward.

"There's a group out there that framed me," Rentaro continued, choosing his words carefully. "Not only did they pin the murder on me; they targeted everybody in the Tendo Civil Security Agency. I'm not some kind of innocent bystander here. I want to catch the guys that framed me. Can you help me with that?"

"You're just gonna run away."

"If that's what you think, then go right ahead and hand me over. But, if you think even a little bit that I'm worth listening to, I want you to wait on that. I know you want to learn the truth about all this, if you can. I took a case from Suibara. He was keeping some kind of secret, and he said he wanted to go through me so he could reveal it to the Seitenshi. A day later, somebody killed him. There's got to be something going on behind the scenes."

"...Two minutes."

"If it turns out there's *not* anyone behind the scenes, you can go ahead and kill me then. Burn me at the stake, draw and quarter me, put my head on a pike; anything."

"Are you...serious?"

Rentaro returned Hotaru's stare and gave her a powerful nod.

"Suibara trusted in me. Now it's your turn. Please."

The two of them looked into each other's eyes for several moments. Rentaro held his breath in silence. A drop of water from the tap fell with a *splip* onto the tile floor by his feet.

Just as Hotaru was about to say something, someone began repeatedly pressing the doorbell. It was the police.

Rentaro closed his eyes and tried to keep his body from shaking. *Time's up, huh?*

Hotaru, all emotion quelled from her eyes, stood up and walked out of the bathroom. She didn't close the glass door behind her, forcing Rentaro to watch the entire proceedings. The layout of this place meant that the main bathroom and the front door were extremely close to each other, so it took only a few seconds for Hotaru to undo the door chain and greet the person outside. He could see Hotaru, but not the policeman she was talking to.

"Are you the girl who called?"

A chill crossed Rentaro's spine.

"Yeah."

"All right," said the clearly doubtful voice of another officer. There must've been two of them. "Um, so…let's cut to the chase. Did you really capture Rentaro Satomi?"

Rentaro jammed his eyes shut, already imagining the next sentence. *Oh, do come in. Want some tea? I have him in cuffs in the bathroom.*

"I'm sorry, that…that was a prank call. I didn't think the police would actually show up or anything!"

Watching Hotaru bow down deeply in a laudable act of apology, Rentaro had to stop himself from audibly saying *Wha?*

"Yeah, I figured," said an officer, not sounding particularly angry about it. "The news said there's a good chance he's dead anyway. But you know it's against the law to waste the police's time like this, all right, kid?"

Hotaru continued to apologize. The policemen continued to give her a mild scolding. They exchanged a few more words. And then they left.

Her sorrowful expression immediately drawing itself back, Hotaru went expressionless once more as she briskly walked to the bathroom. Falling to one knee, she took a key out of her pocket, inserted it into the keyhole in Rentaro's cuffs, and turned it.

"Why…?" Rentaro whispered, deeply moved as he heard metal rattling.

"You're not the guy, are you?" Hotaru replied, refusing to return his gaze.

Of course he wasn't. But how many times had he screamed that before? How many times had she ignored him? Hot tears began to well in his eyes. He wiped them away with the pit of an arm.

Soon, there was another *clink*, and the handcuffs fell to the floor. Rentaro tried to stand up as he checked his wrists. His knees refused to cooperate. He decided not to risk it, instead borrowing a shoulder from the suddenly cooperative Hotaru.

The moment he stepped out of the bathroom, the droning of the insects outside went up an octave in his ear. He was greeted with a tiny, cramped, and disorganized studio apartment. He didn't realize it in the bathroom, but apparently it was the middle of the afternoon outside, the contrast between his poorly lit bathroom cell and the great outdoors reminding him more than a little of his own place.

Taking a closer look, Rentaro realized that all the newspapers and magazines strewn around the apartment had coverage of the Suibara murder in them. THE FALLEN HERO, began one. SATOMI ARRESTED, screamed another. It was like every outlet was falling over themselves to get more sensational with their headlines. Right after the Third Kanto Battle, it was almost as if they printed a new article every time he so much as ate breakfast. He couldn't believe how far the tables had turned in less than a month.

Listening to the strange noises coming from the ancient, whirring air-conditioning unit, he was led to a creaky pipe-frame bed and felt a stiff blanket being pulled over him. There were stains from previous water leaks on the ceiling, bits of paper missing from the walls, and everything was a duller color than when it was first installed.

Suddenly, Rentaro began to suspect something. This apartment was clearly meant for one person. There was a lone single bed in this studio. So she didn't live together with Suibara? Idly pondering this, he removed his shirt in bed, unwrapped his bandages, and examined his side.

The gruesome sight almost made him groan. It was no longer bleeding, but the wound was still a blaze of pain.

"Hey, how did you stop the blood?"

"I stuck a hot frying pan against it."

"Oh, so *that's* what I'm smelling? Were you making some *yakiniku*?"

Hotaru's eyes widened for a moment. Then she let out a light sigh. "I'm amazed you have the energy to mouth off at me," she said. "I dunno if it's luck or not, but the bullet didn't get lodged in you."

"Sounds like luck to me."

"Not to me," she replied, chin stuck high in the air. Then she narrowed her eyes at him again. "That's a pretty funny body you got."

Rentaro followed her eyes down until they reached his cybernetic right arm and leg. They were still a dark shade of black. He had ripped the skin off them while he was trapped in the hotel.

"What *is* that?"

"Suibara never told you? It's a set of armaments from the New Humanity Creation Project."

That made Hotaru open her eyes even wider.

"Wait, so you don't know anything about the New World Creation Project? Or the Black Swan Project, maybe?"

Hotaru gave him a clueless look.

Aha. Suibara must have kept any dangerous knowledge away from her to keep her safe. The fact she wasn't as dead as Suibara was all the proof he needed for that. If she knew everything Suibara did, she would've been part of *their* hit list, too. There's no way she'd still be alive.

Thus, Rentaro reasoned, whoever killed Suibara figured there was no harm in leaving her be.

He noticed a first-aid box tossed at him. It contained a tube of fibrin, a form of biological glue that Rentaro was well familiar with by now. Civsec officers turned to it first whenever they wanted their wounds to heal quicker. It wasn't quite as insta-heal as some of the potions in the RPGs Enju liked, but it patched things up far more speedily than Mother Nature could.

Shutting one eye at the stinging pain in his side, he applied a fibrin glue pad and kept it fast with bandages.

He was over the worst of it. Or so he thought. Then his greedy stomach started to whine at him.

In a few moments, he was pestering Hotaru for some rice water, something that his stomach wouldn't immediately reject. Soon, he was slurping up rice porridge. Considering he hadn't eaten in three days, his gastrointestinal system hadn't faltered on him that badly, enough so that he managed to keep down bread and soup well enough. The bread was only lightly toasted and he wouldn't dare put any jam on it, but the wheat flavor that spread across his mouth with every bite almost made tears come out of his eyes. Before he knew it, he wolfed down the whole slice.

The food in jail wasn't all that bad. But he couldn't remember the last time he had anything resembling home-cooked food. He lay back in bed, his full stomach making him feel tremendously satisfied. The thick, starchy blanket and comically creaky bed seemed fit for a king to him. He could feel himself falling asleep, but there was no time for that.

Nothing had changed for the better at all.

His exploits at the Magata Plaza Hotel the other day seemed like ancient history to him, but the bitter, painful experience he was handed there filled him with impotent resentment.

More to the point, Tina was still with the cops, and Enju was still in the IISO's hands.

Dark Stalker, aka Yuga Mitsugi, told him at the hotel that Enju's new partner was a "buddy killer" and promised her a painful death. He was suddenly very curious about what the past three days were like.

"I still don't trust you," Hotaru said scornfully as she sat down on the edge of the bed. "Can you tell me what's going on already?"

"Well, where should I start…?"

Staring straight up at the ceiling, Rentaro regaled Hotaru with the story of how he accepted Suibara's job, got arrested, and found himself leaping off the roof of the hotel. By the time he was done, Hotaru was at rapt attention, chin resting in her hand and deep in thought.

"So Kihachi got rubbed out by this…group, because he knew a lot about these New World and Black Swan projects?"

"Do you believe me?"

"It's too complex to be made up. Plus, I definitely noticed that Kihachi was hiding something from me. Never imagined it was something this immense, but…"

Seeing her accept this story the police dismissed as absurd gladdened him. It was almost anticlimactic for him. But Hotaru still glared at him coldly, the hostility still not entirely gone from her eyes.

"So what are you gonna do now?"

"What do *you* want to do?"

"That Hitsuma guy's one of them, right?"

"Yeah, probably."

"*Satomi*," Yuga had told him at the hotel, "*we need you as a sacrifice. Tina Sprout's going to be executed. Kisara Tendo's going to be trained to destroy the Tendo family. Enju Aihara's actually got her next Promoter assigned to her already. He's a bad seed. A buddy killer. Worse than you'd ever imagine. And once you're found guilty, the whole picture's complete.*"

Trained to destroy the Tendo family. *That* was what threw him. Kisara wasn't stupid enough to let someone use and abuse her like that. But what about someone whom she'd opened at least some of her heart to? Someone with a clear gift for manipulating people's minds? *There was no telling*, Rentaro thought. And in Kisara's recent social life, there was only one man who filled that bill.

If Hitsuma was part of this criminal group, he could've easily ambushed Rentaro using what little information he gave his civsec boss about his whereabouts. Then he could've interrupted the orders from the police, put Yuga in place, and surrounded the hotel with police just in case. It seemed to fit the picture well enough.

He doubted Kisara would give up his location *that* easily, but if she did, that meant she was wrapped around Hitsuma's finger.

Rentaro shut his eyes tightly, hands balling into painful fists.

I thought I could leave Kisara safely in your hands, Hitsuma. Kisara trusted in you.

He ground his teeth.

And you used her. You've gotta pay.

Hotaru lifted her head up from her thoughts. "I'm going to kill that Hitsuma guy," she said. "And Dark Stalker, too, if he fired the shot."

"Don't."

"Can you tell me why not?" replied a clearly peeved Hotaru.

"Because that won't solve anything. Even if that went without a hitch, you're still a criminal. You flipped a van; you injured three law enforcement officers; and if you did *that*, too, you'd be a double murderer."

"It's not like my enemy was playing fair. Why do *I* have to?"

Rentaro thought Hotaru resembled someone he knew. Now it finally dawned on him.

"Satomi, I just realized. You couldn't punish the mastermind behind the Kagetane Hiruko Terrorist Incident, Kikunojo Tendo. You couldn't punish the mastermind behind the Seitenshi Sniping Incident, Sougen Saitake. But I was able to punish the person responsible for the Third Kanto Battle, Kazumitsu Tendo. Do you know why?

"Don't you understand? Justice isn't good enough. Justice can't oppose evil. But absolute evil—evil that goes beyond evil—can. I have that power."

"No. You can't do that. It's wrong. If someone's unfair to you, you have to be fair back at him. If you wind up turning into a criminal on me, how am I gonna face up to Suibara's grave?"

"Don't give me that lip service. What other choice do I have?"

"The choice of exposing the Black Swan Project, getting evidence, and arresting the perpetrators. That way, they'll round up Hitsuma and everybody else involved in this."

And it'll clear his name if they arrest the real killer.

But it wouldn't be that easy, of course. Suibara lost his life trying to reveal Black Swan to the world. Their dark tentacles had extended themselves not just to Rentaro, but to Tina, Enju, Kisara, and the Tendo Civil Security Agency itself.

He didn't know how much of a bead his enemy had on his movements, but if they failed to fish his body out of the river, they'd be striking back soon enough. And now, there was more than Hitsuma and his police force pursuing him. There was that mechanized soldier, too, the New World update of his New Humanity self.

Frankly, he thought, *I don't like my chances much.*

Surrounded on all sides. Completely isolated. The situation was nothing short of hopeless. If he could, he didn't want to make Hotaru—Suibara's only living memory—cross a bridge as dangerous as this.

"Look, I don't want you to get the wrong idea..." Hotaru turned the cold eyes underneath her chestnut hair an infinitesimal amount toward him, face still blank. "But I need revenge for Kihachi. You're just the bait."

"The bait?"

"Mm-hmm. If the enemy finds out you're alive and starts gathering around your blood, that's perfect for me. All I have to do is take out the people trying to take *you* out."

The sleeves of her jacket sprang up as she swung her hands to her hips. The next minute, she had a pair of jet-black pistols at the ready.

"This battle's how I'm gonna be paying my condolences to Kihachi."

Rentaro breathed an admiring sigh. She didn't pull the triggers, but she'd drawn those guns so fast, you'd miss it if you blinked.

Even before this point, he had imagined she was pretty handy with a gun. *This must've been how she fought in battle, then.*

Her guns were both Gold Cup National Match models, one of the custom government pistol lines manufactured by Colt. They weren't exactly suited for dual wielding, but gun collectors cherished them for ease of handling (even a small girl's hands could wrap around them) and their sheer beauty, making them a world-renowned model. They came with a crisscrossing dual holster she kept behind her back.

Guns still at the ready, Hotaru turned her freezing gaze upon Rentaro. "So let's keep this strictly business, all right? I use you; you use me. There's nothing else to it. If you die, I won't even take a look back. And if the opposite happens, feel free to leave me on the sidewalk."

"No cooperation?"

"None."

Rentaro grimaced. It was a blunt reaction, one that made him wonder if he hallucinated that single moment of empathy she showed in front of the police.

"...All right. Well, you can fight for whatever you want to, but if we run into anyone calling himself Dark Stalker, I want you to let me handle him. He's this conceited little bastard in a school uniform with a pop-up collar."

"Is he good?"

"*Damn* good. He'd be too much for you."

"You mind not selling me short, please?"

Suddenly, something black and heavy flew toward Rentaro. He caught it just in time. It was a pair of nylon hip holsters—one with a gun, the other a knife. The very ones Rentaro confiscated from the SAT trooper in the hotel. The knife was a survival blade from Gerber. The gun was—

"—A Beretta...?"

It must have been a custom job owned by the trooper. It featured a reinforced "brigadier" slide, something that went out of production long ago. Kisara used a custom-line Beretta 90two as her choice of gun, Rentaro recalled. Beretta always devoted as much care to the look of their guns as they did their performance. It seemed like a match made in heaven for Kisara. But would it work for him?

"That's not your gun?"

"Nah, I seized it along the way. My XD's still in evidence storage."

"An XD? That cheap piece of crap? You'll hit more often with a Beretta."

"Yeah, but doesn't the sight system take some getting used to? I mean, say what you want, but I was pretty used to that XD."

"That means *you're* a cheap piece of crap, too."

"I *knew* you were gonna say that!"

Then Rentaro realized he had yet to ask something important.

"Hey, by the way, what kind of Gastrea factor is in your blood?"

Hotaru gave him a sullen, silent glare as she turned her head.

"I don't need to tell you."

Man, she pisses me off. Rentaro decided to check how tight his holsters were instead of engaging her any further.

"I'm not done with you yet," he heard Hotaru say.

"Jeez, girl, there's more?" a fed-up Rentaro replied, only to find Hotaru's index finger sticking right in his face.

"Do *not* call me 'girl.' My name is Hotaru."

"...You're the boss, Hotaru."

"What should I call you?"

"Rentaro works."

"Really? Well, great. Rentaro, then."

Thus, their alliance to defeat their foes and uncover the truth was formed. They weren't exactly the most steadfast of teams, but to Rentaro, she was the only ally he had in the entirety of Tokyo Area. The feeling was probably mutual, too.

"So what're we gonna do now?"

"We start here," Rentaro replied, looking around the room. "I meant to search Suibara's place for evidence anyway. You can help me save some time."

"This isn't Kihachi's apartment."

"Huh?"

"I *said*, this isn't Kihachi's apartment."

"So where are we?"

Hotaru gave an exasperated shake of her head. "Rentaro," she said, "have you seriously not noticed yet? I don't have a Promoter, but the IISO still hasn't taken me away."

"Oh—"

The vague feeling of discomfort stuck in the back of his throat suddenly made total sense. Enju was seized by an IISO agent practically the moment Rentaro surrendered his license. If Suibara was dead, Hotaru should've been expecting a visit from them, too.

"Wh-why's that?" Rentaro dared to ask. Instead of answering, Hotaru pointed outside.

"Let's go outside. It'll be easier to show you."

The moment they were out, Rentaro was greeted with eye-piercingly bright sunlight. The air conditioner that had so kindly kept him cool inside now blew hot, processed air at him, making him immediately break into a sweat. They went down the stairs, each step creaking in dangerous-sounding fashion, and went away from the building a bit before stopping to look at it.

The apartment was tilted to the side, boasting a simple corrugated sheet-iron ceiling and walls. Other similar-looking buildings sur-rounded it. The area must not have enjoyed the benefits of garbage pickup—piles of scrap iron and other junk were all over the place, and the ground was lined with a rainbow of colorful plastic trash. The stench made his nose wrinkle.

Feeling someone's eyes upon him, Rentaro saw a sharp-eyed man staring at him before turning back into his hovel. Judging by his face, he obviously wasn't Japanese. And it clearly was his home, judging by the sounds of daily life coming from it. But why would he leave that "house" of his in such terrible condition? Something told him the landlord probably had at least a couple gang connections.

He thought he was in the Outer Districts for a moment as he took a 360-degree look at his surroundings, but the Monoliths were far away from here. He was inland.

"Why're you living in a place like this?"

"I had to stay in *some* illegal slum or another. It's not like anyone else would take in a lone child without any parent or guardian. I had to get out of our place before the IISO got me. I knew they'd be coming."

Again, Rentaro had to commend Hotaru's coolheadedness and abil-ity to take action. When she learned Suibara was killed, she barely spent a moment mourning him. She got to work. Enju was kind of mature for her age, yes, but that was because she had to experience everything from direct threats like frostbite and hunger to emotional ones like contempt and persecution. There was some truth in the idea that hardship and adversity could make a person stronger, but not even Enju could so sensitively pick up on unseen threats and flee this much in advance. Rentaro wondered what Hotaru must've gone through to reach that point.

"The police are staking out the place we used to live in."

"Oh…"

Rentaro thought for a moment.

"Are you willing to risk that?"

"No. We better not, Hotaru. There's someplace I want to go first."

"Where?"

Rentaro looked at Hotaru.

"The place where Suibara was killed."

2

Shigetoku Tadashima stood bolt upright, notebook in hand, thinking to himself how much he wanted to strangle the person he was talking to.

"But that guy didn't abandon me! He treated my wound and told that police officer to carry me down. I really don't think he's the monster the media's portraying him as… Are you even listening to me?"

"Yeah…"

"Okay. So where was I? Oh, right! I was all groggy from the sleep medication I took, so I didn't make it out of the hotel when the alarm went off. So then—"

"—Um, I think I have enough, thanks," an exasperated Tadashima said, trying to hide the chagrin on his face as he closed his notebook. The somewhat well-nourished woman he was interviewing, sitting cross-legged on her bed, looked a tad disappointed.

"Oh, really? But I haven't even told you a third of what I wanted to!"

"It's been a great help, ma'am. I might have some more questions for you later, but I think we're good for today."

Tadashima seized the moment to salute while he could and left the room.

"What's up, Inspector?" asked Yoshikawa, waiting by the door, the moment he emerged.

"Don't get me started," a fed-up Tadashima said, waving a hand in front of his face. "I know the perp saved her life and everything, but she couldn't heap more praise on his feet if she tried. She's not a witness so much as she is a groupie. Must be that Stockholm whatever in action."

Yoshikawa chuckled. "I'm heading back to the station for now. Are you coming with me?"

"Nah, Hitsuma's called me in. Looks like it'll be me and him in a two-man cell. I'll be the investigator, and he'll just yell at me all day."

"Must be hard keeping your career on track, huh, Inspector?"

Tadashima gave Yoshikawa a bop on the head. "Ahh, quit your bitching. If you wanna say something, say it to *him*, not me. Oof... The guy's a genius, but something about him just bothers me."

Leaving Yoshikawa behind as he rubbed his head, Tadashima left the hospital and caught a taxi to the point Hitsuma had directed him to. It was an enormous skyscraper, easily dwarfing everything adjacent to it. It was matte black, making the inspector wonder if it was made of Varanium, and a guard armed with a pistol was standing in front.

A stone tablet with CENTRAL CONTROL DEVELOPMENT ORGANIZATION carved into it stood in front of the structure. People on the street just called it "the black building." Nobody really knew what went on inside.

Tadashima rechecked the map Hitsuma texted him. This was definitely the place. Reporting to the guard, he showed his badge and was quickly ushered inside without further question. The elevator he boarded seemed to break the sound barrier as it rose, almost making him lose his footing on the way to the sixty-fifth floor.

From that point, a female employee in a lab coat guided him as he went through multiple security doors, each protected by a different kind of card-key lock or biometric scanner. Tadashima grew more and more nervous. He was dressed in the same wrinkled suit he slept in last night over at the investigation team HQ, and the stubble on his face was starting to cross that inscrutable boundary to full-on beardhood. He didn't know where he was being led to, but he would hope for no dress code, at least.

The bulletproof-glass door labeled CONTROL ROOM opened with a hydraulic-sounding *pshhuu*. Behind it, Tadashima could hear footsteps running back and forth and a cacophony of noise.

The sight that unfolded startled him. The gigantic, fan-shaped room was dimly lit, mostly by the seemingly infinite number of holodisplays deployed in every inch of available space. Indicator bars and numbers danced across each screen. It resembled the air-traffic control tower of a particularly busy airport, but the main difference was the huge holodisplay in the center of the room depicting a map of Tokyo Area, monitoring electricity usage region-wide in intense detail.

Tadashima had to fight back the impression that he had somehow slipped into the future.

"What *is* this...?"

"Have you ever heard of the SmartCity concept?"

Startled, Tadashima turned to find Hitsuma in a freshly pressed suit, arms open wide as he walked toward him. Tadashima attempted to jump-start his mind back into action. It had been a while since it worked right.

"Um...wasn't it an old urbanization plan? I think the first Seitenshi proposed it in an effort to optimize electrical demand."

"Precisely, Inspector. Electricity is transported along power lines using high voltages, but a lot of that power winds up getting lost before it reaches homes. Storing it is not only difficult, but produces a lot of waste of its own as well.

"For example, places like large data centers usually keep some of their power supply in an idle state, just in case there's any unexpected server load or heavy access, but they only use around six percent of the electricity sent to them. Twelve tops. All the rest of it is wasted. The SmartCity concept has the city monitor energy usage to distribute power efficiently while avoiding things like blackouts. You remember how strained the grid was around Tokyo after the Gastrea War."

Tadashima nodded silently as he gave another astonished look at the SmartCity nerve center before him. "So you actually finished it, huh?" he said. "It hasn't been in the news for ages. I thought it was canceled or something."

"Well, we didn't want it to become a terrorist target, for one. That's why it's in this nondescript building with a nondescript name."

"Right," Tadashima replied with a shrug. "So what did you want from me? I barely even touch a computer unless I'm doing things like police paperwork. I'm sure you didn't call me here just to show off all your fancy machinery."

"Of course not. There's actually one function of this control room I wanted to show you."

Hitsuma tapped at the central control panel. The system promptly showed a variety of video images, showing a shopping district, a café, a theater, and so forth, most looking down from a very high viewpoint. It was a familiar enough sight to Tadashima.

"Are these surveillance cameras…?"

"Yes. We had these installed in places like rail stations and airports at first, but now they cover all of Tokyo Area in order to quickly spot Gastrea."

"How many cameras do you have for that?" an astounded Tadashima replied. "You'd need thousands. Tens of thousands."

"Too many for human beings to monitor, certainly. That's why we feed the video through the face-recognition system we have here in this control room. If you search based on that, you can do things like this."

One of the images on the giant holodisplay expanded out to take over the whole screen region. "Whoa," Tadashima marveled. There, shot from slightly above a restaurant building, he saw a young police detective in a gray business suit, speedily slurping up ramen from the front-facing bar. He recognized the face right off—despite his three years on the force, he still looked like a raw recruit. In fact, they were just talking a few moments ago.

"Yoshikawa…"

"Exactly," Hitsuma replied as he triumphantly nodded behind him. "And we've got Rentaro Satomi's facial pattern in the database, too. The trap's already been set. Now all we have to do is wait for our prey to show up."

"I see. That's some pretty amazing tech. But I'm impressed you could call on the services of this place without a warrant or anything. Does the investigation team know about this?"

"Actually, no. Outside of myself and my father the commissioner, you're the only one."

Tadashima couldn't believe his ears. He was acting by himself without even the HQ knowing about it? A police department was supposed to be stricter, more bureaucratic than that. Even if this was the commissioner's son, was it really all right to let him run wild like this?

The detective felt something brooding in the pit of his stomach. It told him that the Hitsuma clan was after Rentaro for more reasons than just the crimes he allegedly committed.

"By the way," a voice said from behind, cutting off his thought process, "how's your investigation been going, Inspector Tadashima?" It belonged to a boy in a school uniform, coming out of nowhere in the dimly lit room.

"Oh, you're, um…"

"Yuga Mitsugi. The civsec who ran into Satomi by accident at the Plaza Hotel. Sorry for all the trouble I caused."

Why was *this* boy in the room, too?

"Um, hey…" A clearly agitated Hitsuma greeted Yuga with a cold stare.

"What's the big deal, Superintendent Hitsuma?"

Hitsuma's breezy composure was now a thing of the past. It looked like he was afraid the boy would say something he wasn't supposed to. Did they know each other?

"So, uh, Inspector, how's the investigation coming along?"

The boy's overly familiar speech rankled Tadashima.

"I'm afraid I can't discuss that with the general public."

"Inspector, would you mind telling him for me? It sounds like he'll be offering help to the investigation as a civsec officer."

Tadashima took out his notebook, offended and wondering why anyone asked for a civsec's help with a non-Gastrea case. "I went to the hospital and spoke with one of the SAT officers the suspect tangled with," he stated, "along with a woman hit by friendly fire during the incident. Surprisingly, the woman said that Rentaro Satomi saved her life. She even thanked him for it, saying, 'He can't be the killer. I'm sure there's something else compelling him to do all this.' The SAT officer was just as cheerful with me. He smiled at me and said, 'I'd love to have another match with him.'"

"Ha-ha! Pretty funny civsec, huh? Even as he's fleeing us, he's building a fan base for himself."

Tadashima ignored the equally cheerful Yuga, turning toward Hitsuma instead. "About that, actually. None of it makes any sense to me. He's a murderer. If he wanted to get out of this as safely as possible, wouldn't it have been faster for him to take the woman hostage and barricade himself in a room?"

"I imagine he figured her wound wouldn't make her much use as a hostage," Hitsuma replied bluntly.

"Yeah, but he could've taken one of the SAT officers hostage, too. He also went through the trouble of simply incapacitating the SAT team. For him, that has to be a thousand times harder than just killing them. Don't you think that's strange at all? He's on the run from the law, but he's still taking time out to save people's lives on the way. If he really murdered one person already, would he be this hesitant about killing another?"

"He probably can't shake off the image of himself as the hero of Tokyo Area. And who's to say he *didn't* mean to kill any of the SAT guys? Maybe he meant to and just failed at it."

"You sure seem intent on his guilt, Superintendent."

"And *you* must think he's not guilty, don't you, Inspector? You're the one who interrogated him, aren't you?"

Tadashima rubbed the back of his head. "Yeah, you got me there, sir. But I don't play favorites in the interrogation room. I'm tough with everybody I talk to in there. I can't get a confession out of a criminal if I think he's innocent."

Yuga, to the side, gave out a sudden laugh. "Either way, though, as long as Satomi isn't defanged, he's going to do *something* for us. It's pretty clear searching the river isn't gonna do anything for us at this point. He's alive—I'm sure of it. Heh-heh… This game's only getting started, Satomi."

Tadashima rubbed the top of his arm, feeling something cold and heartless behind the boy's inscrutable chuckling to himself.

3

With a flashing green light and a melody that sounded like a tweeting baby chick, a mass of humanity scrambled across the busy intersection.

The asphalt radiated heat like an oven burner, and everyone in the crowd looked fatigued.

Amid this swell of humanity dodging and weaving around itself in intricate geometrical patterns, Rentaro Satomi's eyes darted to and fro. There was a man with a hurried, restless walk repeatedly looking down at his watch. A couple walking hand in hand together. A mother on the way home from shopping, her son staring into his mobile phone as he walked. Whenever someone happened to size him up, he would unconsciously shudder.

"Keep looking forward, Rentaro," a dry voice next to him said. "Try not to do anything too suspicious." It sounded like the chestnut-haired girl had nothing fun, nothing exciting left in her world.

"Yeah, but it's kind of hard to act normal when you're consciously thinking about it."

"At least you're aware of that. But I don't think you need to worry. People don't care about you as much as you think."

"Why are you finding ways to berate me with everything you say?"

"I'm just trying to help you relax, all right?" the girl replied, not a trace of emotion to her voice. Rentaro fell silent. She was making sense. Even now, the world was in a state of constant flux. It had been three days since Rentaro's alleged death. He recalled how Sumire once told him, *"You know, people care a hundred times more about how they just banged their little finger against the corner of the dresser than about some politician or famous singer dying."*

Everyone walking around in public had their own lives to live. Not a single one of them had any mental capacity to consider Rentaro's role in their existences. He understood that on an intellectual basis, and he kept consciously telling that to himself.

But what if somebody recognized his face? What if someone screamed and ran up to him, grabbing his arms? The nightmarish image kept flitting in and out of his mind, filling him with a dreadful sense of uneasiness.

Soon, they were past the intersection and on their way down a long, wide shopping arcade. Rentaro gave his head a light shake. Something he keenly noticed, now that he was all alone in the world, was how much he appreciated all the people that once supported him in life, tangibly or intangibly. If it wasn't for the warmth of the girl walking next to him, he might have been too scared to so much as walk out the door.

Of course, as partners went, the girl couldn't have acted more disinterested in him. She only saw him as a way to lure over the New World Creation Project soldier in her sights, and it admittedly irritated him a little.

"We're here."

Rentaro turned his head, only to find the bare framework of the new city hall building looming before him. Construction had ground to a halt on the site, the catwalks that lined the outside walls barren of people. Tractors, power shovels, and other bits of construction equipment lay abandoned around the building, like some kind of avant-garde art installation.

The sun was at its highest point in the sky. Rentaro and Hotaru fled under the building's shadow, sweat pouring unbearably out of their bodies. They were in the middle of the city, but it was still oddly quiet. Or perhaps it was their sixth sense creating the tension, warning them of another human being's death in a way difficult to put in physical terms.

"Are you okay?"

"Don't worry about me," Hotaru replied as she walked on ahead. Rentaro grimaced. Did she *really* care about Suibara so much that she was willing to kill in his name? He sighed and followed after her.

The police were finished with the crime scene. There was no clotted blood on the floor, no white pieces of tape marking out evidence locations—but simply standing at the scene made Rentaro's brain vividly re-create the entire incident. He closed his eyes and made a silent prayer for the deceased.

What did you want to tell me, Suibara?

Looking to his side, he saw an expressionless Hotaru standing bolt upright.

"You're not going to pray for him?" Rentaro asked.

"I did all my mourning when he died. I don't have any tears left."

"Oh..."

"So?" Hotaru's chestnut hair swayed in the wind as she looked up at him. "What're we going to do here?"

Rentaro scratched distractedly at the back of his head. "Well," he

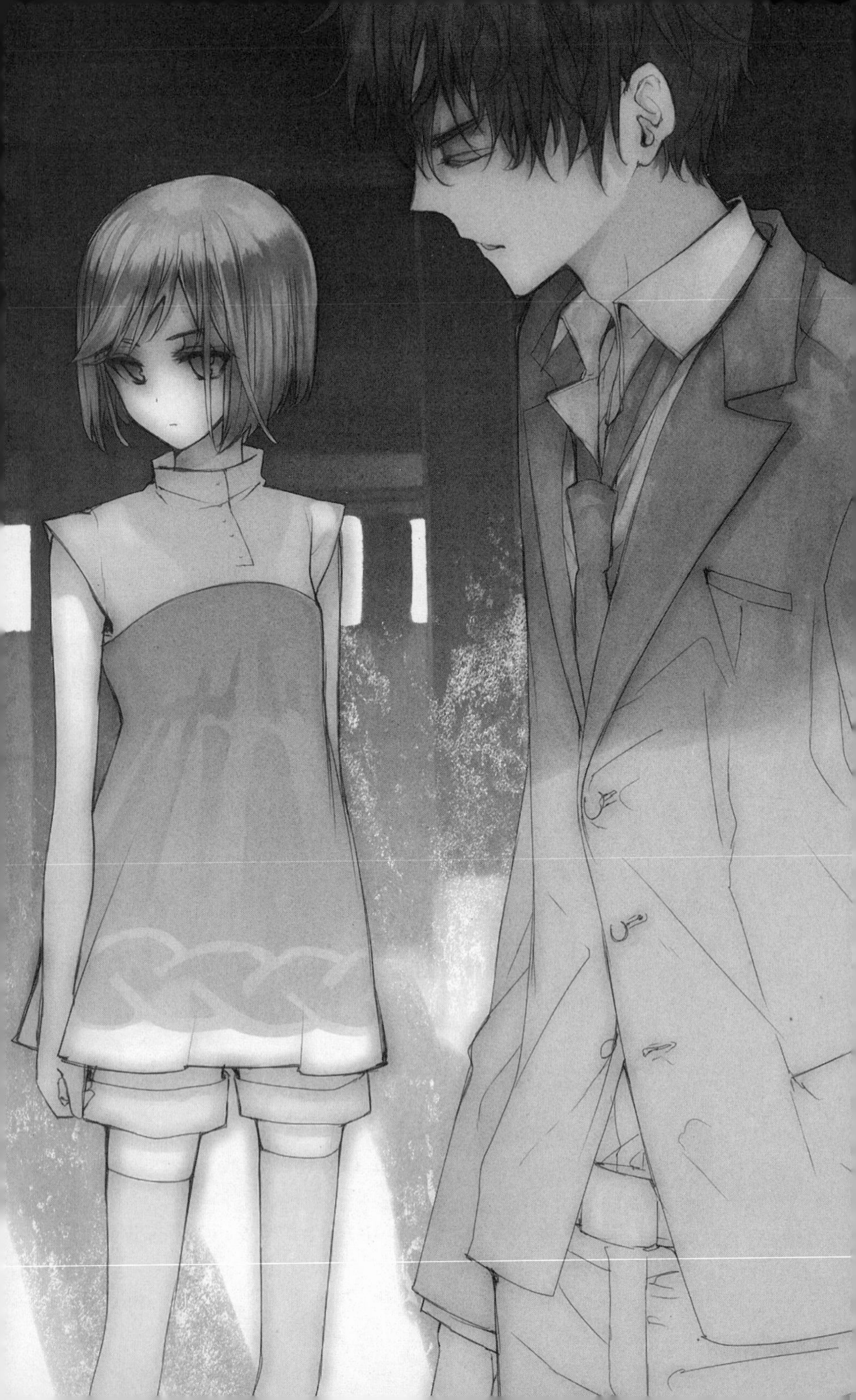

said, "it's not like I had some grand scheme in mind. But you never know what you'll find at the crime scene, you know? Plus, just being here is reminding me of all kinds of things." The fateful night replayed itself in his mind. "The body was still warm when I got here. He couldn't have been dead for long. It was too much of a coincidence that the police just happened to show up at that time. Someone waited until the moment I appeared to call the cops."

Which meant the culprit was someone close to the scene—close enough to visually monitor Rentaro's movements.

Then something flashed into his mind. "Hotaru," he said to the inscrutable girl next to him, "you said you noticed Suibara acting 'strange' around you, right? How was he acting, exactly?"

"He started working solo a lot more. He'd go out more and more often, and he'd never tell me where. He'd try to make up silly little excuses about it. I didn't pry at all. I figured a guy like him just had a bunch of stuff going on in his life."

"I told you about how he wanted to meet with Lady Seitenshi, right? I think he wanted to talk about a pair of conspiracies—the New World Creation Project, and the Black Swan Project."

"Right. And the New World is just an updated version of the New Humanity Creation Project, isn't it? What about Black Swan?"

Rentaro shook his head. "I have no idea. But something tells me that if I can find out, that'll blow the whole door open on this thing."

Suddenly, Hotaru's remarks made a new image of Suibara rise up in his mind.

Are you trying to blow the whistle about something? 'Cause if you have any evidence you can give me, I can make sure it gets to her."

"...I'm sorry. My evidence got stolen."

"Oh, right. When he came to my office, he said that he had some evidence that got stolen from him. That's why he wanted to meet directly with either Lady Seitenshi or her assistant..."

...Then, another voice rose up from the depths of his memory:

"I've been told to ask you this, so I will. Where is the memory card Suibara gave you?"

"Ah..."

Rentaro and Hotaru exchanged glances. They must have come to the same conclusion simultaneously.

"Didn't the assassin at the hotel ask you for a memory card, Rentaro?"

Rentaro thought for a moment, eyes on the ground.

"Yeah... It's weird. Logically speaking, that card must've been what was stolen from Suibara, huh?"

"Wait...so, what, then? Kihachi got his memory card stolen by some evil group, but then that group thinks *you* have it? So who has it now?"

The cry of some irritated-sounding cicada in the distance seemed to rise in volume. The shadows cast on the building uncomfortably adjusted their positions. Now Rentaro was sweating for another reason. He felt ill.

Hotaru suspiciously eyed him. "Rentaro, are you *sure* Kihachi didn't give you anything? Like, anything at all? He didn't slip you something while you weren't paying attention?"

Rentaro briskly shook his head. "No. Nothing."

"Oh..."

"What about you? Did Suibara ask you to keep anything for him?"

"Nothing I can think of."

They were right back where they started.

But Suibara's memory card had to exist somewhere. It was the one thing they could link to everything else in the case. Rentaro decided to file that thought away for now as he mentally switched gears.

"Hotaru, there's something else coming here reminded me of. Do you have Suibara's cell phone or anything?"

"I was kind of hoping you did," Hotaru replied, leaning against a concrete column. "You don't know where it is?"

"No..."

Rentaro had been asked multiple times by police interrogators about Suibara's mobile phone. It was clear, if indirect, evidence that the cops didn't have it. Smartphones had been everyday parts of people's lives for over twenty years now, their functionality and privacy measures both far advanced over the initial generation.

If they could track down the phone, that would earn them valuable evidence, such as his site-access history and call records. The police would doubtlessly do anything to find it.

"The killer must've taken it with him," Rentaro said. "Bastards thought of everything."

"We shouldn't jump to conclusions yet," replied Hotaru as she took out her cell phone, tapping at it a bit before bringing it to her ear. *Must be calling Suibara's line*, Rentaro thought.

Suddenly, he could hear the faint sound of a phone ringing somewhere.

"Where is it?!"

"Ssh!" Hotaru brought a finger to her lips. Somewhere between the quiet, the cicada calls, and the roar of the trucks occasionally passing by the building, they could hear a sound as soft as the cry of a mosquito. Tiptoeing to the edge of the building, they felt the wind blow against their faces as they peered downward from the dizzying height. The sound was coming from beneath them.

Rentaro and Hotaru looked at each other, nodded, and quickly went downstairs. It came from the far end of the building's outer perimeter, and now they could clearly hear it. A pop tune, one whose main melody was familiar even to the chronically nontrendy Rentaro. Wading through the tall grass to the side, they finally found it—a black smartphone, lying facedown, vibrating a little on the ground.

He picked it up just as the vibration stopped. The phone fell silent, and no matter how much he jabbed at the start button, it wouldn't respond.

"The battery must be drained. That sure was close."

"Oh..."

The phone must have fallen out of Suibara's hand as he was shot. If he consciously threw it out of the building as he fell, it'd be a pretty remarkable feat on his part.

Suibara...

Rentaro felt an odd sense of nostalgia as he turned the phone over. The screen was heavily cracked, like someone had taken a knuckleduster to it. It was amazing that the internals survived intact. Looking at the home screen, there was only the barest sliver of a charge left. Uncharacteristically, Rentaro found himself thinking this was the hand of fate at work.

"Let's go find a charger."

Flying into a nearby Internet café, the two of them grabbed a PC booth, settling down on the hard, contoured chairs and plugging the phone into the universal charger on the side of the computer. They waited a few moments, hands clasped in prayer, and then the phone whirred in Rentaro's hand. One percent charged.

Rentaro and Hotaru gave each other a joyous glance. The screen was just as damaged as before, although the touchscreen somehow still worked. But before he could start flicking around the screen, Rentaro's finger stopped. Suibara might be dead, but how permissible would this be—poking around someone's private property just to clear your own name? He might be about to go face-to-face with a Kihachi Suibara he never knew before. Browsing through it might be something he'd eternally regret. Paranoia set in.

Well, he thought as he brought finger to screen, *so be it*.

From there, Rentaro and Hotaru took their time, searching through the phone for whatever clues they could find. But there was nothing particularly noteworthy in his inbox, and his photo gallery mostly consisted of people—all shapes and sizes. Over half of them were of Hotaru. Rentaro could've predicted it, given that Suibara adored her to the point where he had her as his wallpaper.

Then his eyes stopped on a certain photo. It must've been shot on Christmas. Suibara and Hotaru were there, both wearing Santa hats and standing on either side of a fancy cake in the background. Judging by the high angle, it must've been a selfie.

But the biggest surprise in the pic was that Hotaru was smiling. Not exactly *beaming*, per se, but both sides of her lips were curled gently upward as she gave the peace sign to the camera. It made Rentaro feel like a depraved peeper of sorts, and he swiped the photo away before Hotaru could notice his surprise.

With their check of the gallery complete, all that remained to search was the call history. There, they spotted something strange. Twice on the day of the murder, and once the day before, he had spoken with someone identified as "Dr. Surumi" in the directory. Looking further back in the history, they discovered Suibara exchanged a total of twenty-five calls with the doctor, extending back over the past month.

"Do you know who this is, Hotaru?"

"Yeah. Dr. Ayame Surumi. A forensic Gastrea pathologist. They spoke a few times about autopsy findings and stuff as part of our work."

"Wow. Just like the one I know..."

"The one you know?"

"Ah, never mind. Do you know why they'd be talking to each other so often?"

Hotaru thought for a moment, then shook her head. "I can't think of anything. I don't think Kihachi and Dr. Surumi had any kind of private relationship."

"All right. We better check this person out."

"Her office is in a university hospital in District 6," Hotaru said as she stood up.

"She's a woman?"

"Yeah."

"Uh, she wouldn't happen to be pale to the point where you can see her veins, or wear a lab coat so long that it drags against the floor, or call her autopsy room 'the kitchen,' or have a body temperature of around 32 degrees Celsius, or build an expansion to her basement lab so she can have more room for her collection of corpses?"

"What?" replied Hotaru, clearly put off.

"Oh, uh, nothing. I'm sure it's not the same woman. Probably."

"She's absent? Why?"

"Well, that's what I'd like to know," the tired-looking doctor replied, his ample belly fat wobbling as he walked up to them. He couldn't have been an intern, but his youth was evidently clear. "She won't answer the phone, and now I have to fill in for her shifts. I'm practically going out of my mind here."

One eye exhibited a nervous tic as he spoke. It was clear that either stress or fatigue was taking its toll.

Rentaro and Hotaru were in an examination room at Shidao University Hospital. They managed to catch this doctor, who introduced himself as Kakujo, right as he was about to take a well-deserved break.

"Have there been that many Gastrea lately?" Rentaro asked point-blank.

Kakujo nodded broadly and opened his arms wide. "*That many* ain't the half of it! It's crazy! People are spreading all kinds of rumors about how there's something up with the new Monolith 32 they built after the Third Kanto Battle."

That couldn't have been the case. The old Monolith 32's collapse was entirely avoidable, the result of adulteration that reduced the purity of the Varanium inside. The new one was 100 percent Varanium, something Rentaro and the Tendo Civil Security Agency personally confirmed for themselves.

Come to think of it, didn't Enju mention an uptick in Gastrea numbers lately, too? Apparently the trend wasn't exclusive to the Tendo Group's jurisdiction. Where were they all getting in?

"Say," Rentaro remarked, "you mind if I ask you a question? How many ways are there for Gastrea to get into Tokyo Area, anyway?"

"Mmm, good question. Where should I begin...?"

The doctor looked up at the ceiling, pointing his potbelly directly at Rentaro.

"Basically, there are three infiltration routes—air, land, and underground. You sometimes see sea-dwelling Gastrea make it in, too, but they can't be much of a danger if they can't breathe air, you know? Otherwise, the Varanium field weakens once you get about 200 meters underground or 5,000 meters into the sky, so if you can burrow below or fly above those numbers, you can get in that way. Remember back when a pack of really obstinate guys picked up an upward-flowing air current and caused a huge racket around the city? That sorta thing."

The Morphe Butterfly Incident, Rentaro thought, as he nodded vaguely at the doctor. But he didn't voice it. If he demonstrated too much knowledge, Kakujo might start thinking he was a civsec. He wanted to avoid that if he could.

"So how would land-dwelling Gastrea get in?" Hotaru asked from the stool she was sitting on.

"Between the breaks in the Monoliths," Kakujo instantly replied.

"The breaks?"

"Yeah. The Monoliths are built ten kilometers apart from one another, right? So they kind of aim for the places where the Varanium field's at its weakest, usually in that five-kilometer interval right in the middle."

"Do they really succeed all that often?"

"Nah. Probably nine out of ten of 'em die trying—plus, we got the self-defense force patrolling the border, so that one lucky survivor usually doesn't last long, either. They say maybe one out of a hundred land-based Gastrea who attempt the crossing actually make it through. But we're still talking a ton of them, and they have a tendency to try to attack people first, so no matter how much we beat 'em down, they keep on trying to get into Tokyo Area. So that's why, in terms of sheer numbers, it's still the land-based ones we see the most of in the statistics."

"Wow. I see."

"I mean," Kakujo grumbled, "you know how much of a hit the SDF took in the Third Kanto Battle. Something like half the civsecs in Tokyo Area lost their lives. All we got left are people who didn't join the battle or who fled to other Areas, and do you think we could really count on *those* guys? We're still managing to keep this boat afloat so far, but all of us on the ground level are scared stiff that we'll have another Pandemic before long. Plus, the news said that the 'hero of Tokyo Area' guy died in the Plaza Hotel a few days ago. Hey, actually, you look a little like—"

Rentaro scrambled to say something, but a cool, composed voice stopped him from the side.

"I apologize, Doctor, but could you tell us a little more about Dr. Surumi? How long has she been absent from work?"

On the way there, the pair decided that Hotaru would pose as Dr. Surumi's sister. The ruse seemed to be working. Dr. Kakujo abandoned his suspicion and thought a little bit.

"Well, four days, I guess. On a job like this, if you're absent for that long a period of time, you're not gonna last too long. It's tough, but that's how it is."

"Have you contacted the police yet?"

"The police? Nah, nah," the doctor said, smiling as he dodged the question. "The retention rate in this place—ah, you probably don't know what that word means, huh, little girl? Basically, people quit a whole lot around here. Surumi had a good head on her shoulders, so I figured she'd stick around for the long term, but…"

He was doubtlessly right. Performing pathological work on something as hideous as Gastrea corpses would require some pretty thick skin. Sumire, who enjoyed calling it her life's work, was one in a million.

"Is there any chance she may have disappeared, or gotten caught up in something?"

"Hmm… I couldn't really say," Dr. Kakujo replied as he stroked his five-o'clock shadow. "I never thought about that…" Then he slapped a fist against his hand. "Hey, are you guys going to visit Surumi's place after this?"

Hotaru drooped her shoulders in disappointment. She had a natural talent for acting. "I wanted to," she said, "but my sister never gave her address out to anyone in the family, so…"

"Oh, that's fine, I can give it to you. I think I asked her for it when I had to send off some stuff that came to the office for her."

Rentaro wondered whether Dr. Kakujo was allowed to be so cavalier with people's personal information, but he nevertheless appreciated his falling so completely for Hotaru's cover story. Somehow, he doubted he could have convinced him to hand off the address by himself.

The doctor stood up and recomposed himself. "In exchange for that, there's a favor I'd like to ask of you, if you don't mind."

"What's that?"

"Well, Surumi conducted a Gastrea autopsy about a month ago, but the electronic version of her report's disappeared from our database for some reason. I know Surumi printed out a paper version for our records right beforehand, so she might still have it kicking around somewhere. Sorry to bother you guys, but if you see her, would you be able to get that for us? I don't really mind if she wants to quit or not, but we got a legal obligation to keep track of our records, so…"

Rentaro and Hotaru gave each other a glance. Dr. Surumi began making frequent contact with Suibara a month ago, too.

"Sure thing," Rentaro replied, nodding deeply as Dr. Kakujo wrote down the missing doctor's address on a piece of notepaper. The duo was just about to leave when the doctor called to them from behind.

"Hey, you guys don't happen to know what Black Swan is, do you?"

Rentaro and Hotaru both whirled around at once.

"Where did you hear *that* name?"

Dr. Kakujo's brows arched, a little taken aback by Rentaro's sudden forcefulness. "Uh…well, no, I mean, I just remembered it. Surumi kinda mentioned it in passing not long before she left. Like she was kind of brooding over it, you know? It was almost like she was having a nervous breakdown or something at her lab station. And that's not all…"

The corpulent doctor looked honestly bewildered as he spoke. "She said she 'had to burn the vineyard,' whatever that means."

The Shidao University Hospital grounds were orderly and well-kept, complete with artificial lawns and ponds. It would have been an inviting spot to rest and forget about your classes on most days, but to Rentaro, the sight was simply depressing. Hotaru's gait next to his was similarly heavy, almost plodding.

It was clear now that Dr. Surumi and Suibara were working together. But that just led to new problems for them to tackle.

"What the hell is the 'vineyard'...?"

Hotaru, preoccupied with the same question, had already taken out her cell phone, setting it to holodisplay mode so Rentaro could see the screen in the air. The first result was for an English instruction site. The pronunciation made it sound like some Romance-language word, but it turned out "vineyard" was simply a fancy way of saying "grape farm."

"'Burn the vineyard,' though... What could that mean?"

"I don't know."

"That guy said Dr. Surumi started acting weird about a month ago, right?" said Hotaru, her voice free of any intonation. It was a far cry from the forlorn little girl she pretended to be for a moment in the doctor's office. "And now that I think about it, I think I started noticing Kihachi hiding stuff from me a month or so ago, too."

There it is again. A month.

"What happened during that time...?"

Rentaro decided to step back and take an impartial look at the situation. Dr. Surumi and Suibara, two people who allegedly had no personal connection to each other, had talked on the phone twenty-five times in the past month. They started puzzling the people around them with their behavior at about the same time. Suibara was a civsec. The only thing that could connect a civsec with a Gastrea pathologist was...well, a Gastrea.

"Did you and Suibara have any Gastrea encounters in the past month, Hotaru?"

"Yeah... Actually, Kihachi and I ran into one a month ago."

"What kind was it?" an expectant Rentaro asked. Hotaru gave him a vague look of discomfort in response.

"I dunno…just your typical Stage Two. A flying one. It had a see-through thorax, so you could see all its guts and stuff floating around. It had a really long nose, too. Pretty gross."

"Did you kill it?"

"Yeah. Kihachi and I were driving on the expressway and it was flying alongside us. I stuck myself out the passenger-side window and blew it away with a shotgun."

"And then?"

"That's all."

"That *can't* be all, Hotaru."

"There's really nothing else worth mentioning about it. I mean, the Gastrea looked pretty weird, yeah, but you could say that about all Gastrea that are Stage Two or higher. So then we left it to the police and went home, and… Oh, I remember that Kihachi got a phone call, then hurried right out of our place. Now that I think about it, I bet that was from Dr. Surumi."

If the Gastrea looked normal enough but caused Suibara alarm later, the forensic pathologist must have discovered something highly unusual about it. But, just as before, this lead was getting them nowhere. Rentaro felt like they had a pretty decent selection of puzzle pieces, but there was no telling how they fit together to form a complete picture.

It was clear, however, that they now had information their foes absolutely did not want them to know. If the enemy picked up on their presence, they would undoubtedly face the full brunt of their vengeance. Hotaru was sadly not privy to Suibara and Dr. Surumi's first exchange—but then again, if she were, chances were that she wouldn't be breathing right now. A thorny dilemma.

They were now at the end of Shidao University grounds, an ornate cast-iron gate in the red brick wall that surrounded the area marking the front entrance. There, Rentaro noticed a security camera positioned overhead, watching the thin stream of students going in and out. He kept his head down as he passed by, but for a single moment, he couldn't help but look at it out of the corner of his eye. The moment his eyes met the lens illuminated within the domed shell, he felt a chill run down his spine. He hurried his way out of the school.

*　　*　　*

"I found him!"

The tension across the control room was palpable as the operator shrieked out.

"Where?" shrieked Hitsuma, trying to contain his excitement. Instead of replying, the operator put up an image of a gate somewhere in the city on the gigantic main holopanel.

"Where's this?"

"The front gate of the Shidao University Hospital in District 6."

Tadashima watched on, agape. "You're kidding me... So he didn't flee to the Outer Districts? He's been walking around inland the whole time?"

The operator tapped at her panel, highlighting a section of the image. This wasn't the grainy footage of a generation or two ago, too fuzzy to be admissible as court evidence. The video transmitted to the server was clear as day. Nobody had to strain their eyes to decipher the scene before them as, for a single moment, a downward-facing man in black clothing peered at the camera. It was apparently just enough time for the face-recognition program to do its work.

Next, the operator stopped the video and zoomed in on the figure's face. There was no mistaking it. It was Rentaro Satomi.

Hitsuma turned his head left and right, scanning the control room for a certain face. Soon finding it, he sidled up to Yuga. The boy's hands were in his pockets, but the look on his face made it seem like he was about to break into song.

"What is the meaning of this?" Hitsuma said, his voice low enough that only Yuga could hear. "You told me your sniper bullet made a clean hit on him. And now he's up and walking around!"

Yuga shrugged. "Guess it wasn't so clean after all. But what's the problem? This just makes things more fun."

"Fun? You find this *fun*...?"

Having Rentaro alive would not only make the police the laughing-stock of Tokyo Area—it'd also instill a sense of hope in Kisara Tendo, right when Hitsuma thought he had her tamed and obedient.

Before Hitsuma could explode in rage, Yuga used his right hand to point out a section of the holopanel.

"Mr. Hitsuma, that girl there was Kihachi Suibara's Initiator, right?"

He was pointing at the quiet, demure girl with the bobbed haircut walking next to Rentaro. He had seen the face several times in the evidence sheets. There was no mistaking this, either.

"Hotaru Kouro...?"

Kihachi Suibara's Initiator. They had ordered Nest to conduct an undercover investigation, but they had no idea she was working in tandem with this fugitive.

Tadashima approached Hitsuma, saluting. "I'll take a car over to headquarters to request support. In the meantime, sir, I want you to stay in contact with me on the radio and tell me where the suspect is headed." He then briskly walked out of the control room.

Hitsuma watched him go, stony-faced until he was sure the inspector was gone. Then he took out his phone and made a call, his mind running in circles as he listened to the ringing. He couldn't afford to have the police catch Rentaro. He wasn't sure how close this civsec was to the truth, but he'd already caused *this* much trouble for them—it would take a lot more than the status quo to take care of him. He couldn't afford another mistake.

The phone picked up.

"Nest? Can you create a traffic jam for me? I've got a police car that I need to have delayed. Also, *he's* still alive. Get me Hummingbird. We're gonna crush him."

The up-to-now composed Yuga blanched at this.

"Wait a minute, Mr. Hitsuma! Why Hummingbird? Rentaro Satomi's *my* prey. I'm gonna head out."

"People have seen your face."

"My body was specifically designed to be capable of suppressing Rentaro Satomi! Who could possibly be more qualified than I am?"

"Hummingbird's good enough."

"But...!"

"Enough!"

Yuga's mouth stayed open, still hoping to get a final word or two in, but he thought better of it. He left the control room, gnashing his teeth the whole way.

Hitsuma, his breathing accelerated, glared at the close-up of the boy in the holopanel. *If he's pouncing upon us, trying to take us down with him...then it's time to prove to him that dead men really* don't *tell tales.*

4

"Well, here's the place. You can just toss the key back into the manager's room once you're done."

The building manager used a bony hand to give Hotaru the key, distractedly using his other to adjust his reading glasses as he turned and left. Wasn't the manager supposed to accompany them if someone besides the person renting the place came in? He didn't act like he cared to, anyway.

Rentaro gave a look to his "sister" standing next to him. Once she was sure the manager was gone, Hotaru wiped the smile from her face and returned to her usual dour expression. "You got a problem with something?" she asked emotionlessly, once she noticed Rentaro staring at her. "It's almost night. I'd like to get this over with by the end of today."

The yellow sunlight streaming in through a west-facing window felt warm against his skin. They were finally about to be freed from the blazing fire of the afternoon.

They were in the hallway of a high-rise apartment complex. Rentaro looked around. The floor was comprised of two parallel corridors linked by a landing that offered two elevators, an emergency staircase, and another one for regular use. There was also an external stairwell with a ramp. Ever since the Plaza Hotel, Rentaro was in the habit of scoping out the floor plan and potential escape routes wherever he went.

Looking at the nameplate, they saw 1203—AYAME SURUMI written on a faded piece of paper. They had already rung the doorbell several times before visiting the manager's room, but they tried it again once more with a sliver of hope. The artificial chime went *ding-dong, ding-dong* twice, but there was no response from within.

At his feet, Rentaro noticed a dead cicada on the floor, frozen and exposing its grotesque-looking stomach to them. A small army of ants was already on the scene, ready to feast on the meal.

"I don't know if she's holed up in there or she's gone somewhere else," Hotaru said, "but hopefully we can find something about Black Swan."

"Holed up? 'Gone' somewhere? You really think it's gonna be that easy for her?"

"Huh?"

"Hotaru, have you ever seen a dead body before?"

Hotaru looked startled for a moment.

"I'll go in first."

Rentaro unlocked the door and opened it a crack. Then he shivered. Through the crevice, he could feel an unnervingly strong chill—along with the light scent of something rotting.

Pulling the breechblock on the weapon at his hip to ensure he could fire it at any time, he silently went inside.

Immediately to his left was the kitchen, equipped with a semi-circular dining table. Some vegetables lay shriveled on the kitchen counter, and a half-eaten piece of cake was currently serving as an all-inclusive resort for a clan of black ants. She might have been in the midst of preparing a meal—there was a bowl of sliced-up vegetables soaking in water—although the surface was now entirely covered in black mold.

They knew from before that all the apartments in the building contained two rooms and a kitchen. Keeping his guard up and his gun cocked, Rentaro brought a hand to another doorknob and slowly pulled it. He couldn't see inside at first—some curtains had been drawn—but it was her bedroom, as well as the site of her home computer. There was also an air conditioner chugging away as it spat cold air into the room. It sounded unnaturally loud in the otherwise completely silent apartment.

Despite being occupied, the apartment was almost bare of decoration, its colors uniformly beige. There wasn't so much as a poster on the wall, although one shelf rack contained a digital picture frame.

The final room lay beyond. Drumming up all the willpower he had, Rentaro pulled the door open.

There was dust all over the closets and dresser, as well as the large desk that sat next to a bookshelf that occupied an entire wall. But there *wasn't* any sign of a corpse. The rotting smell was already fading away.

So where did that come from…?

Just as he thought about it, Rentaro heard a sound that made him gasp nervously. He ran back to the kitchen, only to find Hotaru frozen like a statue, her eyes focused on a singular point. He realized that, from her position, she could see the bathroom door. Below it, a very dark red liquid was oozing out.

"Get back," Rentaro said, biting his lip to keep his voice from shaking. Taking a moment to compose himself, he gently pushed the door open.

The body was kneeling on the floor, face still under the surface of the water in the bathtub. It was naked, the skin pale and bereft of blood. The long hair from its head floated on the water like algae. The water itself was black in color. On the floor, near the drain, was a pool of coagulated blood.

At Rentaro's feet were three or so fingernails, appearing to have been pulled from the corpse. Torture must have been involved. Judging by how it only took three nails, they must have extracted the information they wanted from her in relatively short order.

Rentaro gave the body a quick once-over, then turned around and opened the closet, finding a large picnic blanket that he then placed the body on. He wondered if altering the crime scene was such a great idea, but he and Hotaru had already been seen together, and besides, the police could figure out when she died and realize soon enough that Rentaro couldn't have been involved.

Somewhere in the midst of this, Hotaru came up next to him. He thought she'd be frozen in fear. He was wrong.

"That's a real pity. We could have gotten a lot from her alive. Guess they beat us to the punch."

Rentaro was shocked. "A real pity? Beat us to the punch? Is that all you have to say? You *knew* her, right?"

"So?"

Hotaru steeled her gaze at him, a little annoyed. Rentaro balled his hands into fists, the anger welling to the surface as he shook his head.

"You're making no sense to me at all…!"

"Why do I need to?" She turned her back to him, then rotated herself halfway back. "You're free to drop out of this, if you insist."

"Like hell I am."

"Oh?" she said, blithely walking into the bathroom to check out the body. "You know, given the time, she's been decomposing pretty slowly. I guess that's because of the AC running."

Rentaro took a deep breath, bottling up his irritation. This girl was deeply involved with the whole case. Being with her got him closer to the truth; being alone kept him firmly away from it. It was theoretically far more efficient than attempting all of this solo. He had to make the best of it.

—*Even if my partner's somebody I absolutely cannot respect as a person.*

It was also very clear now that their foes had no problem rubbing out anyone who got too close to the truth. They definitely weren't out of the shark tank yet.

"All right. Let's split up and search the place. We might find something."

Hotaru walked off in apparent agreement. Watching her go, Rentaro went back into the bedroom. Having a dead body in the bathroom made him all the more reluctant to continue, but continue he did.

The first thing he noticed was the digital frame beyond the door. It was cycling through some pictures with the main university building in the background, presumably from her undergraduate days. It must have been fun for her. She was smiling in each and every one of them. A lot of them also included a man, perhaps a love interest.

Rentaro recalled something Dr. Kakujo told him: "*Surumi conducted a Gastrea autopsy about a month ago, but the electronic version of her report's disappeared from our database for some reason. I know Surumi printed out a paper version for our records right beforehand, so she might still have it kicking around somewhere.*"

Suibara and Dr. Surumi were connected by that Gastrea. It seemed natural to think that autopsy report had something to do with all this.

Sidling into the next room, Rentaro noticed that someone had broken the lock on a drawer in the desk and rummaged around inside. He groaned. Whoever tortured and killed Dr. Surumi must have asked her about that report. A day late and a dollar short, yet again. Their foes thought of everything.

But not even the enemy could be perfect. As long as they weren't machines, they had to make some kind of human error. There must be something. Praying to himself, he methodically took each book off the bookshelf and paged through it. Then he noticed something on the ground in the tight crevice between the desk and the wall. Carefully pulling it out and blowing the dust off, he realized it was a printed-out photograph.

The moment he looked at it, Rentaro's eyebrows arched downward.

The photo depicted a Gastrea in mid-autopsy. The stomach had been cut open, with a mark engraved on the translucent, mucusy organs, like the insides of a squid. Looking closer, he could tell the mark was a five-pointed star, a delicately designed feather on one of the points.

"Hotaru, come over here." He showed her the photograph. "Does this look familiar to you?"

"The claws you see on the side of the photo... They look kind of like the ones on the Gastrea from a month ago I told you about. I don't know what that star's for, though."

"Oh..."

"You think this is what Dr. Kakujo was talking about?"

"Probably. I don't think she had a picture as grotesque as this one sitting around for decoration."

Gastrea may not be your typical wildlife, but they were still the creations of nature. They wouldn't naturally be sporting pentagrams on their stomachs.

As he thought this over, a shrill sound made Rentaro's heart leap. It was the phone ringing from the bedroom. He slipped inside—first his head, then his entire body—and stood gingerly in front of the noise source. It was a landline phone—a rarity, given how smartphones and satellite phones dominated the market.

Rentaro gave Hotaru a silent nod, then slowly picked up the receiver and put it to his ear.

"Hey, this is Satomi, right?"

The heavy, overwrought voice was hard to make out over the non-human pitch. It was someone using a voice changer to disguise his or her real one. Rentaro stared at the receiver for a moment.

"Who...are you?"

"The enemy's about to head your way. Code name Hummingbird. A soldier from the New World Creation Project."

"What're you talking about? The enemy? Hummingbird?"

"You're free to think I'm lying. But maybe it'll make sense to you when I say this: That's the one who killed Kenji Houbara, ex–New Humanity."

"Wha—?"

This was all beyond his understanding, but at least one thing was clear. This was no prank, no pack of lies—the voice on the other end of the line was warning Rentaro about a real, and impending, danger.

"Lemme tell you what Hummingbird can do. You should probably use the time to devise a strategy with that li'l lady you got there with you."

Rentaro fell silent, waiting for him to continue.

"You there? With Hummingbird, you got—"

Then, with a click, the call ended.

"Hey, what happened? Hey!"

"—Lemme have it."

A hand reached out from the side to snatch the receiver away. Hotaru fought with the phone a little bit, but then shook her head and put the receiver down.

"I'm not even getting static. Someone's cut the phone lines, haven't they?"

Hotaru fumbled around her pocket for her cell phone, looked at it, then pointed it at Rentaro. NO SERVICE, it read.

He felt another shiver run down his spine. He knew they had service when they entered the apartment. The room, absent any other activity, was silent.

"Our enemy's here," Hotaru said. "In this building. They're already inside."

The sound of a propeller slicing through the air echoed throughout the cargo room.

Rika Kurume opened the sliding door. The wind blew against her body, the cold air flapping her dress around and almost knocking her straw hat off.

The evening sun, half-hidden behind the Monolith to the west, was bright enough that she had to squint.

She was in the cargo room of a transport plane one thousand meters in the air. It was clear out, with no stratus or nimbostratus clouds blocking her view. The cityscape beneath her looked like an elaborate miniature; there were no people or even cars visible. She could smell a cool clearness in the air.

"Hummingbird—jumping out."

Rika took a step away from the cargo room, then fell backward, leaving her body to the air. She pointed her head down, her long hair forming a comet's tail as she plunged straight toward the ground. The whole time, she was performing a mental countdown. That, plus her experience, told her when she was at the 500-meter point. Then she twisted her body around, spreading her limbs wide like a flying squirrel and pulling the cord on her Ram-Air parachute. It opened, the tremendous feeling of deceleration jarring her body from the harness on her back downward.

It didn't last long. Opening her eyes and looking down below, she saw her feet beat against thin air. Craning her neck back upward, she watched her open parachute grow, bathed in the orange-red of the setting sun.

Making one final check of the city below her, she waved her right arm to the side. A point of light appeared on the roof of one of the many buildings down below, an arrow labeled TARGET marking it out in her vision alongside its vertical and horizontal range. It was being implanted on her retinas by the augmented-reality contact lenses she put on before the drop began.

Rika used her control lines to carefully make fine-tuned adjustments as she descended. Before long, her targeted apartment building loomed large in her sights, both feet pointed at the dead-center point.

No matter how many times she dropped, the force of the impact always tended to make her fall forward. Today was no exception. The parachute settled down on top of Rika soon afterward. Removing the belt and escaping the tangled chute, she put on the straw hat she had stuck between her dress and the harness and hugged her favorite teddy bear against her arm as she patted the debris off her skirt. Then she took a cell phone out from one of her spandex socks and called a certain number.

"This is Hummingbird. I'm safe at the target point."

"Copy that. I'm sending target faces to you now."

In just a few moments, the file was sent over and floating in the air on her holodisplay. There were two photos—a boy slightly older than she was, and a girl slightly younger, captioned RENTARO SATOMI and HOTARU KOURO, respectively.

"Hang on, Nest," Rika said in her high, resentful voice. "Don't you think you're overworking me a little? I just killed some weird old guy a few days ago. You're not giving me much free time between jobs."

The voice on the other end of the line seemed unfazed. *"This is your* mission," it said. *"Stop complaining about it. I've electronically shut off the building from the rest of the world for thirty minutes, just like you asked me to. If you lose that window, we're gonna lose them again, too."*

Rika rolled her eyes, then pointed at the photo of Rentaro with a finger. She gave a light, pity-laden laugh.

"Dark Stalker couldn't kill this target, right? Talk about pathetic."

"Yeah. Dark Stalker actually had a message for you. He said, 'Don't underestimate Rentaro Satomi, or else you might be the one regretting it.'"

Now Rika's laugh was indifferent and haughty. "Oh, what is he, stupid? He screwed up, and now he's making excuses for it? Laaaame... Whatever, though. I'll make this quick."

As Rika spoke, two smaller parachutes settled down on the building roof behind her. They looked like regular old tires at first—each about the size of a flying disc with beveled edges used for high-speed, long-distance throws in disc golf—but there was nothing typical about them.

Rika's brain was implanted with a brain-machine interface (BMI) chip that allowed her to move and operate objects linked to her mind by thought alone. These tires were the "interface" her mind worked with.

"All right, Necropolis Striders—it's time to get up, my beloved familiars."

She brought her palms together. The compact motors within each tire began to whir, and they stood up as if operating by themselves, whirling in a tight circle around Rika. As they did, she reviewed her map of the apartment building, finding the phone line running behind the basement switchboard. It seemed to her that disabling the alarm system would be a good idea, too.

"Right. Let's make sure nothing gets in my way first. Offensive Enchant: Thorn!"

There was the sound of metal piercing rubber as the tires suddenly grew large blades across their entire external surface. In an instant, they had both become sharp, lethal stabbing weapons, cutting grooves on the floor as they continued to wheel their way around Rika.

The assassin pointed at the rooftop door, then sent her Striders away.

"Go!"

On her signal, the shockwave engines installed on each Strider revved into action, propelling them at high speed. They smashed into the steel door, their "thorns" seeking to cut through its weak points like a buzz saw. The sound, and the sparks, were terrific. But before long, the latch and deadbolt were cut clean off, the disabled door slamming inward to the floor.

The Striders, not particularly moved by this sight, used their shockwave engines to pinball their way down the floor, the ceiling, the walls—on their way into the landing, leaving deep ruts wherever their rampage took them.

Soon, Rika could hear screaming and the sound of shredding flesh from a floor below.

The Striders would never stop until Rentaro Satomi and Hotaru Kouro were dead. Whenever Rika activated them, she made sure no one was breathing afterward. Hence the "Necropolis" part. Wherever they went, a city of death reigned.

Before long, Strider 1 sent a signal to Rika indicating it had cut the targeted phone line. Strider 2 was keeping watch at the front door, ensuring no one tried to flee outside. Enjoying the carnage playing out in her mind, Rika adjusted her grip on the plush bear and sang to herself as she walked downstairs.

"Overrr the raaaainbow...♪"

With their phone call cut off, Rentaro and Hotaru found themselves having to come up with a new plan of action. Fast.

"This is bad," Rentaro said. "The guy on the phone suggested he knew *you* were here, too."

Hotaru tried to present a façade of coolness as she thought over the situation. It was difficult given the adrenaline coursing through her, urging her on toward revenge. This was the perfect chance. She never even dreamed she'd have an opportunity to swing the iron hammer of justice so quickly.

Reaching for the pair of government handguns on her back holster, she closed her eyes as she felt the sensation of steel in her hands, praying for their salvation as she undid the safety on both.

Kihachi, I need your strength.

"We better focus on getting out of this building for now."

"No. I'm taking them on. Now I can finally get revenge for Kihachi."

"You're crazy. We have no idea what kind of enemy we're facing or what they're capable of. They'll kill you."

Hotaru sneered at Rentaro out of the corner of her eye. This was exactly the kind of limp-wristed feebleness that got Kihachi killed in the first place.

"I *told* you. The only reason I'm working with you is so I could hunt down the enemies after *your* blood. You've been the best decoy I could ever have hoped for. If you think we've got some kind of partnership going on, let me assure you, it's all in your head. I always hated you anyway."

"Hotaru, this *really* isn't a good time for this, all right? The enemy's probably got you on their hit list by now. If we stand here and argue like this… That's exactly what our enemy wants from us. We'll waste whatever chance we have to win this."

Rentaro extended a hand.

"You need to work with me, Hotaru. The enemy's shut us off from the outside world. If they're willing to do that, then worst-case scenario, they're willing to massacre every man, woman, and child in this building. We need to get everyone evacuated—"

He was cut off by a dry, shrill *slap*. Hotaru, face full of sullen resentment, beat his hand away from her.

"If you're so hell-bent on saving people's lives, why didn't you save Kihachi's?"

Rentaro winced, unable to respond.

"Rentaro, are you *really* the hero? This guy who took all those demoralized civsecs in the Third Kanto Battle and drove them to defeat Aldebaran? Because you don't look like it to me."

He kept his eyes straight on her. "The dead don't care about revenge, Hotaru."

"*I* don't care about *you*. I'm hunting them down, and I don't need your help. Good-bye."

"Hotaru!"

She headed for the door, Rentaro hot on her heels. Out in the hallway, she closed the door behind her and took a deep breath, focusing her mind's eye on her navel. She could feel her limbs warm up, her five senses expanding themselves and releasing their powers.

Quietly, Hotaru opened her eyes. *He's wrong. I'll be fine by myself. I'll prove it by killing my enemy alone.*

She scanned the hallway before her, ensuring nothing was amiss. The phone was dead, but the lights were still on.

Then, above her, she heard a scream and the sound of something being sawed through. She raced up the stairs, two steps at a time, and stormed through the thirteenth-floor doorway.

The smell of blood weighed heavily upon her nose. It was, as Rentaro put it just moments ago, a massacre. Dismembered corpses littered the hallway, dark-red blood tracing its way across the linoleum floor. The ceiling and walls had heavy ruts etched into them, as if a giant was swinging a long broadsword around the hall.

She crouched down to look at the body of a female victim. Her wounds appeared to have been made with a coarse, sawlike weapon. Looking closer, many of the bodies featured missing arms, legs, and heads, with others in a multitude of small pieces. It must have been hell for them. They must have come out of their apartments to investigate the noise and screaming.

Around the corner, she saw an open elevator car with a body preventing the doors from fully closing. Every time the doors attempted to close, they squished against the corpse in gruesome fashion, changing its position just a little each time before opening back up.

Rentaro was right. The enemy was killing indiscriminately. An enemy so completely free of morals like this— *Can I really beat them?*

Hearing a quiet motor nearby, Hotaru turned to find something on top of a body at the other end of the hallway. At first, she thought she was looking at a jaguar gnawing on the flesh of some kind of wild game. It took several moments for her to realize it was a small tire, the size of a flying disc. It was covered in serrated blades, and given that they didn't seem to deflate the tire at all, she figured it must be filled with some kind of reinforced plastic or the like instead. Right now, it was spewing exhaust from two rear-facing pipes as its blades ground their way into the corpse.

Instinctively, she could tell this was it. She had no idea what made it tick, but this machine was the perpetrator of this massacre.

Is that Hummingbird? She shook her head. *No. This isn't even human.*

The killing machine changed position—it had noticed her. By the time Hotaru realized the danger, it was already too late. With a scream wholly different from anything a gasoline engine could produce, it blazed a trail straight for her.

Witnessing the saw blades proceeding toward her at worrying speed, Hotaru crossed her guns together in self-defense. The tire hit them, sending her reeling back as it spun against her defensive shield, sparks flying. She gritted her teeth, attempting to push back with her strength. The distance between them grew, just enough for her to take aim and blaze away with both triggers.

Then Hotaru found herself gazing in wonder again.

Running a zigzag across the hall, the tire dodged every one of her .45-caliber shots, jumping off the floor and latching itself onto the wall. It ran along, not letting gravity affect its joyride as it crossed over to the ceiling and carved out a track for itself, advancing upon Hotaru again.

Hotaru, her aim upset by this unexpected move, instantly leapt to the side. A moment later, the murder machine's claws had sunk into the floor where she was.

She gave a kick, knowing that it could cost her her leg. One of the knives stabbed her in the knee. A groan of pain leaked out from between her gritted teeth.

But her enemy paid the price, too. The tire, taking the full brunt of an Initiator's kick, was sent against the wall, smashing into and almost through it before falling to the floor, twitching in its final death throes.

Hotaru jumped with one foot, healing her right leg instantaneously in the air as she sank both of her heels into the wheel portion of the tire. She landed on it, took out both guns, and fired a flurry of shots at point-blank range. She experienced it all—the noise, the eye-watering flashes, the recoil kicking at her arms, the spent cases bouncing off the walls and floor.

The results pulverized the spokes and smashed into the shockwave engine installed in the hub. At the same time, the slide stop on both guns popped up, indicating she was out of ammo.

There was a moment of silence, the smell of smoke invading Hotaru's nostrils. She resented the heavy panting she heard, only to realize it was coming from her. She wiped the sweat from her brow. The mystery machine was dead. Somehow or other, she had won. If she had her way, she'd prefer this to be the only enemy she had to face.

"Help me!"

Turning toward the sudden shout, she realized a girl was running toward her.

She had all but told Rentaro that she didn't care about survivors. Yet the sight of someone actually making it through this disaster alive still felt like a relief to her.

The girl bounded right up to Hotaru, hugging her as she did.

With a *jnnk* sound, Hotaru convulsed as a shockwave spread across her body.

"Huh?"

Slowly, her eyes fell upon her chest.

The girl, clad in a straw hat and carrying a teddy bear, had removed a knife she had hidden in her stuffed toy. And now the edge of it was—

The girl brought her lips to Hotaru's ear.

"You dummy."

"Ahh…hhh…"

The blade, easily making its way through her tank top, had gone right through her left lung. It was long, black, and over halfway inside her. Varanium, without a doubt.

"Well? Can you feel it? Can you see? How does it feel to be dying?"

"N-no…"

Was this the girl—?

"Good-bye, my splendid princess."

She wrested the knife away from her body. Then, the next point she struck was the heart.

Hotaru's body convulsed as if struck by lightning, while she coughed up copious amounts of blood. The girl took a step back to dodge the stream. The Initiator's vision blurred as she fell to her knees. Her fingertips felt cold. Her blurred eyesight looked up at her enemy. The girl in the dress grinned as she looked back down at her.

The ground approached. Before her face even hit the linoleum, Hotaru's consciousness was torn apart, as she embraced the end of her life.

Hotaru's assailant picked up the fallen girl's hand, ensuring there was no pulse. She checked her pupils, too, just in case. Listening for a heartbeat as well seemed like overkill, so she skipped that step.

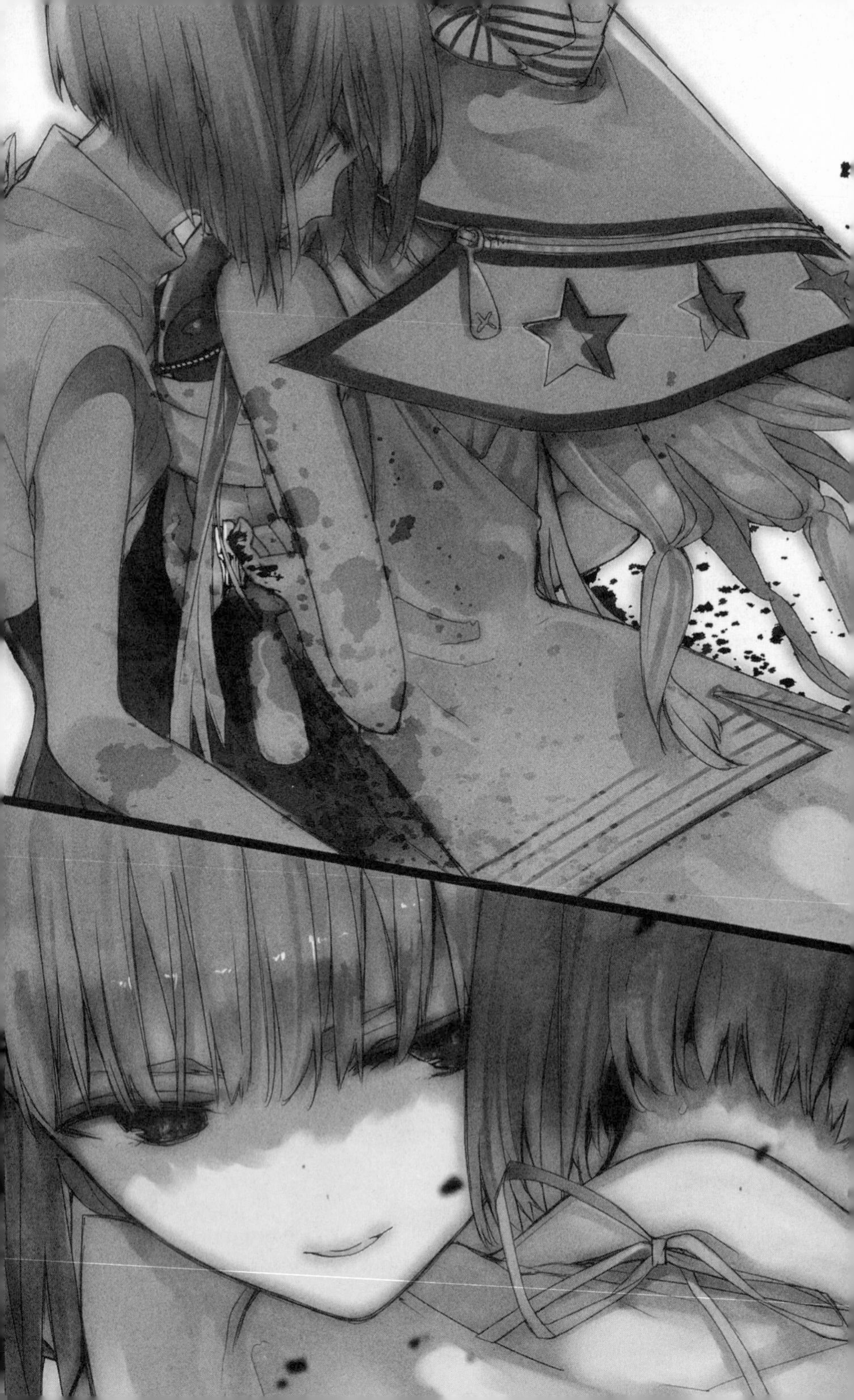

Something about the sight of the body struck Rika as funny. She trampled on Hotaru's fixed expression, stamping on it with her sole.

"Just *onnnnnne leeefffft!*"

Rika turned around and helped herself to the stairway, seeking her final enemy.

5

Rentaro pushed the door's intercom button. The moment the door opened, he took a hand to the edge, pushed himself inside, and readied his weapon.

"Get out. Now. Keep it slow."

The bathrobe-clad old man, nonplussed to be facing the barrel of a gun this time of night, sheepishly went out the door, not quite managing to find the right timing to scream or at least act surprised.

"Could I ask who you are?"

Rentaro ignored the question that finally did come out, prodding the elderly man forward until he was in the elevator. Inside were ten other people from the twelfth floor, all corralled there by him in the same manner.

"Is it money? Do you want money?" "What was that noise just now? Was that gunfire? What's going on?"

"—I don't have time to explain. I'm sending you guys down to the lobby, so just get out of the building and call for help."

A few moments ago, there was gunfire and the sounds of combat from the floor above. The enemy was up there. If he could get these people down, at least they wouldn't run into the guy. That was Rentaro's line of thinking as he pushed the L button and took a few steps back from the door.

Before he could see them off, though, misgivings began to creep into his mind. The enemy cut off the phone lines to prevent him from contacting external help. They'd need switchboard access for that, and that switchboard had to be either on the first floor or the basement. Definitely not on the thirteenth or higher. Which meant there had to be multiple hostiles—one snapping the cords, one engaging Hotaru above him.

The moment before the door closed, Rentaro stuck his arm in to stop it.

"Wait. I'm getting on, too."

The residents of the twelfth floor dolefully glared at him. *God damn it, I'm trying to protect you guys.*

The doors began to close again. This time, Rentaro stopped them because of a voice shouting "Wait! Help!" from across the corridor. A girl in a straw hat, maybe thirteen or fourteen, was making a dash for the elevator, teddy bear at the ready.

"There's some kind of tire monster upstairs! There's dead people up there!"

"Tire monster?" Rentaro exclaimed. Then he had a thought. He put his hand up to around chest level. "Hey, did you see a girl about this tall up there?"

The girl shook her head, tugging at her stuffed animal a little.

"Oh…"

The gunshots and other noise were gone. Whichever way the battle went for Hotaru, it was over. Hopefully she made it.

Looking at the button panel, Rentaro noticed the building had fifteen floors and two basement levels. The occupants of the car, perhaps moved by the girl's disturbing testimony, remained meekly silent. The door finally closed. The L button was lit.

There was a slight sense of weightlessness as the car shuddered into action. The number on the top of the panel began to count downward, far too slowly for everyone's tastes. Nobody said a word. The smell of stagnant sweat permeated the car. Rentaro had a bad taste in his mouth. The silence was painful, and not just because of the lack of personal space.

Rentaro wiped his palms against his slacks, his brain preoccupied with the thought of the elevator jarring to a halt and the overhead light going out. Luckily, it didn't happen. The elevator let out a cheery *ding* as it reached the lobby.

Suddenly, a ferocious sense of dread struck Rentaro, for reasons he failed to articulate.

—Then someone or something smashed into the car with a loud roar, strong enough to put a dent in the door. Gigantic serrated blades made their way through the slit in the middle. Then they began to spin, generating a cascade of sparks. Pressing the DOOR CLOSE button did nothing. It was being pried open.

"Aaaaaaahhh!"

Doom and panic prevailed inside the car. Rentaro jostled his way to the front. *No time to think.* Sizing up the whirling blades wresting the doors open, he rolled up his right sleeve, revealing his cybernetic arm as he held his body low.

Waiting for the moment when the door was open enough, he activated his arm. There was a loud percussion, followed by a single empty cartridge spinning in the air.

"—*Kohaku Tensei!*"

He unleashed his arm, driven by a sudden massive propulsion that sent him into the lobby. The punch, easily a match for the mysterious spinning object, cut through the blades. He could feel the blow hitting home.

The tables were quickly turned. Rentaro's blow, powerful enough to send a microbus into the air, smashed right through the spinning saw, sending it bounding off the floor and into the opposite wall.

"What is that...?!"

Now the enemy was fully in sight. "Tire monster" was the only way to describe it. Its engine revved loudly. An unmanned drone? Or...?

The person who called Dr. Surumi's home came back to his memory. "*The enemy's about to head your way. Code name Hummingbird. A soldier from the New World Creation Project.*"

If *this* was what this Hummingbird was capable of, Rentaro knew someone who had notably similar capabilities. Tina Sprout. She had a brain-machine interface that let her use brain signals to operate autonomous machines—technology that Ain Rand, genius scientist and former colleague of Sumire Muroto's, pioneered and produced. Meanwhile, Yuga Mitsugi—aka Dark Stalker—boasted the same abilities as Rentaro's 21-Form Varanium Artificial Eye, an advanced piece of tech that Sumire expended countless hours of research and effort to complete.

What kind of group would it take to not only copy this tech, but actually upgrade it? Who was behind the New World Creation Project...?

Rentaro had little time to think about it. The tire monster resumed its position. He removed the Beretta from his holster and fired two shots. Shockingly, the enemy zigzagged left and right to dodge them. Rentaro deliberately ignored the gunsights his eye put up for him and fired again, aiming at a fire extinguisher near the hole the tire just gouged into the wall.

The sturdily built Varanium bullet broke through the glass and dented the aluminum exterior. Rentaro kept firing. On the fourth shot, the extinguisher finally gave up the ghost against the supersonic 9-mm Varanium bullets and went flying. He was ready for this.

"Haaahhh!"

The next moment, he closed in on the tire, gun aimed at the engine inside its hub.

"Tendo Martial Arts First Style, Number 12—"

He triggered a cartridge in his arm. The smell of gunpowder burned his nostrils. The monster shuddered in fear, but it was too late.

"—*Senkuu Renen!*"

The entire floor shook as his hand plowed through the tire's engine and sank into the floor itself with a loud bang. The force of the point-blank strike rendered his enemy motionless, the faintly blinking signal light on it fading as it fell to the ground.

Once he was sure it was done for, Rentaro loosened up his body and took a breath. Leaving a BMI-driven machine unattended would be suicide. It was better for him to crush it while he had the chance. It was a lesson Rentaro had to learn the hard way in his fight against Tina.

Rentaro took a look around the first-floor lobby as the smoky mist from the extinguisher began to dissipate. The sight made him furrow his brows. The BMI devices had done in some of the residents who'd noticed early on that something was up and had tried to escape. The bodies were now in multiple pieces and splattered across the walls and floor. Was everyone in the New World Creation Project this heartless...?

Then, remembering his duty, he turned back through the mist, toward the elevator as he waved his arms.

"It's all clear now!"

The people slowly, warily filed out of the elevator car. One of them, the old man in the bathrobe, asked a question.

"Wh-what is this? What's going on...?"

Rentaro shook his head. "I don't know," he said. "All I can say is that the lobby's safe. All of you get out right now and call the police."

"What about you?"

"I'll get as many people out of here as I can until the police come."

It wasn't a very well-made plan, but without so much as an emergency alarm at his disposal, the best one he could think of involved positioning himself and the residents up and down the elevator until police arrived. Considering he was a wanted man, he wasn't entirely sure he had an escape route if the authorities decided to send an army of cops his way, but he wasn't willing to simply leave this hideous murder scene behind him and run. Besides, the whole reason for this massacre was because Rentaro was here, paying a visit to Dr. Surumi.

Rentaro watched the twelfth-floor denizens leave out the front door, then turned around. He noticed someone still on the elevator. The girl with the teddy bear. Rentaro irritatedly waved at her.

"Hey! You get out of here! You want to get killed?"

The girl meekly smiled back. "Let me help, too," she said. "Two people would be more efficient than one, right?"

It was a fairly incredible request to Rentaro's ears. Unless you were trained to do so, or at least had a fairly strong sense of duty, you wouldn't be wanting to help other people in a situation where your own life was in danger. If a lion was chasing you, your main focus wouldn't be on the friend running away with you.

But *this* girl…?

Rentaro was honestly more suspicious than thankful.

The girl gave him a flick of her eyebrows and smiled. "Come on, let's go. Even as we speak, those tire monsters are still running around, aren't they? It'll be twice as efficient with the two of us."

She had a point. Rentaro closed his eyes, took a deep breath, and opened them.

"All right. You can help if you want. I'll get off at the eleventh floor," he said as he entered the car and pushed DOOR CLOSE, "so you take the tenth."

Then he smelled something sweet. Perfume. He didn't notice it when they were packed in like sardines earlier, but she must have been wearing it.

This triggered something in his brain. Something he heard from Sumire at her underground lab when he discussed the murders of Kenji Houbara, Saya Takamura, and Giichi Ebihara.

"I got all curious about these murders, so I had Miori give me some information. There were no witnesses to Kenji Houbara's stabbing at the theater and they couldn't find any fingerprints on the knife, but apparently there was a faintly sweet scent left on the weapon."

—A faintly sweet scent?

Rentaro shuddered.

If the tire monsters were BMI devices like Tina's Shenfield system, there had to be someone nearby the scene controlling them. If Hummingbird was inside the building right now, then where?

The elevator door closed with a clattering sound. Rentaro's pulse quickened, his chest pained. He felt nauseated. His hand, checking the position of the holster around his hips, was drenched in sweat. He looked at the girl opposite him in the car, but the large straw hat made it difficult to gauge her expression. She held the teddy bear in her left hand, and now, with her right hand, she was fumbling around its stomach area.

Taking a closer look, there was an odd indentation in the bear's stomach. Clearly there was something besides stuffing in it.

Rentaro's brain went on red alert. The elevator door was fully closed. The girl moved. Rentaro moved with her. At lightning speed, his gun was drawn and aimed.

But the next thing he knew, his vision was dominated by the barrel of another gun, one aimed squarely at his head.

The girl had a ferociously self-confident smile on her face. "Oh-*hoh*? How come you noticed that, huh? I think this might be the first time I didn't get the first attack on someone. It's kind of novel!"

"Are you Hummingbird?"

"Uh-huh! I'm the second assassin."

Rentaro gritted his teeth bitterly. *I am such an idiot. How could I fail to notice the assassin when she's right in front of me?*

"Listen, um, I kinda lied to you earlier." Hummingbird waited a moment before showing off a mischievous smile. "Hotaru Kouro's actually been cold dead for a while now."

Fury erupted from Rentaro's fingertips to the top of his head. He squeezed the trigger, just as he tilted his head to the side to get out of her sights. His enemy mirrored him, doing the exact same thing. Two deafening gunshots erupted. The heat from the muzzle flash opposite him made him squint his eyes as he felt a sonic boom from the bullet whizzing by his ear at somewhere above Mach 1.

One of the shots ricocheted, zinging between the walls of the elevator car—but by some diabolical coincidence, neither party was injured.

Now it was time to disable the enemy's weapon. Rentaro slapped the girl's thin arm away, smashing the elbow on his cybernetic right arm against the palm of her hand. She yelped in pain as the gun fell. A moment later, it transformed into a maniacal laugh.

What is with *this girl?*

Hummingbird lowered her body, then unleashed a kick aimed at Rentaro's crotch. It was a clean hit. Rentaro fell back just in time to take a blow to a joint right above the arm holding his gun. The pain made him feel like his arm was being twisted off. It made him quickly shut off his pain receptors, but it was just enough to make him drop his own gun.

The girl rammed into him, plastering him against the wall of the cramped elevator and knocking the wind out of him. His back slammed against the button panel, hard enough to make the elevator shudder to life. A cold sweat ran down his side. He was flexing his muscles to the limit, but the sheer unrelenting force his enemy used against him was something no young girl should possess. Desperate, he finally managed to land three knee strikes on her hips, waiting for her to let up just a little bit before sidestepping around and behind her.

Then his brain triggered a danger signal. He reared his head back out of instinct, just in time for Hummingbird's nails to miss the eyes they were targeting. There was no time to even be shocked. He shouted in pain at the blow she then landed on his left calf. The upper-body eye gouge segued perfectly into a low kick.

Taking a dagger out from the teddy bear lying on the floor, Hummingbird held it close to her stomach and rushed forward. There was too little space to escape.

With an electronic beep, the door opened behind him. The elevator was on the fifth floor. Rentaro realized he had an escape path after all.

There was no time to evaluate how practical his plan was. Grabbing his foe by both shoulders, he diverted the kinetic energy of her bull rush behind his back, holding his own body down as he sent her flying in a classic judo-style overhead throw.

Unable to stop herself, the girl flew into the air, a surprised look on her face. She must not have realized what had happened to her at first. Before she could, her tiny body smashed into the opposite wall of the elevator lobby at full speed. It offered Rentaro a perfect chance at a follow-up strike, but his leg was still in pain from the low kick, preventing him from taking nimble action.

Hummingbird leaped back to her feet, hiked up her skirt, drew her auxiliary pistol from a holster strapped to her thigh, and fired. Rentaro hid behind the elevator frame, turning his head against the ensuing blast and rain of sparks. He jabbed at the DOOR CLOSE button. The elevator obeyed after a moment. He pushed the LOBBY button. The elevator began to descend.

He leaned his body against the now-pockmarked elevator wall, just barely managing not to crumple to the ground. Every part of him was screaming. His bandaged wound was about to reopen. For the time being, at least, he was distant from his foe, but the threat was no less present. His mind raced. *What should I do? What should I do?*

Then the elevator rattled like it was the victim of a sudden earthquake, the ceiling light flickering on and off. Rentaro held on to the wall to keep from slipping. Something must've fallen on it from above. But what?

The answer was obvious—Hummingbird had fallen on him from the fifth floor. Rentaro threw his body to the ground, grabbing his Beretta and the gun his enemy dropped, then unloaded both straight upward.

His foe was firing by instinct from above as well. The flying bullets smashed the button panel and shattered the ceiling lights, sending a rain of glass down at him. He tried as hard as he could to fight back. The concerto of crisscrossing gunfire continued on, empty cartridges providing bombastic percussion to the proceedings. A pang of pain as a bullet grazed his cheek. Then, the intense heat of bullet against bone as a ricocheting shot struck him in the knee.

Both of his guns ran out of ammo simultaneously. So did his enemy's. For a moment, there was deafening silence, and the smell of gunpowder assaulting Rentaro's nostrils.

What happened?

After a moment, he heard something heavy thudding against the ceiling above him. Somewhere in the midst of the battle, the elevator had stopped moving. The shot that struck the instrument panel must've knocked it offline. The ceiling lights were gone, except for a single flickering bulb. The space was dim.

Holding a hand against the wall, Rentaro gingerly got himself up and peeled off a dangling, heavily perforated ceiling panel. A prone Hummingbird tumbled into the elevator, groaning once her body hit the floor. Two 9-mm shots in the stomach and one in the chest were staining her dress crimson, her upper body heaving as she gasped for breath. The battle was over for her.

The girl looked up at the ceiling in disbelief. "You…you're kidding me," she whispered. "I was built to…to surpass the New Humanity Creation Project…and I lost…?"

Rentaro looked down silently at her for a few moments.

"…There's a lot I want to ask you. I'll treat your wounds if you don't resist me."

Hummingbird scowled in self-derision, coughing violently in response to the pain in her chest. A fountain of blood shot out, and faint lines of red oozed from her lips.

"Don't be…stupid," she said weakly, her trembling hands tapping against her heart. "They're…monitoring my heartbeat, and if, if they, found out you, helped me… I'll, I'll be rubbed out either way. You… you'll never have any more peace. Even if—if I die…it'll be someone else, next. My friends, will kill…you. It's all the same."

She sighed as she stared upward, resigned to her fate.

"I guess…I guess Dark Stalker was…right after all."

"What do you mean?"

"Dark Stalker…was the only one, who, who recognized…what kind of threat you were. He said you.…you were a genius. He wanted to, to fight you again, and…and he fought our, our leader over it."

"……"

Internally, Rentaro was shocked that someone as breathlessly confident of himself as Yuga was willing to heap that much praise upon him. Maybe Yuga Mitsugi was the greatest threat to his life after all.

Then he noticed Hummingbird's skirt was up, revealing her lily-white thighs. He gazed at them in wonderment. There was a five-pointed star tattooed on one of them, a pair of intricately designed feathers drawn on two of the points. The exact same. Just what he saw carved on the Gastrea in the photo.

"Hey!" he hurriedly shouted. "What's that? What's that star on you mean?!"

Hummingbird simply smiled wryly. "Look...look at what's, what's inside my teddy bear."

Rentaro, despite his suspicion, obeyed. The polar bear, a scarf around his neck, still had an oddly bloated stomach. There must have been another weapon inside. He stuck a hand in, trying to get it out, but it was too big to easily take out of the slit. The bear was soft and fuzzy on the outside, but inside, there was something cold and solid to the touch.

What *is* this? Growing increasingly impatient, he finally just ripped the bear's upper body apart. Cotton stuffing flew out from it, revealing what was inside. Rentaro gulped nervously. The bear's stomach was lined with cords and lumps of what looked like clay. A cheap digital timer was attached to the middle. It had just gone past thirty seconds. The moment he realized it was a time bomb, his blood froze as a dark chill crashed upon his body.

Hummingbird let out a bitter laugh. "If...if my heartbeat, goes down enough, it's, it's set to automatically, go off. The elevator's down, your leg's hurt... I don't think you're escaping. So...can we, can we call it a draw?"

"Shit!"

Rentaro jumped for the door, trying to pry it open. It wouldn't budge. Then he tried jumping for the ceiling, holding his wounded leg in the air. A sharp pain erupted from it, incapacitating him. Twenty seconds to go.

Then, with another loud noise, his vision was jarred up and down as his feet struggled for purchase. It didn't take him as long to realize that something just fell on the elevator again.

Through a hole in the battered ceiling, he could see what it was.

Rentaro and Hummingbird both opened their eyes wide, the con-fused dismay particularly clear upon Hummingbird's face. She let out a scream.

"You, you're supposed to be dead—"

The reply came in the form of gunfire. With a dry crack from the gun, Hummingbird's head exploded in a spray of blood, falling limply against the wall behind her.

A cold voice fell in from above.

"Good-bye, my splendid princess."

"Hotaru!"

The shadow he could barely make out above turned into a silhouette of Hotaru Kouro, her frozen eyes coming into view.

"You... Hummingbird said you were dead..."

Then he shook his head. There were more pressing issues at hand. He looked at the timer. Seven seconds left.

"Hotaru! The bomb!"

"Gimme your hand!"

He lifted up his arm. It was yanked up, hard enough to almost dis-locate his shoulder, as he was pulled into the elevator shaft. His vision suddenly went dark, the sound of the cable groaning at the weight pounding his eardrums.

"Grab on to the wire!"

Rentaro obediently did so. Four seconds left.

With a series of nimble shots, Hotaru fired at the braking devices latched on to the guide rail, destroying them all.

—Three seconds.

Then she took out her knife, using her Initiator strength to snap in an instant the three cords besides the one Rentaro held.

——Two seconds.

Grabbing the one remaining wire with her left hand to secure a life-line, she lifted her legs high and bashed her heels against the top of the car.

———One second.

The elevator car, struggling at this new force applied to it, snapped its remaining wire, tumbling down the shaft like a shooting star. The wire the two of them held shot up in response, zooming up like a bun-gee cord.

Rentaro and Hotaru tried madly to hold on to the torn wire. Below him, he could see the car generating sparks as it plunged down the guide rail. The counterweight scraped against the side of the shaft as it, too, whizzed downward.

Then—the bomb finally went off.

A hot shockwave, too hot for Rentaro to keep his eyes open, slammed up at him. Like a tugboat in a typhoon, they were tossed and roiled as they clung to the wire. Flames shot up the shaft as the elevator began to consume itself, stopping only when they were right at Rentaro's and Hotaru's feet. Slowly, they retreated downward, almost like a living creature licking its wounds in chagrin.

The two of them breathed a synchronized sigh of relief. Hotaru's eyes, now unexpectedly close to his, were wide open with surprise. They looked endearing to him. But the attention made Hotaru avert them in embarrassment. "Let's go up," she said as she pulled the rope, dragging Rentaro along.

They emerged at the fifteenth-floor elevator lobby. The setting sun bathed the area in a bright red, almost too bright to set eyes upon. It was near the end of the day. In the light, Rentaro noticed Hotaru's tank top was torn, shredded, and covered in a rich crimson.

"Did she stab you?"

"It's already closed up."

"Closed up...?"

She had clearly been stabbed right in the heart. Was it too shallow to kill her, though? *No way.* Rentaro shook his head. Hummingbird had said it herself—"*you're supposed to be dead.*" He doubted a gifted assassin like her would fall for a victim playing possum on her.

"Hotaru, what type of Gastrea factor do you have?"

Hotaru stared silently at Rentaro for a moment. Then she shook her head lightly, perhaps realizing there was no way to hide it any longer.

"It's a *dugesia*, a type of flatworm."

"*Dugesia*...?"

Rentaro had heard of this. He hadn't read all those nature books in the Tendo family library for nothing. It was a type of planarian flatworm, a small creature with astonishing regenerative skills and the ability to weather just about any kind of famine. They could famously form two distinct and healthy flatworms even if cut in half, making them useful for experiments in natural regeneration.

"So that means you can…"

"Basically, I have enhanced regenerative skills. Most Initiators can close up their wounds and heal even if their injuries would kill any normal person. In my case, my ability's strong enough that I can push back against Varanium inhibiting that."

Rentaro sighed in amazement. The natural world always had a way of aweing him like that. Twice in the past, Rentaro had personally witnessed people healing themselves at astonishing speed. The first time, it was Rentaro himself—the AGV test drug from Sumire helped him overcome mortal injury and fend off Kagetane Hiruko. But that drug had the Russian roulette–like side effect of turning 20 percent of its patients into Gastrea. Rentaro using all five of the syringes given to him and still not making the transformation was something of a miracle. It wasn't exactly safe for everyday use.

The second time he saw regeneration like that was with Aldebaran, the enemy he fought in the Third Kanto Battle. Those ominous memories were still fresh in his mind. The high-powered EP bomb developed by Shiba Heavy Weapons eventually blew it to smithereens, but that battle couldn't have been a closer call than it was.

"That's so…powerful. Why'd you hide it from me?"

Hotaru shook her head in frustration. "It's not the cure-all you probably think it is," she replied. "The human body's a lot more complex than a flatworm's, so I can only regenerate so much at a time. If someone lit my dead body on fire with gasoline or decapitated me, I'm not gonna be able to make up for that. It's not like I can put up a resistance while I'm dead, so I need to make sure my enemy doesn't know about that ability. It's hard to work into a battle strategy. I kept it a secret from you because if someone tortured that info out of you, that'd mean trouble for me."

I see, thought Rentaro. *That makes enough sense.* When two Initiators fought against each other, even a single blow could be lethal, no matter what the ability. If her foe knew about her innate skills, that could easily be used against her. As a result, Initiators generally stayed tight-lipped about that sort of thing. Loose lips sank ships in this business.

"Wow... Well, I guess I see now. I thought you really hated me for a while."

"There was that, too."

"......"

"What?"

Rentaro scratched his head, forcing himself not to pursue this line of conversation. He removed the outer jacket of his uniform and tossed it at Hotaru. "Here," he said, "put that on. Your clothes are all bloody. You can't go walking around like that."

Hotaru gave Rentaro's jacket a light sniff, then winced. "It smells terrible. Why does men's sweat have to be so stinky all the time...?"

"Okay, give it back."

"Well, I'll put it on if I *haaave* to."

Rentaro rolled his eyes and turned around. She was *so* annoying to deal with.

"Oh, uh, thanks."

"Huh?"

"Nothing. Let's go, Rentaro."

Her cheeks were red, perhaps because of the evening sunlight she was drenched in, as she marched off. "Wait a sec," Rentaro said, stopping her as he pointed at his left leg. "Lend me a shoulder."

Hotaru watched him silently for a moment, walked back, and just as silently offered her shoulder. He sheepishly accepted. She was unflinchingly cold to him, but for whatever reason, her skin felt hot to the touch.

Wisely opting to leave the elevator for someone else to worry about, the pair of them limped down the stairs and out the main entrance. The front was lined with people. It was only a matter of time before the police showed up. Wary that someone would notice him, Rentaro hid his face, pretending to be unconscious as Hotaru dragged him along. She keenly picked up a taxi and directed the driver to the apartment she was hiding out in.

The middle-aged driver gave the two extremely disheveled passengers a dubious look, but his sense of professionalism willed him to gently bring the car into motion regardless.

They could hear sirens far away, and before long, a small squadron of police cars came in from ahead, lights flashing. As they passed,

Rentaro and Hotaru instinctively ducked from the windows. The Doppler effect made the sirens sound almost comical as they faded away behind them. Cautiously, they sat back up and looked toward the rear. The police were now pouring into the apartment building they had just left. Just in the nick of time.

Rentaro loosened up, the mental strain exiting his body—but then the driver's eyes met his through the rearview mirror. He looked startled for a moment but quickly averted his gaze, as if he had just witnessed a couple making out at the bar. The odd response made the hairs stand on Rentaro's nape.

That stare indicated the driver had just connected a vague memory with his current reality. And his eyes darted away right afterward. From the backseat, Rentaro sensed danger. What did the driver just remember—? What else *could* it be? His face matched the fugitive's from the news. Otherwise, why would he awkwardly take his eyes away like that?

And of *course* Hotaru had to give him the exact address of her apartment before hopping in. The idea that the driver would drop them off then *not* exercise his civic duty to contact the police seemed far too optimistic to him. In fact, he might even drive his taxi right to the police station instead of taking them over. If he did, they were finished.

The taxi stopped quietly at a red light. Hotaru sat there, picking up on Rentaro's nerves and waiting to see what happened next. She knew the driver was on to them. The tension was at the boiling point. Just a light prod could make it explode.

The light turned green. The driver stepped on the gas. Rentaro could feel the inertia drive his body into the seat a little.

"Um, sir...?"

Rentaro shuddered. His body tensed up, as if a judge just sentenced him to death.

"Would you mind," the driver continued, "if I talked to myself for a little bit? I know this isn't exactly a glamorous job I have, but y'know, I was seriously thinking about joining the self-defense force a month ago. At *my* age, you know? Like, you remember how they expanded the age limit to accommodate for just about anybody during the Third Kanto Battle? I figured, y'know, maybe I needed to take up arms and fight to defend this city, too, so..."

Then the driver fell silent. "Uh, and then what?" Rentaro dared to ask.

The steering wheel squeaked a little underneath the cabbie's grip. "Ah, it didn't work out in the end," he said mournfully. "I was too scared. I lost my wife and kid in the war ten years ago, so I figured I had nothing left to lose, but…you know, I wound up marrying another widow, someone just like me. We live in a pretty humble place, but we're happy, y'know? …So I just couldn't go through with it. Not if it meant losing something again. If I'm doomed to die, I wanted it to be together with her."

"…Nothing wrong about that. That's a natural reaction."

The taxi entered a tunnel. A steady stream of orange lights whizzed by, weakly illuminating their faces at regular intervals.

"Do you have any family, civsec?" the driver asked. He had no doubts about Rentaro's job position, at any rate.

After a moment figuring out what to say, Rentaro decided to just shake his head, not bothering with pleasantries. "They're all dead."

"You weren't scared of that Aldebaran guy at all?"

"Well, sure I was."

Hotaru looked at Rentaro, mouth slightly open.

"That wasn't something anyone should have to experience. And compared to the work it took, I've gotten far too little appreciation for it."

"So why do you do it?"

Rentaro thought for a little, then shook his head again. "I don't know," he admitted. "But I was the only one there who could, really, so…"

"Oh…"

The driver clammed up again. Rentaro grew anxious, squirming in his seat as he wondered if he had offended the cabbie somehow. But the words that finally greeted him weren't what he expected.

"I guess the kinds of people we call heroes are pretty much like that, huh?"

The driver smiled at him through the mirror.

"Don't worry. I've been terribly forgetful as of late, y'know. By the time I drop you off, I'm probably going to forget I even had anybody in this car."

"Oh… Uh, well, thanks. I really owe you one."

Rentaro didn't know what he could say after that. So he kept quiet. His conversational partner joined him. The atmosphere was far gentler now. He closed his eyes.

He was no hero, no savior of humanity. That much he was sure of. But if what he did helped others smile just a little more, enjoy that little bit more of happiness—didn't that mean there was some greater meaning behind the path he took, at the end of it all?

Nothing at all had improved with his situation. Enju was still a ward of the IISO. Tina was still locked up in jail somewhere. And Kisara was still wrapped cruelly around Hitsuma's finger. The thought of Hitsuma taking advantage of her trust in him filled his mind with rage, but it wasn't like he could storm the police headquarters with guns a-blazing. That would just add to his already-long rap sheet. His only hope was to follow Suibara's trail down whatever he was investigating and catch the people who put him in this mess.

He managed to dispatch Hummingbird. The girl who almost certainly killed Kenji Houbara. Judging by the sniping skill he showed off at the Plaza Hotel, Dark Stalker must have been Giichi Ebihara's killer.

Which meant, by the process of elimination, that someone whose name he didn't even know must have assassinated Saya Takamura.

So, two killers left. And the one Rentaro really had to watch out for was Dark Stalker. One thing the battle with Hummingbird made clear was that he didn't have to dread them so much after all. They were strong, but beatable. And sooner or later, he'd make that clear as black and white to them.

The fury in his stomach warmed his entire body as Rentaro contemplated his enemies, wherever they lurked, across the Tokyo Area landscape.

6

A loud *wham* echoed across the control room, making the operators sit bolt upright in their seats.

Atsuro Hitsuma, not caring about the pain in his fist as he slammed it against the terminal, winced as he scrunched his eyebrows downward, all but crushing the cell phone in his other hand. "All right," he managed to squeak out. "Let me know if anything happens." Then he stormed out of the control room.

As he walked along, he bashed his fist against a vending machine down the hallway. "Shit... Shit! This is ridiculous! He got Hummingbird?!"

"Oooh, Mr. Hitsuma, you're gonna have to answer for that, huh?"

Hitsuma rolled his eyes toward the voice. A completely unfazed Yuga shrugged at him, apparently enjoying the show.

"I told you that you should've let me take care of him. Hummingbird just didn't have what it takes."

"Whether she did or not, could *any one* of us have predicted that she'd lose? She had a one-hundred-percent mission completion rate!"

"One hundred percent of a bunch of small-fry hit man jobs. How could anyone be proud of *that* record? That's all she had the capacity for, really."

Yuga's reaction to his colleague being killed went far beyond indifference and into the realm of coldhearted callousness.

"Rentaro Satomi... God."

"So is it clear who we're dealing with now, Mr. Hitsuma? Next time, why don't you—?"

"—No! Not yet! We still have Swordtail! And I'm done screwing around. It's no mercy from here on in! I have to get them killed!"

Yuga wrinkled his nose as he chuckled. "Well, do what you like," he said chidingly. "But hasn't Inspector Tadashima been calling for you?"

Hitsuma blinked, stood up, and looked at his watch. The idea of having to act cool and deal with him when one of his top assassins was dead didn't exactly appeal to him, but he couldn't delay the inspector any longer. It could lead to some completely avoidable misunderstandings.

"You hold down the fort here," Hitsuma grunted as he passed by. Yuga responded with an uncharacteristically stern face.

"Mr. Hitsuma, about that inspector... He's pretty angry, all right? Make sure you keep your guard up."

"Tadashima is?" Hitsuma shook his head, dismissing this warning. "I don't care. He's almost up for retirement anyway; he's not gonna risk his pension trying to rock the boat. There's no way he'd ever come near the truth. That's why I chose him as my partner."

"Well, hopefully so. Just watch he doesn't trip you up, all right?"

*   *   *

The smell of defeat was in the air.

The steering wheel of his beloved car creaked in his hands as it thundered down the road. He had the accelerator all the way down, forgetting the fact he was on duty, and he was well beyond the highway speed limit. Dark Stalker, one of his men, was openly revolting against him. If he couldn't count on Swordtail to quiet things down, the organization might start asking some very unwelcome questions.

"God damn you, Rentaro Satomi…!"

Hitsuma found himself having trouble dealing with his emotions. If he met with Tadashima like this, he might notice something was up.

So he decided to take a quick breather in order to release some of his stress. *I have enough time for that,* he figured, as he spun the wheel and got off the highway, turning across several narrow roads until he reached a street lined with bars and restaurants.

He stopped in front of a dingy-looking building. Going up the stairs, he glanced at the nameplate of the Tendo Civil Security Agency. He opened the door, using a key he had made for him, only to find the office brightly lit by the evening sun through the window.

Deeper inside, behind an ebony-colored desk, Kisara Tendo sat with her back turned to him. Stealthily, Hitsuma crept up to her, then brought his hands around her head.

"I've come to see you, Kisara."

The girl in black, only noticing him once he spoke, sluggishly raised her head to meet Hitsuma's gaze. Her eyes were glassy and devoid of life. They were turned toward him, but they didn't actually seem to be looking at anything.

"Oh…Mr. Hitsuma," she slowly intoned. It was a 180-degree difference from her usual lighthearted self.

"What were you looking at?" Hitsuma said, smile deepening as he followed her eyes. "…Oh, did it show up?"

The soft chiffon fabric shone beautifully, extending out across the pleated skirt. It was a full-length dress, as pure and white as a young woman's chastity. The mannequin it was on had its head covered in a see-through veil that ran down to the shoulders. It was the wedding dress Hitsuma bought for her—one he spared no expense on.

Kisara had been like this ever since she heard Rentaro died at the Plaza Hotel. Pre-wedding jitters, perhaps, or something like it. Hitsuma appreciated how pliable it made her.

His previous research indicated that Rentaro had feelings for her. Hitsuma could have any woman he wanted. To him, taking Kisara for his own had deeper meaning. The moment Rentaro was dead and this girl was his, his revenge would be complete.

"We should hurry with the ceremony, Kisara," he said, a twisted smile on his face as he ran his hand through her black, silken hair.

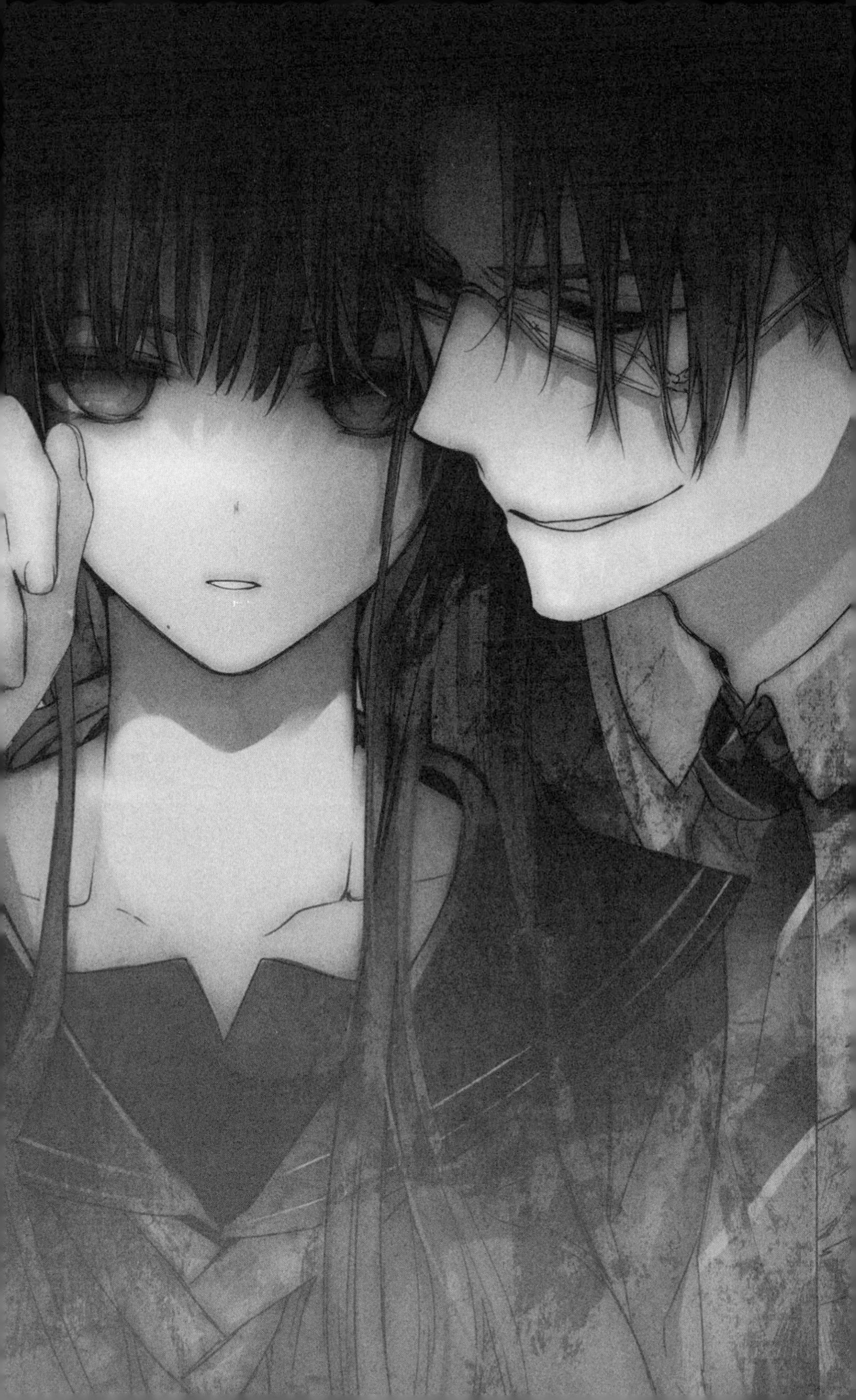

AFTERWORD

To a writer, the plot is something like the blueprint of a story, something they use as a springboard to weave the entire tale together.

In my case, I start by saying to myself, "I want to do *this* kind of scene!" then backtrack in my mind in order to figure out how "this kind of scene" would ever happen. It's called the inductive method. The opposite, where you start at the beginning and go on to the conclusion, is called the deductive method, and I could never use it very well. Whenever I try to write deductively, my hands just freeze. It reflects my deficiencies as an author, of course, but it has its advantages as well—the inductive method is a pretty logical approach, and getting it right allows you to write consistent, logical stories.

On the other hand, once your story setting grows complicated enough, going on induction means a nearly infinite number of things have to be decided upon early, usually causing my mind to overflow. (In my case, I have a thing about making my text as easy-to-read and visually engaging as possible as well, which doesn't do much to improve my writing speed either.)

With this volume, I knew I'd be having trouble ever since I tossed the plot I had spent considerable time working on into the trash after just such an overflow. Still, I had no idea I'd take up *this* much time for it.

It was a difficult birth to be sure, but still, we finally managed to get it out to the public. Sorry to make all of you wait. As long as my readers enjoy it, there'd be nothing in the world that'd please me more.

My thanks go out, as always, to my editor Kurosaki, a deeply well-educated person who apparently even wrote about opera in the past. They also go to Saki Ukai, a person who does nothing but smile stiffly whenever people say "I thought you were a guy" at autograph sessions (multiple times at one!), as well as everyone in the editorial department involved with this book. I appreciate it.

Finally, one more note to readers: Shiden Kanzaki, a detestable author who trolls his readership with promises of boobs and Lolita innuendo then blasts them in the eyes with decapitated heads and oozing guts with every page—a marketing approach unlike anything seen before—is getting even more detestable going forward. I think I'll get the next volume out faster, anyway. Check out Dengeki Bunko's webpage or my Twitter account for publication details—that way, you'll be sure you'll know about it first.

Thank you again for reaching out and picking up this volume. May God shower His blessings upon everyone who reads my work.

Shiden Kanzaki

BLACK BULLET

VOLUME 5 RELEASED
CONGRATULATIONS!

HELLO THERE! I'M MORINOHON, ARTIST FOR THE MANGA VERSION OF *BLACK BULLET*. THE NOVEL YOU'RE READING RIGHT NOW COMES OUT THE SAME DAY AS VOLUME 2 OF THE MANGA. GREAT NEWS, HUH? I HOPE YOU'LL CHECK OUT RENTARO'S AND ENJU'S ADVENTURES IN COMIC FORMAT, TOO!

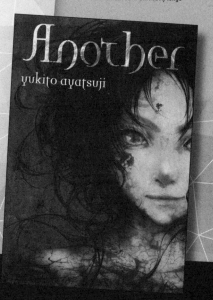